Lyn Andrews is one of the UK's top one hundred bestselling authors, reaching No. 1 on the *Sunday Times* paperback bestseller list. Born and brought up in Liverpool, she is the daughter of a policeman and also married a policeman. After becoming the mother of triplets, she took some time off from her writing whilst she raised her children. Shortlisted for the RNA Romantic Novel of the Year Award in 1993, she has now written twenty-nine hugely successful novels. Lyn Andrews divides her time between Merseyside and Ireland.

By Lyn Andrews

Maggie May
The Leaving of Liverpool
Liverpool Lou
The Sisters O'Donnell
The White Empress
Ellan Vannin
Mist Over the Mersey
Mersey Blues
Liverpool Songbird
Liverpool Lamplight
Where the Mersey Flows
From This Day Forth
When Tomorrow Dawns
Angels of Mercy
The Ties That Bind
Take These Broken Wings
My Sister's Child
The House on Lonely Street
Love and a Promise
A Wing and a Prayer
When Daylight Comes
Across a Summer Sea
A Mother's Love
Friends Forever
Every Mother's Son
Far From Home
Days of Hope
A Daughter's Journey
A Secret in the Family

lyn andrews

A Secret in the Family

headline

First published in 2009
by HEADLINE PUBLISHING GROUP

First published in paperback in 2010
by HEADLINE PUBLISHING GROUP

3

ISBN 978 0 7553 4611 0 (A-format)
ISBN 978 0 7553 5750 5 (B-format)

Typeset in Janson by Avon DataSet Ltd,
Bidford-on-Avon, Warwickshire

Printed in the UK by CPI Group (UK) Ltd, Croydon, CR0 4YY

Headline's policy is to use papers that are natural, renewable and
recyclable products and made from wood grown in sustainable forests.
The logging and manufacturing processes are expected to conform to
the environmental regulations of the country of origin.

HEADLINE PUBLISHING GROUP
An Hachette UK Company
338 Euston Road
London NW1 3BH

www.headline.co.uk
www.hachette.co.uk

A Secret
in the Family

Part I

Chapter One

Liverpool, 1959

'NO MORE FLAMING SCHOOL! WE'RE free at last, Dee!' Jean Williams tore off her much hated school beret and threw it in the air, her blue eyes dancing with delight and relief. Oh, this final year had seemed to last an eternity but now it was over. Now she could look forward to a future that held the promise of some excitement. After all, times had changed. Young people now had opportunities their parents had never dreamed of. Everything was different, the fashions, the music; there was the chance to travel, even to learn to drive a car of your own.

All around them girls of their own age, mainly in groups of two or three, streamed out of the ornate iron gates of Blackburn House and on to the pavement where the old ash and beech trees provided some shade from the hot sun. All were chatting animatedly about their plans, hopes and dreams for the weeks ahead as they headed towards the various bus stops, their schooldays behind them now.

'Except for our exam results, don't forget we have to come back for them,' Jean's best friend, Dee Campbell, reminded her.

Jean shrugged and slung her battered schoolbag over her shoulder. She linked arms with her friend and the two girls crossed the road, heading towards the bus stop. They both lived in Cobden Street in Everton and had been friends since the age of five. In appearance they were as different as chalk and cheese. Jean was small and inclined to be a little plump, with large blue eyes and fine shoulder-length straight blond hair. Denise, or 'Dee' as her family and friends called her, was tall and slim with a mop of thick, dark curly hair and penny-brown eyes. By dint of hard work and sheer good fortune they had both managed to pass the eleven-plus exam and had chosen to attend the same grammar school.

Jean tossed her blond ponytail with an air of indifference. 'Well, I'm not going to start worrying my head about exam results!' she stated firmly.

Dee frowned and looked thoughtful. She had always been the more serious of the two. 'You'd better. After all the sacrifices that have been made so we could go to grammar school in the first place, we'd both better get good results or we'll never hear the end of it.'

At that Jean grimaced and nodded slowly; there was a lot of sense in what Dee said. ' "The way I've scrimped and saved and done without meself so you could have a decent education and make something of yourself! You've had far more opportunities than our Margaret has!" If I've heard that once from Mam I've heard it a hundred times.'

Dee smiled. Jean was a good mimic: she had Ada Williams's strident tone to a T.

Jean had never found schoolwork easy. She had never aspired to become a teacher or some other type of professional person. 'Anyway, I'm not going to need half a dozen O Levels to be a hairdresser, now am I?' she continued. It was still a great bone of contention in the Williams household that Ada and Harry's second daughter, despite the grammar-school education, would not be applying for a position in the offices of one of Liverpool's many commercial establishments. Financially, higher education in the form of university or training college had been totally out of the question, but Ada had hoped that Jean – providing she got the qualifications – would try for something like the civil service, which was deemed very prestigious. Jean, however, had been adamant. She didn't want to work in a stuffy old office. Two years ago she had decided that she wanted to be a hairdresser and she'd stuck to that decision. She'd told her mam that time and time again and her elder sister, Margaret, had backed her up. Finally her father, worn out by the constant arguments, had agreed, although his decision still rankled with her mother, who never missed an opportunity to make her feelings on the subject known.

'You're not going to get much of a break though, are you?' Dee reminded her. Unlike her friend, who was due to start work as an apprentice hairdresser in a shop on Everton Road in two weeks, Dee would have to wait for the results of her exams before she could be formally accepted for the commercial course in town which would start in September, giving her the summer free.

'I don't mind. I've got my overalls and other stuff to get and the sooner I start work the sooner I'll have some money of my own – not that you could call two pounds ten shillings any kind of a decent *wage*. It will just about cover my bus fares and lunches,' Jean answered a little glumly.

'You'll get a rise each year,' Dee reminded her. 'And you'll earn good money when you've qualified. And they aren't going to charge to train you like some of those fancy places in town do.'

'God! Don't remind me. When Mam found that out I thought she'd have a heart attack. At least our Margaret put her straight.' Jean shook her head, remembering the tirade that had followed the information that large hairdressing establishments charged an often hefty premium before any indentures could be signed. It was her older sister's common sense that had prevailed on that occasion. 'She doesn't have to train in a big fancy place, Mam. One of the smaller shops around here won't charge. I bet they'll be only too glad to have someone like our Jean brushing up and holding pins or doing the shampooing for them while she learns.' And so it had proved. Mrs Nelson, proprietor of Sadie's Salon on Everton Road, had readily agreed to take on such a willing girl of good family and educated to a higher level than most.

Jean's forehead creased in a frown. 'I can't help wondering why our Margaret keeps backing me up. It's not like her. You remember how she carried on when she found out I was going to Blackburn House? She tormented me for ages.'

Dee grinned. 'I would have thought that was dead obvious. She's looking forward to years of free hairdos. You'll need someone to practise on, don't forget.'

'I just hope she stays as *supportive* if I make a mess of her hair,' Jean replied scathingly as the bus rounded the corner and they quickened their steps.

The sun was still beating down hard as the girls alighted on the corner of Everton Road and West Derby Road. Cobden Street, like many streets in the neighbourhood, consisted of two rows of small, soot-blackened, two-up two-down terraced houses with a yard at the back. The narrow streets were interspersed with corner shops and pubs, the two most notable of the latter being the Gregson's Well and the Boar's Head on the corner of Wilmott Street. Everyone made an effort to keep their homes as clean and tidy as possible but as the houses were over a hundred years old and every family suffered to some extent from overcrowding and the ever-present shortage of money, it wasn't easy. Some of the younger children were playing football in the cobbled roadway and Elsie Harper and Betty Kemp, two of their neighbours, were standing gossiping outside Marsden's corner shop.

It was the kind of street where everyone knew everyone else, which Dee often thought had its advantages and disadvantages. In times of trouble or hardship everyone helped out, which was great, but the downside was that it was difficult to have much of a private life.

'We're in for an interrogation now,' she muttered to Jean as they drew closer to the two women.

'Ladies of leisure now, you two?' Elsie remarked jovially.

Jean shook her head. 'Not for long, Mrs Harper. I'm starting work in a couple of weeks, didn't Mam tell you?'

'She did and I wish you luck, luv,' Elsie replied.

'We'll know where to come when we need our hair done for a special occasion,' Betty added.

'I don't think Mrs Nelson will be letting me loose on the paying customers at first,' Jean said good-naturedly.

'At least I'll be able to give Mam a hand until I go on my course,' Dee informed them.

Betty nodded. 'You've both done well for yourselves.'

Dee smiled. 'We'd best be getting home now.'

The two women watched them as they resumed their journey, thinking it was a great thing to have a grammar-school education, something none of their respective offspring had achieved.

'I hope Mam's not gone and done a pan of scouse for the tea, it's too hot,' Dee remarked, pushing a few damp curls from her forehead and fanning herself with her discarded beret. 'Are you coming in? Our Graham's got Ritchie Valens's record "Donna" and you can try that new lipstick I got in Woolies last week. It's called "Pink Meringue".'

As Jean envisaged a lecture from her mother about schooldays being the happiest of your life and that in a month's time she would be wishing she was back there, followed by the usual litany of complaints about her father – mainly that he wasted too much money on drink and the horses – she felt that half an hour spent listening to Dee's brother's records and trying on a new lipstick was infinitely preferable.

No smell of cooking pervaded the air as she followed her friend down the dark, narrow lobby and into the cramped kitchen, one wall of which was completely taken up by the old fashioned, cast-iron range.

Flo Campbell looked up from her task of slicing tomatoes and smiled at the two girls. She was tall and thin and her hair was now more grey than the rich dark brown it had once been; it was tortured into tight, frizzy curls by the old-fashioned metal curling pins she put in every night. She was, as she frequently declared to her friends and neighbours, a 'martyr to her nerves', although both Dee and Jean privately thought she seemed to be able to conjure up these attacks of 'nerves' at will. Thankfully, Jean noted she seemed perfectly fine today.

'So, that's it then. No more school. You're "workers of the world" now,' Flo commented, smiling as she wiped her hands on her apron.

'That's it, Mrs Campbell, and I'm really looking forward to it,' Jean replied brightly. 'No more awful school blouses and skirts, I'm going to have a smart overall, probably pink, although Mrs Nelson, who has the shop, said I can have whatever colour I want.'

'That's good of her. I'm sure you'll do well there,' Flo replied encouragingly, pulling apart the head of lettuce preparatory to washing it. 'I thought a nice salad would be a bit of a treat, seeing as the weather's so warm and it's a bit of a special occasion. Of course her next door said when I was buying the ham in Pegram's did I not think it was a poor meal to give a man after a day's work, but you'd never take notice of anything *that* one says. It's a well-known fact that most of what's put on the table in that house fell off the back of a lorry! Have you been home yet, Jean?'

Jean shook her head. 'No, Dee's going to let me try her new lipstick.'

'And we're going to listen to some of our Graham's records,' Dee added.

'Well, don't be deafening us all and don't go scratching any of them. I don't want any fights and arguments when he gets home.' Flo's smile belied her sharp words. 'Did you see any sign of our Davie in the street?'

Dee shook her head. She was certain her ten-year-old brother hadn't been amongst the lads playing outside and she'd distinctly heard noises coming from the back yard that suggested he was lurking somewhere close by.

'Typical! I wanted him to go down and get me a bar of soap from Marsden's. Your da used the last bit of it this morning and I forgot to put it on my list.'

'I bet if you said he could get himself a packet of sweets for going for the soap he'd appear like magic,' Dee said loudly, her eyes on the door to the scullery.

'A packet of sweets! He can make do with whatever he can get for a penny and think himself lucky,' Flo replied sharply, following her daughter's gaze.

The two girls grinned as Davie, hair standing on end, smuts on his face and grey woollen socks sagging around his ankles, appeared in the doorway.

Flo pursed her lips. 'Would you just look at the cut of him! You look like one of those tatters that are always falling out of the Boar's Head on Saturday nights! Go and clean yourself up,' she instructed.

Davie grinned, thinking he had the perfect excuse. 'How can I, Mam, when there ain't no soap?'

'Don't be so hardfaced, meladdo! Pull those socks up and comb your hair or there'll be no sixpence for the pictures tomorrow morning,' Flo threatened.

The girls laughed and were about to go upstairs when to her dismay Jean heard her mother's familiar tones as Ada called down the lobby.

'Looks like she's come to see what's keeping you,' Flo muttered to the girl before calling: 'In here, Ada, luv!'

Ada bustled into the kitchen, puffing a little, her round face red with exertion and the heat. A big woman with tightly permed light brown hair, she was enveloped in a wrap-over pinafore over a faded print dress. The two women had been friends and neighbours for years and neither stood on ceremony.

'God Almighty, but this heat is getting me down and the damned range doesn't help! It's as hot as the hobs of hell in that kitchen! So, this is where you've got to, Jean. I thought you'd gone off into town to celebrate your "freedom" as you call it! She won't be calling it that in a few weeks, Flo, you mark my words!' All this was uttered without a pause for breath while Flo indicated that Jean's mother sit down and prepared to pour her a cup of tea.

'I just called in for a minute, Mam, honestly,' Jean explained.

Ada ignored her and fished a crumpled envelope from her apron pocket. 'Have you had one of these, Flo? It came in the afternoon post but seein' it was sort of "official" I never opened it straight away.'

'What is it?' Flo asked, taking the envelope and handing over a cup of tea.

Ada sipped the tea gratefully. It was far cooler in Flo's kitchen as the range wasn't lit and the scullery and yard doors were wide open, as was the front door. 'Read it, luv,' she urged.

As her mother scanned the letter Dee looked at Jean questioningly. Jean shrugged. Usually the only 'official' things that came in the post were bills and no one was ever eager to open those.

'Dear God! At last!' Flo cried, handing the letter

back. 'Well, I never thought the day would arrive.'

'What is it, Mam?' Dee asked.

'They're finally going to rehouse us,' Ada informed them. 'After all these years of being crammed like sardines in a tin and without a decent kitchen or bathroom we're finally going to get a new house.'

'Where? When?' Jean cried, holding out her hand for the letter.

'It doesn't say exactly when but we're to have a new three-bedroomed house in Kirkby, with all mod cons too. Oh, just think, Flo, a proper kitchen with units and those new Formica worktops that just need a bit of a wipe over. A new cooker, no more dirty old ranges. No dark, smelly scullery. No privy in the yard. A proper bathroom *inside* and a bit of garden front and back.' Ada closed her eyes and sighed deeply at the prospect of such luxury.

'Did you get a letter too, Mam?' Dee asked.

Flo shook her head.

'You will, luv. I bet it'll come in the morning post tomorrow,' Ada said confidently. 'Haven't they been promising us this for years? These houses are long overdue for demolition.'

'But what about my job, Mam?' Jean cried, looking despairingly at Dee.

'What about it?' Ada asked.

'Kirkby's miles and miles away! I don't even know exactly *where* it is,' Jean replied.

'I think it's out beyond Fazakerley. I think it's in the country,' Dee ventured.

Jean looked horrified. 'How am I going to get to work from out there?' she wailed, seeing her apprenticeship slipping away.

'Oh, don't go getting all airyated, Jean! There's bound to be buses,' Ada snapped irritably. She hadn't thought about how Jean, Margaret or Harry, who worked on the docks, would get to work.

'If it's that far out it will cost a fortune in fares and I'm not going to be earning much. I'll have nothing left, Mam, out of my wages. Nothing at all!'

'Don't get upset, Jean. They haven't said exactly when we will be going to move, it could be ages yet. You know what the Council is like, dead slow and stop,' Dee tried to reassure her friend. She was wondering how she too was going to get to town for her commercial course and then, hopefully, to a decent job in Liverpool city centre.

'Dee's right. How long have we been waiting to be rehoused? Years and years and it could be years yet before it finally comes off. And they can't just dump us out in a country place with no transport.' A thought occurred to Flo and one that was disturbing to say the least. 'I hope to God they don't expect us to manage without any amenities. I don't think my poor nerves could stand that!'

'Of course they won't, Mam!' Dee said firmly. 'Let's just wait and see what Da has to say. You know how sensible he is and he might know more about it than we do. If he doesn't he can find out – he can go and see Fred Thomas, he's our Councillor and he's bound to know.'

Flo nodded slowly. What Dee had said was right. Fred Thomas was the man they all trusted. He'd been their councillor for years; he would know all about this matter.

Ada heaved herself to her feet. 'Well, I think it's great news, Flo. We're finally going to get a house we can be proud of. A house it will be a real pleasure to live in. There's bound to be a few difficulties and inconveniences at first but we'll get over them. Lord above, we won't know ourselves. Come on, Jean, you can help me get the tea started.'

When the two had left, Davie was dispatched to the corner shop and Dee helped her mother to set the table. Her brother Graham and her father would be in from their work soon and then this matter of the rehousing could be discussed in more depth.

Chapter Two

———◆———

WHEN HE ARRIVED HOME Bob Campbell was
weary. It had been a long day, full of problems
and harassments. Beneath his bowler hat, which
denoted his position as a foreman or 'blocker man' on
the docks, his hair was stuck to his head with sweat. On
the way home he'd refused the offer of a quick pint
with Harry Williams in the Gregson's Well, knowing
that with Harry it wouldn't stop at one pint, not on a
Friday night. When he got home he was looking
forward to having a wash, then his meal, a quiet half-
hour with the *Echo* and then it would be time for 'Any
Questions' on the radio (for as yet no one in Cobden
Street had a television set). Maybe he'd go down to the
pub for the last half-hour, just to be sociable.

'That looks very appetising, luv,' he remarked to his
wife as he took off his jacket and placed his bowler on
the dresser. Either Flo or Dee had spread the kitchen

table with a clean white cloth and laid out plates of ham, salad and sliced hard-boiled eggs. There was a big plate of bread and butter in the centre of the table, alongside the fancy china salt and pepper cruets decorated with the gilded words 'A Present from Llandudno'. Beside them was a new bottle of Heinz salad cream.

'Well, it's too warm to be cooking and I thought it would make a change seeing as how Dee left school today,' Flo reminded him. 'And there's tinned peaches and evaporated milk for pudding,' she added.

Bob smiled fondly at his daughter who was pouring hot water from the kettle on the gas ring into the teapot. She'd changed out of her school uniform for the last time and was wearing a pale green and white striped shirtwaister dress, the skirt of which stood out stiffly with the tiered layers of net petticoats beneath it. She'd tied back her hair with a white ribbon and wore white plastic earrings shaped like daisies. Sixteen, as pretty as a picture and all grown up, he mused. 'I can't believe how the time has flown,' he said aloud, shaking his head before going into the scullery for a wash.

In the tiny room at the back of the house he found his eldest son stripped to the waist and vigorously towelling his face and neck.

'That loading bay was like a furnace this afternoon, Da! And as for the dust . . .' Graham moved aside and handed his father the towel. At eighteen he was taller than Bob; he had the same thick curly hair as his father but without the strands of grey that now ran through Bob's.

Bob nodded sympathetically. He wished the lad could have got a better job than working in the deliveries department of Robinson's Animal Feed Factory but Graham hadn't been as fortunate as Dee where education had been concerned; he hadn't passed the eleven-plus. Besides, he didn't often complain. Most of the time he said it wasn't a bad job, the lads he worked with were a great bunch and there was often overtime to boost his wages – most of which were spent on clothes, records and going into town to one of the many new coffee bars or skiffle clubs.

'It was no picnic at the docks either but at least on the river there's a bit of a breeze. Thank God I wasn't working down on the Hornby Dock; they had a cargo of grain in and the dust from that would half blind and choke you. I suppose you're off out later?'

Graham grinned. 'I'm meeting a couple of the lads and we're going to a club. We've heard there might be a chance of us playing there next month.' Like countless others, Graham and a few mates had formed their own skiffle group. 'I hope Mam's ironed my best shirt. I forgot to ask her before I left this morning.'

'Well, if she hasn't it's your own fault and don't go upsetting her by asking her to do it after tea, wear something else,' he advised. Flo had her work cut out keeping the house clean and tidy and seeing that they were all well turned out, which wasn't easy given the lack of facilities in these old places.

'Had a busy day, Da?' Dee asked when they were finally seated.

Flo slapped Davie's hand as it shot out to grab a slice of bread. 'How many times have I told you not to snatch? Wait until the plate is offered to you,' she admonished sharply.

Bob gave his youngest son a warning look. Flo seemed to be a bit on edge. 'No more than usual but I'm glad it's only a half-day tomorrow. So, what are you going to do with yourself for the next few weeks?' he asked Dee.

Dee was pouring the tea. 'I'll be able to help Mam more and I thought I'd try and get myself a Saturday job in Woolies or Boots, somewhere like that. I'm going to need a bit of money for notebooks and things if I'm accepted for this course.'

Bob nodded his approval. Like Ada he would have preferred Dee to have applied for the civil service but she had said it would be more sensible to learn short-hand and typing which, with the five O Levels she hoped she would have, would afford her far more choice in the way of job opportunities. He had had to agree for he prided himself that he was far more forward-thinking than those who said education was wasted on girls because in the end they only got married, had children and stayed at home. The women of Flo's generation had never had such opportunities, they'd been leaving school at the age of fourteen when the storm clouds had been gathering over Europe and had become wives and mothers while a war was being fought.

Dragging himself out of his reverie he noticed that his wife was unusually quiet and was pushing the food around on her plate: both signs that something was worrying her. Something which if left unaddressed usually led to one of her bouts of 'nerves'. He sighed. She wasn't the easiest of women to live with. Too skittish and highly strung was how his mother had described her all those years ago, and having to live through the wartime Blitz on Liverpool hadn't helped. 'Has someone upset you, Flo? Apart from meladdo here and his lack of manners, that is?' he asked quietly.

Graham glanced quickly from his father to Dee. God, he hoped they weren't in for one of her 'turns'. Best not even mention the flaming shirt now.

'Jean's mam was up here earlier with a letter she'd had from the Council,' Dee informed him.

'And?' Bob probed.

'They're going to be rehoused. I expect we all are. They've been offered a new three-bedroomed house out at Kirkby.'

Bob put down his knife and fork. This was great news surely? They'd all been promised new and better houses. This entire area was long overdue for demolition. 'Well, it's about time! I never thought we'd see the day.'

Flo shook her head and looked flustered. 'That's all well and good but it's miles and miles away. How is everyone going to get to their work? Poor Jean was very upset, she's supposed to be starting her job the week after next and you know they're only paying her buttons while she's training and . . . and then I've been thinking, we're not used to living in the country. We've always lived in town.'

'When I've been out in town with my mates how the hell am I going to get home to *Kirkby*?' Graham interrupted, completely ignoring the fact that this outburst would only make matters worse.

'Cor! What if there're no schools!' Davie added, looking highly delighted.

Dee glared at them both. Wasn't it obvious that Mam was working herself up into a right state? 'Well, I think it's great news. It will be so much better for all of us but especially Mam. We'll have far more room, everything will be brand new and it will be so much easier to keep clean.'

Bob smiled at his daughter. 'You're right, Dee.'

'Just to put Mam's mind at rest, I suggested that perhaps you and Mr Williams could go along and see Fred Thomas. He's bound to know more about it all. It probably won't be for ages yet and he might know what else there will be, apart from new houses.'

Bob realised that his wife had raised some perfectly valid questions. Of course he could understand her apprehension about living in the country but they'd get used to that. In fact he'd enjoy having a bit of a garden and all the peace and quiet, but there was the question of the amenities. 'That's a sensible idea, Dee. Now don't go getting yourself all worked up about it, Flo. As soon as I've had my tea I'll get changed and drag Harry out of the pub and then we'll go along to Fred

Thomas's place on Everton Road. And I want to hear no more out of you two!' he admonished his sons.

'Let's finish our meal and then I'll help Mam wash up,' Dee added, thankful that her mother did now look a little less agitated.

When they'd cleared the table and washed up, Davie was allowed out to play and Graham went to get ready to go out. Dee was finishing up in the scullery when her father put his head around the door.

'Are you off now to see Mr Thomas?'

Bob nodded. 'We'll get it all sorted out, Dee. I don't want your mam to worry. We should all be looking forward to a new home, I really do think it's good news.'

'So do I and I bet most of the women in this street will think so too. I'll try to get her to relax a bit.'

Bob smiled at her fondly and kissed her on the forehead. 'That's my girl.'

When he'd gone Dee suggested that her mother sit down with her copy of *Woman's Weekly*. 'You like the short stories in that, Mam, and you always say you never get a minute's peace to read them. It will help to take your mind off things until Da gets back. I'm going to see how Jean's getting on,' she urged before she went down the street to the Williamses' house.

Obviously a few other people had heard the news for Elsie Harper, Betty Kemp and Madge Daly were on Elsie's doorstep deep in conversation, while their younger children were playing around the street lamp.

'Has your mam heard the news, Dee?' Madge called.

'Oh, yes. Did you get a letter from the Housing, Mrs Daly?' Dee enquired.

'I didn't but both Betty and Elsie did.'

'I told you the rest will be in the post, Madge,' Betty interrupted. 'I can hardly believe it! Me dream's out! A brand-new house!'

'And the kids will have a garden to play in instead of a dirty old street,' Elsie added before exhorting her youngest son to stop poking around in the gutter.

'I'm grid fishin', Mam! Someone's dropped a couple of ha'pennies down it,' Tommy Harper yelled back.

Elsie raised her eyes skywards and shook her head but she wasn't going to let Tommy's transgression spoil the moment.

Dee could see they were all excited so she determined to say nothing to put a damper on it. 'It's great news, isn't it? I'm just on my way down to see Jean. Her mam got a letter today too.'

Ada's kitchen was never as tidy as their own on a good day but now chaos reigned. The dirty dishes were still on the table; Margaret had been trying to find a missing earring and in exasperation had tipped out the entire contents of the dresser drawers on to the rug in front of the range and was on her knees rummaging through the mess. Young Peter was complaining vociferously and tearfully to his mother that what she had called a pile of 'tatty old paper' and had used to light the range had in fact been his much loved copies of the *Beano* and *Dandy*. Ada herself was sitting at the table with her head in her hands and a half-cold mug of tea before her. Of Jean there was no sign.

'It's just like Fred Karno's Circus in here!' Dee exclaimed to no one in particular.

Ada looked up. 'You can say that again, Dee! If you don't shut up about those blasted old comics I'll swing for you, Peter Williams, I will! And you, my girl, can put all that stuff back or I'll tip the lot into the fire!'

'Mam, they were a good pair of earrings! Rolled gold they were. Frank bought them from a proper jeweller's and he'll expect to see me wearing them tonight,' Margaret complained, casting an imploring look up at Dee.

'Then you should have taken more care of them!' her mother retorted.

Margaret glared at her.

Dee had always thought Margaret was an attractive girl, in a showy sort of way, but at nineteen and now courting steadily Jean said her sister thought of herself as 'sophisticated'. They had giggled a lot about that. 'Where's Jean?' she asked.

Ada pointed to the ceiling. 'Upstairs, sulking! What did your da say about this rehousing lark? Did your mam tell him?'

Dee nodded. 'He was getting changed when I left. He's going to see Mr Thomas. He said he was going to take Mr Williams with him.'

'If he can drag him away from the saloon bar of Gregson's!' Ada said scathingly. 'Fat lot he cares about me sitting here worrying my head about it all!'

To forestall the impending tirade on Harry Williams's character Dee headed for the stairs.

Jean was sitting on the bed she shared with her sister, looking decidedly miserable. Dee sat down beside her and put her arm around her.

'It's not *that* bad!'

'It is!' Jean protested. 'Nice new house, but no shops, no pubs, no coffee bars, no schools, probably very few buses and so no job. And our Margaret doesn't help. She said she's not moving. Frank Woodward's asked her to marry him and she says she will and she'll move in with him and his mam. She said she'd die of boredom in the country. Wouldn't we be better off staying here and putting up with this old house, Dee?'

Dee sighed. 'I think everyone is getting themselves into a right state about it. We should all look on the bright side of things. It might be years yet and they might provide everything we have around here and even if it does take a bit longer to get to work, is that so bad? Not when we will have a proper bathroom and kitchen and a parlour that hasn't got to be used as an extra bedroom so the only "living" room we've got is the kitchen. We'll have a garden to sit in on warm summer evenings like this. Just think how great it will be to look out of the window and see trees and fields instead of the dirty back-yard wall and the jigger and the sooty factory chimneys. Won't it be a real pleasure to come home from a day's work in the city to peace and quiet?'

Jean managed a wry grin. 'Peace and quiet? With that lot down there?'

Seeing her friend was at least making an effort Dee smiled at her. 'Is your Margaret really going to marry Frank Woodward? His mam is a bit of an old tartar, or so I've heard?'

Jean giggled. 'I heard that too. She'll have her work cut out with that old one but it's her life. I suppose he'll be buying her a ring any day now and then all we'll hear is how wonderful "my fiancé" is!'

'Still, you'll get to be a bridesmaid and you'll get this room to yourself.'

Jean looked around at the untidy bedroom and brightened. 'I will. She can take all this stuff with her and then we'll see how Frank likes having all her things strewn around everywhere.'

Dee pulled her to her feet. 'Come on, lets go down and give your Mam a hand to clear up, then we'll go back to our house and wait to see what Da's found out.'

The bar of the Gregson's Well wasn't very big and at this time on a Friday evening it was busy. Bob peered through the crowd and spotted Harry leaning against the bar in conversation with Fred Harper, Jack Daly and Ernie Kemp.

'Changed yer mind, Bob?' Harry grinned as Bob made his way over.

'Not really. I'm on the way to see Fred Thomas.'

'Might as well have a pint first, now yer're here,' Harry urged.

Bob nodded. 'Half of bitter then, Red, please,' he

asked of the landlord Arthur Hathaway, known to all as 'Red' on account of his shock of auburn hair.

'What's so important that yer're off to see Councillor Thomas?' Harry pressed.

'This news about us being rehoused. Flo's getting herself into a state about going to "live in the country".'

'What's up with her?' Jack Daly asked, finishing his drink and signalling Red to fill up his glass. 'Our Madge is over the moon about it, didn't even nag about me coming in here.'

'She's getting worried about the distance and lack of amenities.'

Jack and Harry exchanged glances. 'Ah, take no notice, Bob. Tell her how lucky she is, how lucky we all are. Those houses should have been pulled down years ago.'

'Aye, I always said it was a shame Hitler's bloody Luftwaffe didn't demolish them. That was the only good thing to come out of the Blitz, all the slums that got destroyed,' Ernie Kemp put in.

Harry frowned at him. Bob hated talking about the war. In fact he avoided the subject whenever possible, particularly the Blitz. He assumed that Bob's memories were too traumatic.

Bob ignored the comment, instantly pushing the memories of that week-long bombardment from his mind. 'Well, I think she's actually got a point. Moving out there is going to cause a few inconveniences for us all.'

'It'll cause me more than just a bit of "inconvenience". What am I going to do for customers? Bloody Council will have me in the workhouse!' Red stated gloomily.

'Don't you start an' all! They won't be demolishing the entire bloody neighbourhood, you'll still have customers.' Harry thought this whole subject was becoming a bit depressing.

Fred Harper looked thoughtful. 'Might be a good idea to go and get things cleared up, Bob. You know what the women are like, once one starts moaning and complaining—'

'And the last thing we need is someone putting the mockers on it all. We should have a party to celebrate our good luck,' Ernie interrupted. 'You're just the feller to get it all sorted, Bob. You know how to talk to that feller Thomas.'

They all nodded their agreement. Bob Campbell was much respected. It was a well-known fact on the docks that he wouldn't take a 'back hander' and he was fair in his dealings with the men.

Bob finished his drink. 'I told Flo I'd get you to come with me, Harry.'

Harry looked disgruntled, thinking that was a bit high-handed, but then he shrugged. He supposed he'd get no peace from either Ada or Jean if he refused.

'Come back later and let us know how you get on so we'll be able to pass it all on to the wives,' Jack Daly called as Bob and Harry left the bar.

Chapter Three

◆━◆━◆

IT WAS AFTER NINE when Bob, accompanied by Harry Williams, finally returned home. Davie had been duly dispatched to bed, under protest, and Flo and the two girls were leafing through some old magazines.

Flo jumped to her feet when she heard the front door open. 'Go and put the kettle on, Dee, quickly now!' she instructed. Biting her lip she searched her husband's face for signs of what she felt certain would be bad news. Her stomach was churning with anticipation. 'Well, did you see him? What did he say?'

'We did and he was very reassuring,' Bob replied, taking off his jacket.

'If you ask me our Ada's stirred up a storm in a teacup over all this!' Harry added irritably. 'Trust your mam to go off at a tangent over nothing.' This was directed at Jean who he felt had played no small part in all this fuss.

'Sit down, Harry, and have a cup of tea,' Flo urged, feeling slightly relieved.

'Fred Thomas told us that we are all to be rehoused but that it won't be happening overnight so we'll have plenty of time to prepare for it and get used to the idea. They're already building out at Kirkby but it will take time. There's a Protestant church and school, St Chad's, and other schools will be built, as will shops and all the other amenities. So there's no question of us being dumped in the middle of nowhere with no facilities. There's already an industrial estate out there and that's being enlarged so there will be jobs available on the doorstep for those that want them,' Bob informed them.

'What about buses?' Flo asked.

'There will be regular bus services into town. It will take much longer, there's no getting round that, but as the man said, the advantages outweigh the disadvantages and I agree with him.'

'You women have been complaining for years about the overcrowded conditions you have to put up with, so you should be thanking your lucky stars for getting new modern houses, not moaning and whining about moving.' Harry hadn't been thrilled about being dragged away from his pint and the convivial company in the pub to refute what he considered to be unjustified complaints.

Seeing her mother's lips tighten into a line of disapproval Dee hastened to avert an argument. 'Everyone was just worried about getting to work but

30

now that it's all been sorted out I'm sure there won't be any need for us all to fret.'

'Like I said, trust our Ada to make a mountain out of a molehill.' Harry remarked drily, draining his cup and getting to his feet. 'Well, I think that after all that palaver we're entitled to go and catch last orders, don't you, Bob?'

'Oh, honestly, Da! That means I'll have to go home and explain it all to Mam!' Jean cried, exasperated.

'Go and tell her to come up here, Jean, and you two get yourselves off to the pub, we won't want you under our feet. We've got plans to make. For a start neither of us has enough furniture for a big modern house,' Flo ordered briskly.

Jean looked at Dee in amazement at this complete change of attitude but Dee just shrugged. Her mam's moods could often change like this.

When Ada arrived she was very relieved to see that Flo looked far happier. 'I'd have got here sooner, Flo, but both Elsie and Betty stopped me. Everyone's delighted, it will be the talk of the street for weeks and I must say I'm relieved to hear everything is going to be just fine.'

'I feel much better myself now, Ada, although earlier I was starting to think back on all the happy times we've had in this house . . .'

Ada shook her head. 'Don't go getting too sentimental, Flo, just remember how overcrowded we all are, how hard it is to keep the place clean, no proper kitchen or bathroom. There will be plenty of happy times to look forward to in the new house.'

Flo put the kettle on. Ada was right. Now, they had better start to make plans as would all their neighbours. It really was a piece of good news.

Things settled down again after the initial flurry of excitement had passed up and down the street. Jean, accompanied by Dee, went to the hairdressing wholesaler's in Williamson Square where she bought two bright pink 'shortie' overalls edged on the pockets and cuffs with black.

'I'd wear an old dark coloured pencil skirt with them if I were you, dear. Otherwise you'll ruin your good skirts with tint and the Lord alone knows what else. Are you sure you wouldn't be better off with a full-length overall to start with?' the woman who served them had asked.

Jean had shaken her head firmly. She didn't want to start work looking drab and old-fashioned. She'd wear her flat black ballerina-style shoes and a black straight skirt with the overalls. She also bought a good pair of cutting scissors and a pair of thinning scissors, the price of which amounted to more than she was to be paid for a week's work. It had been made clear to her that she would be expected to attend the City College of Crafts and Catering in Colquitt Street one afternoon a week, most probably on Wednesdays which was Mrs Nelson's half-day closing. This didn't seem at all fair as it only left her with Sunday off, but when she'd complained her mother had told her sharply that if hairdressing was what she wanted to do she would have to make the necessary sacrifices.

Before Jean's first college session the two girls met for coffee in the El Cabala in Bold Street.

'If I'd gone on complaining about having to go to college on my afternoon off she would have said, "Well, you wouldn't listen to me,"' Jean confided.

'It won't be for ever and I can meet you at lunchtime and we can go for a coffee. I'll be at the place opposite,' Dee reminded her.

Dee had written to half a dozen shops applying for a Saturday job and to her relief was taken on by Boots the Chemist who had large premises in Church Street. She hoped she would be kept on at least until Christmas as the money would come in very useful. Like many other girls and women they both made many of their own clothes; needlework had been on the curriculum at school and Flo had a second-hand Singer sewing machine. All the department stores sold paper patterns and there was a vast choice of materials in all the stores and the small specialist shops. It was a far cheaper alternative to buying things ready-made and, as Dee often remarked, you seldom saw anyone wearing exactly the same thing as yourself.

True to her word, Margaret Williams had accepted Frank Woodward's proposal and was now sporting an engagement ring, although you had to get a magnifying glass to see the diamond, Jean had noted to her friend – although not within earshot of her sister. Both Jean and Dee thought she was completely mad to consider getting married at nineteen.

'What's she done with her life? Not much so far and once she's settled in with him and his mam I can't see there being much to get excited about,' Jean commented. She had great plans for when she had finished her apprenticeship. She didn't intend to stay on working for Sadie Nelson. Pauline, who also worked there and who was termed an 'improver', having nearly finished her apprenticeship, had told her that you could get great jobs in big hotels in the popular holiday resorts, at Butlin's holiday camps and even on passenger ships.

'I suppose it's all a matter of what you really want out of life,' Dee mused. She stirred her coffee thoughtfully. 'I suppose we'll get married too – eventually. I mean we wouldn't want to end up as old maids.'

'No, but I think about twenty-five is time enough. We want to do well in our jobs, have a bit of money to spend on ourselves. We'll have had time to enjoy ourselves and find out what life's all about. We could even save up and go away on holidays, wouldn't it be great to go somewhere abroad?'

Dee caught her enthusiasm. 'We could go to France or Spain or Italy – or ever Portugal. See how people live there, how they spend their time, what they eat, what they wear.'

'I've heard that girls are really fashionable in France and Italy.'

Dee nodded. 'All the really fabulous shoes and bags come from Italy.'

'Or we could take driving lessons. Maybe even afford a small car? Just think, Dee, we could go off to a different place each Sunday!'

Dee laughed. 'I think that might be just a bit too ambitious. Not learning to drive but buying a car. We don't know anyone who has a car.'

'We don't know anyone who has a television. Wait, I tell a lie. Our Margaret says Frank's mam is thinking of getting one. Oh, let's forget about our Margaret. Why don't I come up to your house tonight? I could put some big rollers in your hair, that would straighten it out a bit, and I can practise putting it up into a beehive.'

Dee grimaced. 'I'm sure all that back-combing doesn't do it much good, let alone all the hair lacquer you need to keep it in place. It's so stiff that not a hair would move in a force-nine gale and it's murder to get out!'

Jean tutted and cast her eyes to the ceiling. 'Honestly, Dee! You have to keep up with the trends. You only have to brush it out properly every couple of days and when you wash it, if you put Borax in the rinsing water the lacquer comes out.'

Dee didn't look convinced. Her thick, naturally curly hair didn't lend itself to the straight bouffant styles now coming into fashion, styles that relied heavily on vigorous back-combing and liberal applications of very sticky lacquer which came in plastic bottles and left a flaky white residue behind on your hair after brushing.

Margaret Williams on the other hand was only too pleased to let her younger sister practise on her. She had always liked to think of herself as being very fashionable and she loved the new styles. Also now that she had to save every penny towards her wedding, she couldn't afford to pay to go to the hairdresser's.

After her first couple of weeks working for Mrs Nelson, Jean had to admit that, as her mother had warned her, it was extremely hard work. Most of her tasks seemed very menial: sweeping up, cleaning mirrors and washbasins with Vim and a damp cloth, folding towels, taking the wet ones and pegging them out on the line in the tiny back yard. Washing and drying the plastic curlers used for perms with their fiddly rubber-band-type fasteners. Refilling the shampoo, setting lotion and lacquer bottles from the big containers kept in the back room. Holding hairpins and rollers for both Sadie and Pauline. Basically she just watched as they cut, trimmed, wound perms and applied tints, dyes and bleach.

Sadie still did quite a lot of finger waving and pin curling on her more middle-aged customers, who didn't think they were getting good value unless their set lasted a full week. Both Jean and Pauline found this tedious but it was still part of their training, as was the equally old-fashioned and seldom-called-for razor cutting known as 'shingling'. Pauline said she could do two roller sets in the time it took Sadie to do one of those antiquated things. Jean hated the slimy feel of the thick liquid setting lotion that was a necessary part of this procedure and the fiddly process of winding up strands of hair in a pin curl or reverse pin curl and clipping it in place. Then the whole head was enveloped in a large hairnet and the customer sat under the hood of the hairdryer for at least half an hour with the setting on nothing less than medium. Strips of cotton wool were carefully placed around the customer's forehead and ears as the pins got very hot – Jean couldn't imagine how they stuck it all. It seemed like sheer torture. Beside all that the fairly simple process of setting the hair on rollers, back-combing, smoothing over and spraying with lacquer was much easier, no matter what Dee said.

At the end of long hot Saturdays serving behind the counter in Boots, Dee also often felt too tired to get changed and go out. She consoled herself that at least by staying in she was increasing the small amount she had in her Post Office Savings Account. She wanted a smart coat and new shoes for the autumn.

When the day finally arrived for them to go back to school and collect their exam results Jean was working so Dee promised she would collect her friend's as well as her own. As she explained this to the headmistress she wondered why they had ever been in awe of this small, weary looking woman. Was it because now they had left Miss Swainson was treating them not as rather tiresome schoolgirls but young women?

After a quick, slightly stilted conversation with the headmistress, Dee tucked the two sealed envelopes into her handbag.

Once outside she took out the envelope with her name on it and ripped it open. She let out her breath in a sigh of relief. She had passed all five subjects. More than relief, she felt elated – all that hard work and revision had paid off. She could give herself a pat on the back, she had qualifications and that would make Mam happy. She wondered how Jean had got on but she would have to wait until this evening to find out.

Flo had indeed been delighted when she'd arrived home with her news, saying that when she finally received the official certificates they would have them framed and could hang them on the wall in the parlour of the new house. Dee had just smiled; she really wasn't very enthusiastic about that idea.

She went to the corner of the street at teatime to wait for her friend. Jean got off the bus looking tired. Her overall was rolled up and tucked into the basket she used for work instead of a handbag. The baskets were all the rage and were called, for some unknown reason, 'chicken baskets'. Her short-sleeved white top was clinging to her with perspiration but her blond hair was up in the current beehive style and she wore large black and white plastic hoop earrings. Dee thought she looked quite stylish.

'I came up to meet you. I thought you might want to open this before you got home.' Dee handed her the envelope.

'What did you get?' Jean asked, eyeing the envelope cautiously. She had been so set on making a career of hairdressing that she hadn't really worked very hard for her exams and for a while now she'd been feeling a bit apprehensive about the results.

'I managed to scrape through all five so I'll be able to start my course,' Dee replied, falling into step with her friend. She didn't want to enthuse too much about her success.

Jean ripped open the envelope, glanced at the contents and pursed her lips. 'Oh, hell!'

'What?' Dee demanded.

'I failed four and passed one. I'm going to get a dog's life from Mam now.'

Dee felt sorry for her. 'Try to impress on her that they're not all *that* important now you've got your job and you're doing so well. Didn't Mrs Nelson say she'd never had anyone who was so quick to pick things up? And look how well your Margaret's tint turned out. She's delighted with the new colour and hasn't she been urging your mam to let you have a go at giving her a decent perm instead of those Twink things she puts on herself and which don't last long? Look on the positive side, Jean, and make *her* look on the positive side too.'

Jean managed a smile. 'You were always one for looking on the bright side of things, Dee. Come on, let's get this over with. I hope it will be a five-minute wonder. At least the damned exams are over and done with. Maybe we can get just on with our lives now.'

Chapter Four

———◆———

ADA DIDN'T HIDE HER anger and disappointment when she heard the news. 'All that expense and sacrifice! I'm really disappointed in you, Jean.'

'But, Mam, I've got the job I really want and I'm good at it, you know I am,' Jean pleaded.

'That's not the point. It's the sheer waste of an opportunity and a good education. You could have done better, you just didn't try! You didn't put enough effort into it.'

Jean bit her lip. 'I'm sorry, Mam, really I am, but I'll make a good hairdresser, I promise.'

Ada shook her head. 'I should have listened to your da but I wanted you to do well. He's not going to be very happy either, not after having to cut down on his beer and cigarettes for all the time you were at that school. You could have got that job with Sadie Nelson if you'd gone to a secondary modern, that's what he'll say.'

Jean tried to brighten the mood. 'At least you've got our Margaret's wedding to look forward to.'

Ada nodded and managed a smile. That was true. She was pleased and excited about the coming event, the first wedding in the family.

To Jean's relief the exam results were soon forgotten as her training progressed and plans for Margaret's wedding became the main topic of Ada's conversation. The date had been set for the end of January which, as Margaret had confided to her mother, wasn't an ideal month but there didn't seem much point in delaying it when she was moving in with Frank and his mother so they didn't have to save up for furniture and things. Frank was an only child and despite the fact that Mrs Woodward was a widow, they had a comfortable home.

In the Campbell household it was Dee's commercial course at Machin and Harpers Secretarial College that was the topic of interest. The course, which Bob had saved up for, would last nine months and although the girls only attended in the mornings they were expected to learn their shorthand strokes and grammalogues and if possible practise their touch typing each afternoon or evening. Flo had managed to find an old Underwood typewriter in a second-hand shop and so Dee spent at least an hour a day hammering away on its ancient keys in her bedroom. She had had to make a sort of apron that fastened with two pieces of ribbon at the back of the machine, which covered both her hands and the keys and she diligently practised learning the position of all the keys from her instruction manual.

Thankfully she had managed to keep her Saturday job at Boots which helped with the new clothes she felt she needed as all the other students were smartly dressed. In fact 'Appearance and Behaviour' had been the subject of an entire morning session.

In December when Dee and Jean were getting ready to go to the cinema to see Charlton Heston in *Ben Hur*, which they'd been told was a fantastic film and bound to win a few Oscars, Jean confided that Margaret had bought an outfit and some new underwear, which she was calling her 'trousseau', from the Freeman's catalogue run by one of the girls she worked with; she was paying it off each week. She had also seen a wedding dress in a small shop next to Owen Owen's in Clayton Square. She wanted a short veil and a head-dress of artificial flowers. She'd also seen a pair of white stilettos with pointed toes and a bow on the front in Saxone which would finish the ensemble off. Ada had gone with her and the dress had been ordered and paid for, Harry having had a bit of a win on a horse.

'Won't she freeze in white lace at the end of January?' Dee asked as Jean sat at the small dressing table in Dee's bedroom applying yet another coat of Max Factor's black mascara to her eyelashes, a procedure which entailed wetting the block of mascara and then coating the bristles of the small brush that was provided and applying it carefully.

'I did say that a heavy satin would be warmer but I was ignored, as usual. We'll both freeze because I'm to have something similar in lemon lace. *Lemon*, on me! I ask you. It's a colour I never wear, it makes me look washed-out. It would look great on you.'

'Did you get no say in it?'

'Fat chance! Mam said it's *her* big day, I'm to have what she chooses. It's a terrible waste because I'll never wear it again and it's going to cost two guineas. Da's not very happy as Mam's spent all his winnings.'

'You could dye it. There're those Dylon cold-water dyes now.'

Jean brightened. 'I could. Maybe I'll dye it black. I suit black and a little black dress will take you anywhere.'

Dee laughed. 'Where do we go that calls for black lace dresses? We're too young for clubs and hotels and the like.'

'There's always the Grafton and the Locarno. When we get this flaming wedding over and done with, we'll have a really good night out. We can start saving up after Christmas.'

Dee's eyebrows rose. 'Just don't ask me to go to the Loc, it's a right rough house! There are always gangs of Teddy boys outside and so all the fellers are searched before they go in for flick knives and other weapons.'

'Well, the Grafton then? They usually have something special on for Saturday nights.'

'If we haven't moved, that is,' Dee reminded her.

'No one's heard anything more about that yet. Mam says she thinks it will be another year before we have to start packing up – hopefully. She says she's got enough on her plate with this wedding, although it's not going to be much of a do as far as I can see. After the church bit everyone's coming back to our house. No reception in a hotel or even a room over a pub because our Margaret says she doesn't want Da's hard-earned money wasted on booze for half the neighbourhood when Mam could make better use of it when we actually do move.'

'She's got very sensible and considerate all of a sudden,' Dee remarked.

'She's got flaming miserable all of a sudden, that's what I say. Anyway, Mam said we'd never live it down if people weren't asked in for a drink so I suppose there will be a bit of a knees-up. Would your Graham and his mates come and provide some music?'

Dee grinned. 'You mean the Flatliners Skiffle Group?'

Jean nodded, giving her hair a last quick spray of lacquer.

'I suppose so, but I've never heard them play. They could be terrible. We might be better off with records,' Dee warned.

'They can't be all *that* bad. They've played in a couple of coffee bars.'

'I don't think they've ever played in the same one twice though, but I'll ask him. Don't go telling your mam they're great, just remember our Graham is no Lonnie Donegan!'

Jean frowned. 'They won't expect to get paid, will they?'

'I've no idea. If they're going to ask for money I'll

just tell him it can be their wedding present to your Margaret and Frank Woodward. Now, do you think we can get a move on or we're going to miss the start of the film?'

When the girls had gone out Flo went down to see Ada and found her old friend sitting at the kitchen table with a writing pad and pen, her forehead creased in lines of concentration.

'It's not like you to be writing letters, Ada,' she commented, pulling out a chair and sitting down.

'If it was just a letter I wouldn't be so mithered. No, it's lists for our Margaret's wedding. Now that the dresses are ordered I thought I'd better get down to business.'

'I thought you said you were going to have the do here in the house?'

Ada nodded. 'We are. Thank God she doesn't want anything fancy. It would make a big hole in my savings for stuff for the new house. So, it's just family and friends and of course we'll have to have the neighbours in the evening.'

Flo smiled. 'I'll give you a hand to move stuff around when the time comes and I'll go with you for your outfit.'

Ada smiled back. 'I'd be glad of that, Flo, luv. I always think two heads are better than one for things like that.' She shook her head a little ruefully. 'Do you remember when Harry and me got married, Flo? My poor mam, God rest her, was so hard up she had to borrow a coat and hat.'

'I remember it well, Ada. It was my mam's only decent hat she borrowed. There wasn't much money around in Napier Street in the twenties and thirties when we were growing up. Half the men in this city were out of work.'

Ada had put down the pen and had a faraway look in her eyes. 'Old Mrs Fallon lent her the curtains from her parlour windows for the occasion; we had none.'

'And I walked to work instead of getting the tram and did without my bit of carry-out for lunch to help to save the money for a decent dress so I could stand for you,' Flo added. 'Times were really hard when we were young, Ada. There were a lot of kids in our class who came to school barefoot.'

'Thank God we at least had shoes.'

'And thank God things are so much better now. We can put decent meals on the table, we've got fairly comfortable homes and we can give our girls a good start. Your Margaret will have a far better wedding than either of us had.'

Ada picked up the pen again and sighed. 'Right. Now, there's the flowers, she'll have to have at least two cars, I'll have to order a cake . . .'

'I'll put the kettle on while you start with the guest list, Ada, and go on from there,' Flo suggested, getting to her feet. This would be a big occasion for her friend and she would help out as much as she could.

The weather towards the end of January was bitterly cold and on the morning of the wedding it was bright and sunny but the light dusting of snow that had fallen during the night had frozen, making the pavements treacherous for pedestrians. As Flo made her way gingerly down the street to help Ada set the table and lay out the refreshments, she was doubting the wisdom of Margaret's choice of a lace wedding dress.

'It's nice and bright but the roads are like glass, Ada,' she announced, entering the kitchen and noticing that at least this morning it was tidy, although privately she wondered just how they were going to fit everyone in. Of course she and Ada had cleared out most of the furniture from the small parlour but it would still be a terrible crush.

'I told her to put a vest on under that dress but she'll have none of it. She'll be going off on her honeymoon with pneumonia, you mark my words, Flo. Our Jean said she's going to wear a white cardigan over her dress and she doesn't care what it looks like, she'll take it off when she gets to the church,' Ada informed her, looking harassed.

'I shouldn't think it will be very warm in there either. Where is Jean?'

'Upstairs doing the bride's hair. Thank God I had the sense to put a hairnet over mine last night, all it will need now is a bit of a brush before I put the hat on.'

Flo began to lay out Ada's best dishes and her own, which Dee and Davie had brought down last night. The trestle table had been covered with a clean white sheet over which Jean and Margaret had quite artistically laid wide strips of blue and silver ribbon.

There were sandwiches and sausage rolls and small pork pies cut in half, all garnished with bits of parsley and covered with clean, damp tea towels. There were small side bowls containing pickled onions, Branston pickle and pickled red cabbage. There were also plates of small fancy cakes and two big dishes of sherry trifle. The two-tiered iced wedding cake on its hired silver stand had pride of place in the centre of the table.

'At least you've got that nice wool costume so you won't be cold, Ada. I always think that russet brown is such a *warm*-looking colour and it goes lovely with cream.'

Ada nodded, looking pleased. It had been a bargain in Blackler's department for the 'fuller figure'. It had been a sample, the assistant had informed her. 'I've had Harry's suit and overcoat cleaned and his shirt has been washed and ironed. Our Peter has polished his shoes so he should look presentable.'

'Dee's got her new red coat and that red and black check dress she made looks well on her. She's got a black pillbox hat and black patent shoes – mind you, she'll have to take care she doesn't break her neck on those stiletto heels. I honestly don't know how these young girls walk in them, Ada, and they have a habit of getting stuck in gratings and in the old tram lines. At least Margaret's got the cars to take you all up to the church and then bring you back here.'

'I'll bank the range up before we leave so it will be nice and warm for when we get back and Dora Bellingham from number ten is going to come in and heat up the soup. A bowl of hot soup will go down a treat on a day like this. Now, I think that's just about all we can do for now. I'd better go and see how they're all getting on up there. What time are your Graham and his mates going to arrive?'

'About half past six, I think, and I've already told him that we don't want to listen to all this modern stuff. "Mam, we can play things other than 'Rock Island Line' and 'Cumberland Gap'," he says, so I told him they'd better play something a bit more "traditional" for us older ones,' Flo informed her friend before tying on her headscarf and buttoning up her coat, ready to go home and chivvy her own family along. They all had to be at the church before eleven o'clock and it was fast approaching ten now. She hoped Margaret had a good warm coat for the honeymoon in Morecambe for the weather wasn't showing much sign of getting any better, she mused as she made her way back up the street.

By eight o'clock that evening the party was in full swing. The new Mrs Woodward, still in her wedding dress but now minus her veil and head-dress, was dancing happily with Frank while his mother was sitting in an armchair in the corner of the room chatting happily with Dora Bellingham, whose mother she had known years ago. Graham and his mates had been installed in the parlour and, despite Flo's advice, were sticking to Lonnie Donegan's repertoire, to which the younger element was responding enthusiastically.

In the narrow hallway Fred Harper, Jack Daly, Ernie Kemp, Ted Bellingham, Bob Campbell and the bride's father were discussing the merits – and demerits – of various members of Everton Football Club, pint glasses in their hands.

'I tell you, Ernie, that feller couldn't kick a ball into the goal even if the posts were as wide as the Mersey estuary! He's as much use as a wet *Echo*!' Ted Bellingham pontificated.

'It was the ref's fault, Ted! Me brother yelled himself hoarse. "Put yer bloody specs on, ref!" and "Get that feller a white stick!" he bawled,' Ernie replied.

Ted continued, 'And as for that long streak of misery on the wing, acting on he's injured when he was only tripped up! The feller behind me had the right idea about him. "Hit him with yer handbag! Yer big tart!"'

Bob grinned. 'Ah, well, lads, there's always next week. Anyone for a refill?'

This query was greeted enthusiastically. 'I'll come with you, Bob,' Fred Harper offered. 'We'll have a job to fight our way back without spilling anything.'

'And will yer tell your Graham and the lads to either play something quieter or give it a rest altogether for a bit. I can hardly hear meself speak,' Harry added, grinning. He'd already had what Ada would consider to be far too many pints.

When the two men reappeared and the band had decided to take a break, talk turned to matters of work and Bob's opinion was sought about the rumoured new working practices that might be introduced. He was a foreman on the docks, after all.

'I only know as much as you. The management's not known for confiding in the likes of us,' he answered Ernie Kemp.

'True enough, but you would give us the nod, like, if you do hear anything?' Ernie pressed.

'We're working at full capacity. I can't see that there should be any worries about lay-offs.'

'Christ! Don't even mention the word. We don't want to go back to the bad old days. Lay-offs, strikes, lockouts, that's what went on when we all first started. Nothing got really settled until the war and then we had to work day and night to keep things going. "Reserved Occupation"! Oh, aye, they bloody needed the dockers then.'

The others nodded in agreement and Bob frowned. He hated any talk of the war but it wasn't just because of the terrible images of collapsing, burning buildings and dead and injured civilians, or the violent explosions that rocked the city and the noise of the anti-aircraft guns. He had other memories that he wanted to forget.

'Da, can we squeeze through, please?' Dee's voice thankfully put an end to the conversation.

'What's up, Jean? The happy couple aren't leaving already, are they?' Harry demanded of his daughter who was following Dee.

'No. But it's so hot and crowded in the kitchen that we've come to sit on the stairs. Mam and all the other women are in there and they'd give you a headache.'

Harry grinned at her. 'Ah, take no notice. Leave them to their jangling.'

'I'd stay out of Mam's way if I were you,' Jean warned. At the rate he was going her da would be collapsed in a heap before the bride and groom left.

'How much has he had?' Dee whispered as they settled themselves on the stairs after chasing off some of the younger kids who had been perched there.

'Too much. She'll kill him and so will our Margaret if he disgraces them in front of Mrs Woodward,' Jean replied darkly, handing Dee a bottle of Babycham. 'I managed to get us both one.'

'Thanks. It's not bad, better than sherry,' Dee remarked after taking a sip.

'Push up, girls!' Graham Campbell instructed as he and his mates joined them. 'Da told us to give it a break for a while, some of the old ones were complaining about the noise. Not very grateful, are they, considering we're playing for free.'

'Well, Mam did tell you there would be no money involved,' Dee reminded him. 'Think of it as good practice.'

'I think you're quite good,' Jean added and was rewarded by grateful looks.

'I think that when you start up again you should play something they can all have a bit of a waltz to. Get the women out of the kitchen and slow down the drinking there.' Dee indicated with her head the group of men, which included her father, although she had never in her life seen her father the worse for drink.

Graham grinned at his sister. 'Ah, leave the fellers alone, they're enjoying themselves.'

Dee laughed. 'Trust you to side with Da.'

'Well, us men have to stick together. I bet the women are all pulling us to bits something shocking back there in the kitchen.'

'Don't they always?' Jean said flatly before asking Graham just what they did intend to play that would keep their parents happy.

The older women had the kitchen to themselves and had settled down with a freshly made pot of tea to discuss the events of the day. Ada had finally discarded her new hat – it had been carefully placed on the top of the dresser so nothing unfortunate could happen to it – and Flo had eased off her shoes, which had started to pinch.

'You'll never get them back on again, Flo,' Betty Kemp said knowingly.

Flo rubbed her big toe. 'I'm not bothered, Betty. I'll walk home in my stockinged feet if I have to.'

'Just take care none of those fools out there in the lobby step on you,' Madge warned. 'Both our Jack and your Harry have had more than enough.'

Ada nodded. 'I'm past caring, Madge. I'm just glad everything has gone off so well. She can't say we didn't give her a good send-off.'

'Better than most of us had,' Dora put in, handing around the cups of tea.

'You know, Ada, I was just thinking that this will probably be the last celebration we'll have in this street.

In some ways it's a real shame that we're all being moved,' Elsie said.

'A real shame! Are you mad, Elsie? I'm really looking forward to going and I've almost saved up the deposit for a new three-piece suite,' Betty informed them.

'What I meant was that we've had some good times in Cobden Street. Weddings, births, the VE Day party. That was a really great night.'

The others nodded.

'Do you remember us all scratching around for stuff to make sandwiches and cakes?' Dora asked.

'And spending hours making all that red, white and blue bunting to decorate the street?' Flo added. 'And that feller at the pub providing the ale.'

'And Nellie Stanwick, God rest her, belting out all the old songs on their piano that the fellers had dragged into the street,' Betty said happily.

'Ah, now, don't go getting all sentimental!' Ada interrupted. 'There were funerals, times when money was very scarce, these old houses were freezing in winter and we had to take the washing down to the washhouse in the pouring rain and break our backs scrubbing and cleaning to try to keep things half decent. I won't be sorry to leave all that behind.'

Betty was about to reply when young Tommy Harper staggered into the kitchen looking decidedly pale.

'What's up with you?' Elsie demanded.

'I feel terrible, Mam, honestly!'

Elsie was on her feet. 'Just what have you been up

to? I thought you and Davie and Peter have been very quiet.'

Tommy looked sheepish. 'It was just for a bit of a laugh, Mam!'

Ada too got up. 'What was? Where's our Peter?'

'In the yard and it wasn't my idea, Mrs Williams.'

Elsie grabbed her son by the shoulder. 'What's been going on out there?'

'It was just bits in bottles that had been left, Mam. We didn't take no full ones.'

'Do you know what they've been doing, Elsie? The little horrors have been drinking the dregs left in the beer bottles,' Ada announced before going through the scullery and into the back yard, followed by the others.

Peter Williams was half sitting, half lying against the yard wall and young Davie Campbell was standing beside him, swaying slightly and looking green.

'In the name of God, would you look at the cut of him!' Ada exploded.

'It wasn't my idea, Mam. Pete said seeing as everyone else had a drink we should . . . Oh, Mam!' Davie Campbell clutched his stomach and was promptly sick.

Flo glared at him. 'You disgusting little horror! I'm going to get your Da out here to sort you out!' She turned to Ada. 'I'm so sorry, luv. I'll get Bob to sort him out and then I'll get a bucket of water and clean up the mess. I'm mortified!'

'And you can send Harry out here too, he can deal with meladdo there,' Ada snapped. She too was mortified by her son's behaviour.

When Flo went inside she found Dee and Jean in the kitchen and Graham and his mates could be heard tuning up in the parlour.

'What's the matter, Mam? Why are you all out in the yard?' Dee asked, seeing the expression on her mother's face.

'Is your da still in the lobby? Our Davie, Peter and Tommy have disgraced themselves! They're drunk, the three of them.'

'Who got them in that state?' Dee demanded.

'They've been drinking all the dregs people have left and to cap it all our Davie's been sick all over the yard. I'll kill him! Your Peter can't stand up and Tommy Harper looks as if he'll be sick too any minute,' Flo fumed.

Dee and Jean exchanged glances. 'I'll go and get Da. We don't want to spoil Margaret's day. They'll be leaving soon for the honeymoon.'

'I'll come with you but I don't think Da's in any fit state himself to deal with our Peter,' Jean said darkly.

When informed of the condition of the three young miscreants Bob immediately took charge. 'I'll sort this out. Harry, you'll have to stay here to wave Frank and Margaret off or they'll know something is wrong. Jean, you tell Ada to come back inside. I'll get Peter up to bed and then I'll take our Davie home. There's no use bawling them out, I doubt they'll even remember it, but by God I'll have a few words to say to our Davie in the morning!'

'Thanks, Bob. Know . . . can . . . rely on you.' Harry

was hanging on to the banister rail and Jean raised her eyes to the ceiling.

'And if they think they feel ill now it's nothing to how they'll feel tomorrow!' Fred Harper added, following Bob and the girls towards the kitchen.

Bob hoisted a now unconscious Peter over his shoulder. 'Don't worry, Ada, I'll see to him. Then I'll be back to take that young hooligan home.'

'Da's in no fit state himself, Mam,' Jean informed her mother. 'You go back in, we don't want our Margaret to get upset. She's in the parlour so she won't see anything.'

Flo cast her friend a sympathetic glance as Fred took charge of his son and left by the back-yard door. Dee sighed. 'I'll give you a hand to clean this up, Mam,' she offered as Jean steered her furious mother back towards the scullery door.

'Thank God at least we can rely on your da, Dee,' Ada said over her shoulder.

'Amen to that,' Flo replied, rolling her sleeves up and looking around for Ada's yard brush and a bucket.

'Well, those three won't forget this wedding for a long time,' Dee said grimly.

Chapter Five

———◆———

THE LETTER ANNOUNCING THE date and details of the move to Kirkby finally came in the middle of September. Jean was doing very well with her training and Dee had finished her course and had obtained a job as a shorthand typist in the offices of a shipping company in India Buildings. She earned a wage of five pounds a week which, she had been informed, would increase to six pounds ten shillings after she had completed a year and her work was deemed satisfactory. At college she had been warned that she would be classed as a 'Junior' until she was eighteen so she hadn't been expecting much more.

'It's not bad to start with, Flo,' Ada had commented when Flo had passed on the information.

Flo still had mixed feelings about the move though Ada was looking forward to it, but both had done some careful planning and budgeting to ensure that when they finally reached their new homes there would be money available for new curtains and the extra furniture they would require, although Ada said she was certain she would still have a couple of rooms that would look a bit bare. It would help if Harry didn't insist on his bit of pocket money for beer and cigarettes and then there was the money he wasted on the horses. Flo was thankful that Bob had never smoked and only ever gambled on the Grand National and the Derby and then it was only a couple of shillings each way. She knew she could always rely on Bob, he'd never let her down or caused her any worry, everything he did was for the family. He did enjoy a few pints occasionally, but she couldn't complain about that and he earned more than Harry Williams. Now Dee would be earning too, which would help, as did the money Graham gave her for his keep. Ada had lost what Margaret had contributed when she'd got married.

'We'll manage, Ada. At least all our new rooms won't look cluttered.' Flo looked around her small kitchen. With the crockery, pans and utensils, the coal scuttle, fire irons, Davie's comics and toys, the books on gardening that Bob had started borrowing from the library, Dee's paper patterns and magazines and Graham's copies of *Mersey Beat*, it never seemed to be as tidy as she would have wished. 'Sometimes this place looks like a junk shop. In the new house I fully intend to keep all the kitchen things in the kitchen and make the kids keep all their stuff in their own bedrooms. I'll get one of those new coffee tables so Bob can keep his books on that.'

'It sounds very nice, Buttermere Close,' Ada said, rereading the letter from the Housing Department. She was very thankful that both she and Flo were to have houses in the same street, if indeed it was a street. The Williams family had been allocated number six and the Campbells number ten Buttermere Close, Northwood, Kirkby.

'It does. Bob said we might make a trip out there on Saturday afternoon just to have a look around, like. Why don't you and Harry come too?'

Ada nodded thoughtfully. 'That's a good idea. I'll tell him it's the sensible thing to do, get the lie of the land, so to speak. He can find out what number bus we have to get – and no doubt he'll want to see how far it is to the nearest pub,' she finished scathingly before getting to her feet. 'I'd best go and do something about getting the vegetables peeled. I'll have our Peter in from school before I know where I am.'

Jean had arranged to meet Dee for a cup of coffee in the Kardomah Café in Lord Street, which was about halfway between her college and Dee's office. She had been delighted that her friend had got a job but was a little envious that although she had been given a rise of one pound a week her wages were still very low compared to Dee's.

'Just think of all the things you'll be able to buy,' she'd said when Dee had told her.

'I'll have to give Mam some money for my keep and I'll have bus fares and lunches.'

'But you'll still have pounds left over. It will only

take you a couple of weeks to save up for a really good coat,' Jean had replied.

Jean found an empty table in the window and ordered a coffee. She finished a bit earlier than Dee and had taken her time walking up, looking in all the shop windows in Bold Street and Church Street on the way, but it was still a few minutes before her friend arrived.

'Well, how is it going?' she asked as Dee took off the jacket of her grey suit and placed it over the back of the chair. With the plain grey pencil skirt she wore a short-sleeved pink jumper and a pink, black and grey scarf tied loosely around her neck. Jean thought she looked very smart.

'Great. I'm getting to know everyone and where everything is. They don't seem to expect too much of me yet. I've only had half a dozen letters to do this afternoon.' She frowned. 'I hope I'm going to be kept busy or I'll lose my shorthand speed.'

'That suit looks really smart. The pink livens it up.'

Dee leaned forward and looked a little excited. 'I went out in my lunch hour today and I saw the most gorgeous suit in C&A's. It was like those Chanel suits that you see in the more expensive magazines. It was emerald green with navy braid and had a navy blouse with a floppy bow at the neck and the jacket edges were held together with a gilt bar brooch. I might get it next week. I'll have been paid twice by then and I've already got navy shoes and a navy bag. You should see the style of some of the girls in that place, especially the secretaries.'

Jean smiled wryly. 'This time next year you'll have more clothes than you know what to do with.'

Dee bit her lip. 'Don't forget there's the wear and tear on my clothes. I'll have to look smart,' she said. 'You *will* earn a good wage, Jean, and sometimes I wish I could wear an overall. If you're not careful you can get filthy from the carbon paper and when you have to change the typewriter ribbon you just can't touch anything until you've scrubbed your hands. They are literally black with ink! And don't forget now you're starting to get tips.'

'And I'm going to need most of them for the increase in bus fare,' Jean reminded her.

Dee sipped her coffee and nodded. 'Mam's talking about going out to have a look at the place at the weekend.' She grinned. 'You've got froth on your top lip.'

Jean wiped her mouth with the paper serviette. 'I wouldn't have minded going to see the place myself but I'm working, of course! Sometimes it's so dull at Sadie's. I mean, most of the customers are not exactly young.'

'I'll go with them and I can report back to you,' Dee promised.

It was a small group who boarded the bus on Saturday afternoon for Dee, Graham and Davie accompanied Flo, Bob, Ada and Harry.

'It's going to take ages. We seem to be going all round the flaming world!' Graham muttered ominously to Dee as the bus left Fazakerley Terminus. It had taken them almost half an hour to get this far.

'Don't start on about that!' she hissed back, although she was ruefully calculating how early she would have to set out to get to work on time. She had further to travel than either Jean or her brother.

The bus made its way between open fields and Flo and Ada exchanged glances but finally they reached Kirkby and both women were surprised to see the large modern housing estates, schools and rows of shops.

'I didn't realise it would be like this. It doesn't look bad at all, Ada,' Flo remarked.

'Haven't we been telling you you were worrying about nothing?' Harry said, noting that thankfully there were pubs too although not nearly as many as there were in the city itself.

When they alighted on the corner of a long road of brand new semi-detached houses Harry stopped a young girl who was passing.

'Could you tell us where Buttermere Close is, luv?'

She pointed towards the direction she'd come from. 'Just down there. It's the first on the left. Some of the houses are still empty, are you looking for someone?'

'No. We're coming to live here,' Flo informed her.

'It's not bad here. The houses are great. We come from off Scottie Road and me mam wasn't happy at first but she's got used to it now. She says she still misses Paddy's Market and she always goes into town to do the Christmas food shopping in St John's Market.'

'Where are the nearest shops?' Dee asked.

'There's some at the end of this road but most of them are in the town centre. There's one of those new supermarkets there and there's a great market too on a Saturday, the stuff's dead cheap. It's not far on the bus. I'd best get off now. Ta-ra then.'

Dee grinned at her mother. 'That sounds good, Mam. We never had a supermarket before.'

'I've heard that those places just encourage you to spend more than you intended to,' Ada remarked darkly as they walked in the direction of their new homes. All their lives they had shopped daily in the small local shops and both she and Flo were suspicious of change.

'Oh, Mam, this is just great!' Dee exclaimed as they walked up the cul-de-sac that was Buttermere Close. 'Look at the big windows, we'll get plenty of light in all the rooms.'

'You have to admit, Flo, it's really lovely and quiet and everything is so fresh-looking,' Ada added.

'And each one's got its own back garden. That one's even got a tree in it! I hope ours has got a tree too, Pete and me will be able to climb it,' Davie enthused.

'And you'll probably fall out and break your neck! Besides, your da has plans for the garden,' Flo informed her son. But she had caught Ada's enthusiasm – compared to Cobden Street, Buttermere Close looked so clean, so much more refined.

'I've always wanted a bit of a vegetable patch,' Bob mused. The houses certainly were a huge improvement on those in Cobden Street. It was a pity they didn't yet have the keys, he would have liked to have looked around inside.

The same thought had occurred to Ada but she wasn't going to let it prevent her from going and peering in through the windows of number six. 'Come and have a look through the windows, Flo. At least we can see what the kitchen and the front room are like.'

The two women felt quite elated as they walked up the path. They had to stand on tiptoe to see into the kitchen but glimpsing the light-coloured walls and the units with their worktops and the modern stainless-steel sink the two women cried out with delight.

'Oh, Flo, just look at all those gorgeous matching units with Formica tops! No more mismatched cupboards or old food presses and that sink is positively *sparkling*!'

'Look at the cooker, Ada! No more having to rake out the old range or blacklead it. Just a wipe with the dishcloth to keep it clean and I'm sure there's enough room for a small table and chairs.'

Ada couldn't believe their good fortune, in fact she felt quite dizzy. 'It's just like a little palace, Flo, that's what it is!'

Dee and her father peered into the front room.

'Look, Da, it's got a modern tiled fireplace and isn't it *huge*?' Dee exclaimed.

'It won't look quite as huge when the furniture is in but it's a very good size.'

'Our carpet is going to look like a postage stamp in there.' She laughed but her father had turned away and was looking speculatively at the small patch of garden, already planning on where he would put some rose bushes.

'Wait until I tell Jean all about it.'

He nodded. 'It's really lovely and I'm so happy your mam seems to think so, that's the main thing. She deserves a decent place to live after all these years.'

Dee slipped her arm through his. 'So do you, Da. You've worked hard to keep us all and you've always given us the best you could afford.'

He sighed heavily. 'It's the least I could do in the circumstances.'

Dee looked up at him, puzzled. She thought it an odd thing to say and she thought she'd heard a note of what sounded like guilt in his voice. Or had it just been regret that they hadn't had a house like this years ago?

Seeing the expression on his daughter's face, Bob pulled himself together. He smiled at her, looking more cheerful. 'Right then, I suggest we have a walk to see how far the local shops are and then we can ask where the school is, not that our Davie will be too keen to find out about that.'

It was certainly much quieter, she thought as they walked down the road, but they'd all get used to it in time. They would all have to look on it as a fresh start.

The peace of Buttermere Close was looking increasingly appealing, Dee thought on the morning of their departure from Cobden Street as she helped Flo to move the tea chests and cardboard boxes into the lobby so the removal men, aided by her father, could load them on to the lorry.

'I just hope you can remember where everything is, Mam, when we get to the new house. I did suggest marking each box,' she reminded Flo as they manhandled a tea chest containing pots and pans through the doorway.

'Oh, it just seemed like extra work but now I'm beginning to think you were right, Dee. I wonder will we ever get ourselves sorted out,' Flo replied distractedly.

Dee grinned at her. 'Of course we will, Mam. There's so much more space.'

Through the open front door they could hear the activity in the street outside. Quite a few families had already gone and everyone had turned out to wave them off and today it was the turn of the Williams, the Dalys and of course themselves.

'The lads want to know is there very much more, Flo?' Bob called as he picked up three large boxes.

'About four more tea chests and some suitcases and the mop and brushes, they wouldn't fit in anywhere,' Flo replied, pushing a wisp of hair out of her eyes.

Jean appeared in the doorway. 'Mrs Campbell, Mam said have you got any string or is it packed?'

Flo looked at her, harassed. 'Ask our Davie, he was in charge of tying things up, he's good with knots, that's if you can find him. How are things going at your house, Jean?'

Jean rolled her eyes. 'Don't ask! It's bedlam down

there. Our Peter's getting under everyone's feet and our Margaret's turned up to help although I'd say she is more of a hindrance. When I left she was going on at Mam for throwing some of her old things out. She didn't want them, she wouldn't take them with her to Frank's, so what was Mam supposed to do? Our removal van is supposed to be coming after lunch but Mam's nowhere near ready. I've got all my stuff packed and I've done as much to help as I can but you know Mam, always on the last minute.'

'She'll manage, she always does. We'll arrive before you so tell her to come down to me for a cup of tea before she starts unpacking,' Flo instructed.

Dee laughed. 'That's if we've managed to find the kettle, the teapot and the cups by then.'

Davie appeared at the top of the stairs clutching the box into which he'd packed all his books and comics.

'Be careful you don't fall with that and when you've taken it out to the van will you find some string for Mrs Williams?' Flo instructed her son.

'Won't it seem strange waking up tomorrow in a different house?' Jean said to Dee as Davie went in search of the string.

Dee smiled and Flo paused. 'I suppose it will.' She glanced around the dim, narrow hallway still half full of their belongings. It looked so small and dilapidated. 'You know, Jean, your mam and me have some fond memories of these old houses. When I was waving Betty Kemp off last week I got a lump in my throat thinking of how in a few months everything will be just rubble. It will look as if no one has ever lived here. One part of me will be sad to leave.'

'Oh, Mam! Don't go talking like that. Think about the future, we're going to a lovely new house,' Dee urged.

Jean too smiled at the older woman. 'Dee's right, Mrs Campbell, just think about your gorgeous new kitchen. I'd better get back now before Mam and our Margaret come to blows. See you later on in Buttermere Close!'

Dee squeezed her mother's hand. 'It's going to be great, Mam, just wait and see.'

Part II

Part II

Chapter Six

<hr />

1962

THE CONDUCTOR HELPED BOTH Flo and Ada off the bus with their bags of shopping.

Ada thanked him before turning to her friend as they started to walk home. 'If we didn't have to feed that lot we'd be rich, Flo.'

Flo nodded in agreement. 'Still, prices aren't too bad at the market and I got two pairs of stockings for Dee for one and six a pair. They're normally three shillings.'

'Make sure you get the money for them. I could do with every penny if we're going to get a television set for this Christmas.' It was a source of irritation to her that despite the fact that she now had a fridge and a twin-tub washing machine, all on hire purchase, Flo also had both appliances and a television set. Of course Bob had a better job and she had Dee's and Graham's

73

money coming in regularly while she had the whole family to keep on just Harry's wage and the bit Jean gave her. She'd been nagging Harry for ages to go and see about getting a job in one of the factories on the industrial estate. There were plenty of jobs to be had and she'd heard that the money was far better than anything you could earn on the docks but he was reluctant, saying he was too old to change his habits now.

In the two years since they'd been rehoused both women had come to feel they had been very fortunate. Of course things were much better now. The slum areas of the city were being cleared and new houses and flats built, jobs were plentiful, wages were higher and the days of rationing were a distant memory. The country was finally beginning to recover from the disastrous war years, although the precarious state of peace was foremost in everyone's mind at the moment as relations between Russia and America were verging on the downright hostile over both Berlin, where the Russians had blockaded the city, and Cuba where there were now Russian missiles sited just miles off the American coast.

'I'm not looking that far ahead, Ada. What with those nuclear missiles in Cuba and that Mr Khrushchev telling Mr Kennedy if America attacks Cuba there will be a war. My poor nerves are in a shocking state, I can't forget the last war.'

'Harry says if they start dropping them nuclear bombs *no one* will survive this time. Look at what happened to the Japs at the end of the last war with those atom bombs.' Ada shuddered, recalling the horrors of the aftermath of the atomic attack on the cities of Hiroshima and Nagasaki. 'I don't understand it all but wouldn't you think they'd all have more sense? Everyone of our age has had enough of war; it's only the young ones who've never gone through it who don't realise what it's really like. All they're interested in is dolling themselves up and going out enjoying themselves and listening to the likes of the Beatles and Gerry and the Pacemakers and that Elvis Presley.'

Flo stopped and put down the heavy bags. 'I'll have to have a bit of a rest, Ada. My arms feel as though they're being pulled from their sockets. I should never have bought so much tinned stuff, but there was a special offer on it.'

'There's always a special offer on something in that supermarket,' Ada commented. 'Well, there's bound to be something on the news tonight about the state of things.'

'I'll send our Graham down to tell you if there's anything on the telly about it,' Flo promised, picking up her shopping again. 'How's your Margaret doing?' she asked to take their minds off the precarious state of world peace as they resumed their journey home.

'She's fine now that she's over the morning sickness stage. She'll be giving her job up in a couple of months and Frank's mam is so delighted she's going to be a granny that our Margaret doesn't have to lift a finger. Gladys Woodward's got her spoiled. Isn't it today that your Dee was going for that interview?'

Flo nodded. Unlike Harry Williams, Dee had applied for a job in a big factory on the industrial estate. There was a vacancy for a secretary to the works manager and after over two years of working for the shipping company, she felt she had enough experience to apply. She was also tired of spending all that time travelling into Liverpool, and the expense, and the wage being offered was far more than she was currently earning.

'She was going at half past ten. She's going into work this afternoon. She was owed half a day.'

'When will she know if she's got it?' Ada queried. Dee would be doing well if she got the job. A secretary, no less, and earning ten pounds a week. Jean still had another year to do as an apprentice, then two years as an improver. She couldn't look to be earning nearly as much as Dee until she was well turned twenty-two. Oh, Jean was shaping up to be a very good hairdresser, she already had some of her own customers, mainly young women, but it still rankled with Ada that she hadn't taken full advantage of the education she'd received.

'I'm not sure if they'll write and let her know or offer her it on the spot,' Flo replied as they turned into Buttermere Close. 'But I hope she's got the kettle on, I'm parched and I'm fair worn out carrying this lot.'

As she walked into the kitchen and put down the heavy bags Dee came downstairs. She had changed out of the dark green and black bouclé wool suit with the shorter-length pencil skirt and hip-length semi-fitted jacket she'd worn for her interview. The black shoes and bag and three-quarter-length black gloves she'd worn with it had been put away and now she was wearing a brown and cream checked skirt, brown jumper and chisel-toed brown shoes with a low heel. A necklace of chunky cream beads brightened the outfit up. Jean kept Dee's hair well trimmed and she straightened it each night by winding it up on big rollers (which unfortunately were not the most comfortable things to sleep in). Each morning it was back-combed, then smoothed down and held off her face with a coloured bandeau.

'The kettle has boiled, Mam. I'll make you a cup of tea and then I'll help you put all that stuff away before I go to work,' she offered.

Flo sat down thankfully on one of the chairs which matched the small Formica-topped kitchen table. 'Thanks, luv. This doing a weekly shop instead of a daily one does give me more time and it's supposed to save money, but I often think I buy more stuff than I really need.'

Peering at the amount of tins in one of the bags Dee grimaced. 'You've certainly gone a bit mad with the corned beef and luncheon meat.'

Flo nodded. 'I know, but it does come in handy for your da's carry-out, and our Graham's. How did it go, the interview?'

Dee smiled delightedly. 'Great. They were all very nice. I had to take a letter and a memo and then type them but that was no trouble. And they had a lovely brand-new Olympia typewriter too.'

'So, what did they say? Will they let you know?' Flo pressed.

'I got it, Mam! I'll have to give a week's notice so I'll be starting a week on Monday. It only took me ten minutes on the bus to get there and I'll save a fortune on fares.' She poured two cups of tea and sat down opposite her mother. 'I'll be sharing an office with the production manager's secretary but she's really nice. She's older than me. She's married but we got on great. Mrs Ellerby is her name but she said I was to call her Celia. She said I was by far the nicest of the girls who had applied and that her boss had told her that seeing as she would have to share the office, her opinion on my suitability was important. And you'll never guess, Mam? We actually have someone from the canteen who brings our tea morning and afternoon – on a tray! We have to serve it to our bosses but we get a cup too and biscuits. Talk about "coming up in the world"!'

Flo looked amazed. 'Well now! I'm delighted for you, Dee, really I am, and I'm so proud of you. Works manager's secretary, no less.' Then she frowned. 'I wouldn't go on too much about it all to Jean.'

'Oh, Mam! Jean's not like that and wasn't I delighted for her when she had the opportunity to enter that competition in Manchester for the North-West Apprentice of the Year and she was in the top three? She should have won it, in our opinion. Pauline said the girl who did win didn't have half as much flair or expertise as Jean, it was because she worked in Andre Bernard in Liverpool.'

Flo still didn't look convinced. 'Well, that's as may be but I know for a fact that Ada's never really forgiven her for not going into the civil service.'

'Jean would have *hated* the civil service and all this comparing us is just . . . nonsense!'

Flo sniffed. '*I'm* not the one who compares but you know what Ada's like.'

'Mam, it's a silly attitude to take. There will always be people who are better off or who get good jobs or who marry well – whatever that means. We should be happy with what we've got.'

Flo nodded and sighed. Dee was right but she knew Ada wouldn't look at things in that light. Even the fact that Ada was having to wait until Christmas to get a television was causing her friend some annoyance.

'Right. Let's get this stuff put away and then I'd better get going. I'll have to give in my notice but I think they already suspected I was going for an interview,' Dee said, opening one of the cupboards on the wall and putting the tinned stuff away.

When Jean arrived home later that day she found her brother diligently doing his homework in the front room, which was something new. Her mother was in the kitchen preparing the meal but looking far from pleased.

'What's up, Mam?' she asked, taking off her coat to reveal a navy overall trimmed with white. She'd soon discovered that pastel colours quickly got stained and looked shabby. Her hair was back-combed and flicked out at the sides and she wore big navy plastic earrings shaped like stars.

'I had a note from the school about meladdo in there,' Ada replied darkly.

'What's he done now?' Jean asked, easing off her shoes.

'It's more like what he hasn't done!' Ada snapped. 'Like any homework at all for the past three weeks! Just wait until your da get's in, that lad is going to get a right telling-off. He told us they'd had something called an "exemption" since half-term as Mr Rowlands, his teacher, was on jury service. The little liar! I don't know how he dreamed *that* up.'

Jean filled the kettle; she was dying for a cup of tea but it was obvious she was going to have to make it herself. 'I bet he didn't. He hasn't got either the brains or the imagination. I bet it was someone else in the class. Didn't you mention it to Mrs Campbell? Surely if it had been true their Davie wouldn't have homework either?'

Ada shook her head. The thought hadn't crossed her mind. She went to the kitchen door. 'If he carries on like this he'll finish up as thick as the wall and then all he'll be fit for is the dole or worse!' she uttered loudly so her errant son in the front room would hear her words.

'He won't try that on again, Mam. Not now he knows they'll send a note home. Do you know how Dee got on at the interview?'

'No, I haven't heard, but she'll probably get the job. Set the table for me, luv?

'I hope she does. She won't have as far to travel,' Jean replied.

'Isn't that something I keep telling your da,' Ada retorted.

Jean could see that nothing would please her mother in the mood she was in so she set the table in silence and then went in to remonstrate with her younger brother.

'What's wrong with you?' she demanded. 'You've gone and put Mam in a terrible mood. Surely to God you didn't think you'd get away with such a pack of lies?'

Peter Williams looked up at her with indignation. 'It wasn't all lies! Mr Rowlands *was* on jury service – well, when we were on half-term he was and Johnny Arkwright said we could get a couple more weeks out of it.'

'And I suppose if Johnny Arkwright told you to put your hand in the fire you'd do it?' Jean snapped.

'I'm not that daft!' her brother protested.

'Really?' Jean replied sarcastically. 'Well, you're in for it when Da get's home.'

'Da always goes to the pub on Fridays,' Peter reminded her.

'So?'

'Well, he's always in a better mood when he gets home.'

Jean shook her head. 'I wouldn't bank on it. If there's no good news on this Russia/America thing they'll all be in terrible moods. I know Mam's worried to death so you picked a bad time to misbehave.'

Peter chewed the end of his pencil. He hadn't thought of that. All his mates were wondering if there would be another war. They'd grown up listening to tales of the last one and watching films like *The Dam Busters* and viewed it as exciting, but the adults didn't seem to think so at all.

The news that evening was better than anyone had expected as the world took a step back from the brink of nuclear war. Nikita Khrushchev had announced that the Russian missiles deployed in Cuba would be dismantled and shipped back to the USSR.

Ada had heard it on the news on the radio but Bob Campbell had come himself to relay the BBC Television's bulletin to her.

'Thanks be to God! My nerves have been strung out like piano wires for days,' she told him.

'It's been terrifying all right. I've been trying not to think too much about it. War is terrible, it changes people. People act out of character, do things they'd never do in normal times. All of us who came through the Blitz know we wouldn't have had a hope in hell's chance of surviving a war like that, Ada.'

'And I still have the occasional nightmare about the Blitz,' she confided. 'Do you think those fools down the pub will have heard?'

'Bound to. News like that travels fast,' Bob replied.

Ada cast her eyes to the ceiling. 'Then I suppose he'll be late. He'll have something to celebrate.'

'We all have, Ada,' he reminded her.

After he'd gone Ada thought how considerate he'd

been to come and put her mind at rest but that was Bob Campbell all over. He was steady and reliable and she had great respect for him. He was a saint compared to Harry – Flo was certainly fortunate.

When Harry finally arrived home, somewhat the worse for wear, Ada shook her head in resignation. 'Don't tell me – you were celebrating the news! Well, your dinner's ruined but that's not my affair. I suggest you get to bed and sleep it off,' she snapped.

Harry grinned at her lopsidedly. 'Yer're lucky to get me home this early, Ada, luv.'

'Don't you "Ada, luv" me! There's "celebrating" and "celebrating" and you always take it one step too far!'

Harry hung on to the back of the armchair for support. 'It's not every day that a man get's a bit of luck . . . like . . . like what I've had.' He was trying not to slur his words.

Ada was getting exasperated. 'What bit of luck?'

'Ask me who's won the Irish Sweepstake?'

She stared at him hard. 'What?'

'Me! I have! We're in the money, girl! I've won a thousand pounds!'

Jean gave a shriek and jumped to her feet. 'Da, you're not making this up, are you?'

'Would I make . . . make something like that up?' Harry protested.

Jean grabbed her mother around the waist. 'Mam! Mam! He *won*, he's really WON all that money!'

Ada could hardly take it in. 'Glory be to God! A *thousand* pounds!'

Jean caught her father's arm and pulled both her parents into an impromptu dance. 'We're rich! We're rich!'

Ada began to laugh. 'I'll never moan about your gambling again, Harry, and I think we can overlook your little "celebration" tonight.'

Jean laughed with her. 'We'll have our own celebration, Mam. Where's the sherry bottle?'

Harry slumped down on the sofa, grinning at them both. 'Didn't I tell you I'd win a fortune one of these days? But don't be giving me none of that sherry, it tastes like paint stripper!'

Ada beamed at him. 'It's "paint stripper" or nothing.'

Harry capitulated. 'Ah, just a drop then to help me sleep.'

Jean shrieked with laughter. 'When have you ever needed anything to help you sleep, Da?'

Ada looked totally bemused. 'Well, I'm going to have a large glass, I'll never sleep tonight I'm so excited. I can't get over it, I really can't! Us having a *thousand* pounds! We'll never be hard up again!'

Chapter Seven

———

DEE COULDN'T BELIEVE IT when Jean told her the news, having run the short distance to the Campbells' house next morning before she left for work.

'You're joking? A *thousand* pounds? On the Irish Sweepstake?'

'It's true! I can't take it in myself and Mam said she hasn't had a wink of sleep all night what with Da snoring his head off and her thinking what would be best to do with the money. I've been awake too, I'm just so excited! I feel as if I'm on cloud nine!'

Dee hugged her friend. 'Oh, that's great news, Jean!'

Flo looked amazed but delighted. 'Well, you just never know the minute! She won't have to wait until Christmas to get that television set now – but she doesn't want to go mad with the money.'

Jean nodded. 'That's exactly what she said to Da this

morning, although I don't think he was in a fit state to be taking much notice of her. So, we're going to have a bit of a family conference about it tonight. Well, I'd better dash off now or I'll be late.'

After she'd gone Flo turned to her husband, who looked as stunned as she felt. 'I must go down to congratulate Ada.'

'I'll call in to see if she'll let him out later tonight, after the family conference, so I can stand him a celebratory drink. It's not every day your mate comes into a fortune and I'm delighted for them,' Bob said, kissing Flo on the cheek.

By the time Flo had cleared up and got through all the essential chores it was nearly midday. Peter Williams, his misdemeanour forgotten in the excitement, had spent most of the morning in Flo's kitchen telling young Davie what he expected for Christmas, now that his da had plenty of money.

'Do you think they'll move, Mam? Buy a house of their own in a good-class area of the city?' Dee asked her mother.

Flo was sceptical. 'It might seem like a fortune – and it is a lot of money – but you'd have to pay three, maybe four times that much for a house in a posh area, so I don't think that will be on the cards.'

'They could use it as a deposit on a house,' Dee replied.

'No, they won't saddle themselves with a mortgage debt like that at their age. Besides, Harry won't even change his job, let alone go taking a big step like buying a house, and can you honestly see Ada and Harry fitting in in somewhere like Childwall or Allerton or even out in Formby?'

Dee nodded, feeling quite relieved. She knew it was selfish but she didn't want her best friend to move away.

When Flo walked into Ada's kitchen she was informed that Harry had gone out for 'a hair of the dog' but with strict instructions not to be out all afternoon. He would need a clear head for important decisions were going to have to be made.

Flo hugged her old friend. 'We're all delighted for you, Ada! I have to admit that you could have knocked me over with a feather when Jean told me but congratulations! It's great news! And that lad of yours seems to have a good idea of what he wants,' she added as Ada filled the electric kettle.

'What he wants and what he gets are two different things!' Ada replied. 'I'm that excited I've hardly had a wink of sleep, Flo, thinking about it. It's a huge weight off my shoulders knowing we'll have no more money worries and will be able to afford things I never dreamed of being able to buy outright and not on hire purchase.'

'And did you come up with any ideas about what to do with it?' Flo sat down at the kitchen table as Ada put two mugs, the bag of sugar and the milk bottle on the table. Flo smiled to herself, thinking how well the milk bottle and bag of sugar would look on the table in a house in the likes of Childwall. Ada didn't go in much for niceties such as milk jugs or sugar basins.

'The first thing is to decide how much of it we should save. I know Harry, he'll go spending it like it was water and it won't last for ever! Then we should give some to our Margaret, to help with the baby, like. She'll miss her wages when she gives up work.'

Flo nodded and stirred her tea thoughtfully. Ada was being sensible, but then, like themselves, the Williamses had never had much money to spare. 'You can get your television set now. That won't make too much of a hole in it.'

'And I'll pay off all the hire purchase. I don't like being in debt, Flo. And this morning I've been thinking about our Jean. Even though I didn't want her to do it, I have to admit that she's stuck at this hairdressing—'

'And she's good at it, Ada,' Flo interrupted.

Ada nodded. 'She is. So what I'm going to suggest is that we set her up in her own business.'

This was a huge surprise to Flo. 'You mean buy her her own shop?'

'No, not *buy* somewhere. We'll rent some premises but buy all the stuff she'll need. I always wanted her to make something of herself, Flo, you know that. Look at how well your Dee's doing. I never had the opportunity or the education but she has: she's had the schooling and she's getting the training and now we have the money.'

'But Jean still has three years to do before she's qualified,' Flo reminded her friend while wondering if Ada wasn't being a bit too ambitious. You needed a good head on your shoulders to run a successful business and Jean was only nineteen.

'I'd thought of that. That Pauline she works with is fully trained, maybe she'd come and work for our Jean?'

Flo sniffed. 'I can't see Sadie Nelson being delighted about losing two of her girls.'

Ada wasn't to be deterred. 'That's not my problem. Anyway, we'll have to see what both Harry and Jean think.'

Flo got to her feet. 'No doubt Jean will be up to tell Dee all about it tomorrow, but I'm delighted for you, Ada, I really am, and you should treat yourself. You deserve it. You've thought of everyone except yourself. Get yourself a really smart winter coat and a nice hat for best. I'll go into town with you next week, if you like,' she offered.

Ada smiled at her. 'I might do that. Just think, Flo, I could even go to the likes of Hendersons or the Bon Marche! I've only ever been able to afford to shop at Blackler's or T. J. Hughes.' The thought brought a flush of pleasure to her plump cheeks that she, Ada Williams, formerly of Cobden Street, could now afford to shop in two of Liverpool's most exclusive shops.

As Flo had predicted Jean came to see her friend on Sunday morning. It was a cold but bright autumn day and they decided to go for a walk.

'Wrap up well!' Flo advised her daughter as Jean had on a black and white checked coat, black boots and gloves and a white woollen scarf wound around her neck.

They walked to the edge of the housing estate where there was a narrow path that skirted the side of an adjoining field and led through a small copse, and then back to the main road. The dead, brown and russet leaves that had fallen from the trees crunched beneath their feet and the almost bare branches stood out against the pale blue sky. It was a lovely late autumn day but neither of them really noticed.

'I'm still trying to take it all in,' Jean confided.

'You mean about them setting you up in your own business? Mam told me what your mam was planning.' It sounded very exciting to Dee but also a little daunting for someone of Jean's age.

Jean nodded. 'Mam keeps going on about me "making something of myself" and it *is* a great opportunity.'

'But?' Dee prompted.

Jean looked perturbed. 'But I'm worried that I haven't enough experience, and what if it's not a success? I don't want to let them down.'

'You've always said you wouldn't stay on working for Mrs Nelson after you've qualified, like Pauline has,' Dee reminded her. She could see her friend's point of view but it was an opportunity that wasn't open to many people of their class.

'I know and Mam is suggesting I ask Pauline to come and work for me so one of us will be fully qualified, but it's such a big step.' Jean kicked at small pile of leaves and they rose in a tiny dusty cloud around her feet.

'What does your da say?'

'Not much. I think Mam's already made his mind up for him. They're going to save some of it, give our Margaret something for the baby, buy a television, pay off the hire purchase and Mam's going to treat herself to a good coat, and our Peter will probably get extra stuff at Christmas.'

Dee shoved her hands more deeply into the pockets of her coat. 'Is there a sort of "time limit" on this business thing?'

Jean shrugged. 'She's talking about looking for suitable premises after Christmas.'

'Then at least you'll be able to enjoy the holiday without running around looking for shops. Look on the bright side, Jean. Just think, this time next year you could have your own shop and your own staff and customers. You'll be able to decide on things like decoration, what age group you want to appeal to . . .'

Jean brightened up at the thought. 'Young people mainly and I'd go to all the exhibitions and competitions so I'd know the latest trends.'

'And don't forget you could pay yourself a decent wage, once you got established.'

That was something Jean hadn't thought about. 'I could! Nothing mad, of course, but a lot better than I'd get from Sadie Nelson, and if I'm really successful I wouldn't have to worry about money in the future.' At last Jean began to see the positive side of this idea of her mother's.

'I think that we're both going to have a great

Christmas and New Year. I have my new job to look forward to and you'll have a new business to set up – your own business! It might well be useful for you to take some sort of course at night school to help with things like book-keeping and invoicing. I was thinking that I might go for something myself. Maybe a foreign language. We could go together.'

'What will you need a foreign language for?' Jean asked, surprised.

Dee shrugged. 'You never know. I might get the chance to travel one day or maybe get a job in an embassy. These days the opportunities are endless; one of the girls I was at college with, Anna Rimiti, got a job in the embassy in Rome. She spoke fluent Italian. She was half-Italian, her da came from Livorno originally, but she always said if you had a couple of languages you could easily work abroad. I've had a few postcards from her and she's really enjoying it.'

Jean looked at her friend closely. 'I never thought you were so ambitious.'

Dee smiled at her. 'Why not? You have to look on life as a bit of an adventure, especially when you're young.'

'Pity our Margaret didn't have the same attitude. There she is stuck in that house in Everton with Frank and his mam and now with a baby on the way. Oh, she thinks life is just great now. She can buy what she likes, Frank takes her out a couple of times a week, she's waited on hand and foot by her ma-in-law but just wait until she has the baby! All that will go out of the window.'

'That's just what I mean. She's only twenty-two and she's been nowhere, done nothing and she'll have no opportunities in the future, not bringing up a child.'

'Or children. I bet she has more than just one. I suppose we are lucky, Dee,' Jean conceded.

'Or maybe we just had a bit more sense. I'm not saying that I wouldn't get married or have children, but we don't want to end up like Margaret. We should both see a bit of life before we settle down.'

Jean felt she was right and now, the more she thought about having her own business, the more excited she was at the prospect. She would make a success of it and then she would be an independent young woman of some means. The idea appealed to her greatly. Dee was right, they should both be ambitious.

It was nearly lunchtime when they returned home and it was turning noticeably colder.

'Come in and we'll have a warm drink. Mam will have the dinner on,' Jean predicted.

The girls found Ada looking through a brochure of electrical appliances while the pans of vegetables simmered on top of the cooker and the smell of lamb roasting came from the oven. Harry was in the front room with the Sunday papers after telling his wife that a man needed some peace and quiet, even if he had just won a small fortune.

'Picking out the television set, Mrs Williams?' Dee asked, smiling.

Ada smiled back as she got to her feet to check on

the progress of the joint. 'I am and I've a busy week ahead of me.'

Dee grinned. 'Isn't it great? We're all really made up for you.'

'Has she told you about our plans for her?' Ada asked, basting the meat with a large spoon.

'Of course I have, Mam. We've been talking about it all morning. We'll start looking for suitable premises in a good area after Christmas but to start with I'm going to put an order in at the newsagents for the *Hairdressers Journal* and some other trade magazines to give me an idea about what's new in the way of equipment and how much it costs. I'll sound Pauline out about coming to work for me too. Then in January we're both going to go to night school. I'll look for a course that will be useful to help me with the business side of things and Dee's going to do a foreign language. Oh, we've both got great plans for the future, Mam,' she announced, her eyes sparkling.

Ada beamed at her, delighted she was now so enthusiastic about the whole idea. She'd seemed a bit bemused, not to say dubious, about it both last night and first thing this morning but obviously a talk with Dee had changed all that. There was no stopping the young ones these days. The thought that now they could provide for their children's future filled her with a sense of satisfaction and pride.

Chapter Eight

IN NOVEMBER DEE GOT TICKETS for her firm's annual Christmas Staff Dance and asked Jean to accompany her.

'We can take a guest and as you're my best friend I want you to come with me,' she explained.

'Is it a big posh do? Will we have to wear evening dresses?'

'From what I can gather it's quite a big occasion, all the staff go including the managers and their wives, but I don't think we'll have to wear proper evening dresses, not long ones anyway. Something "dressy", Celia advised, but we'll want to look our best so I think I'll buy something new.'

Jean nodded and then looked closely at her friend. 'I know you, Dee Campbell, you're up to something.'

Dee grinned and blushed. 'It's just a dance, Jean.'

'You can't fool me. Is there someone "special" – other than me – going too?'

Dee put down the fashion magazine she'd been idly leafing through. 'Oh, all right. There's a lad who works in the drawing office who looks nice. I've never spoken to him but Celia said his name's Billy Grainger.'

'And is he going?' Jean asked, smiling.

Dee looked a little apprehensive. 'I hope so but I don't know for certain.'

'Then why don't you ask him?'

'I can't do that! I've just told you I've never spoken to him. What would it look like? What would he think of me?'

Jean could see her point. 'Well, can't you get Celia Ellerby to make some discreet enquiries on your behalf? There's no point in buying a stunning new outfit if he's not even going to be there.'

Dee seized on the idea. She'd seen him in the staff canteen a few times and he really did look nice. This dance would be the perfect opportunity to get to speak to him and maybe have a dance with him. 'I'll see what Celia can find out.'

Jean grinned at her. 'I'm starting to look forward to this night out. I can't wait to see this Billy Grainger. I think it's going to be a great Christmas.'

Ada had bought herself a new dress and was greatly looking forward to watching the Queen's broadcast on her new television set on Christmas Day.

On Christmas Eve, after she'd got an over-excited

Peter to bed and had done as much in the way of preparation for next day's dinner as she could, Flo and Bob arrived for a celebratory drink and some mince pies.

'Doesn't the place look nice, Ada? That's a great tree,' Flo commented, congratulating her friend on the smart new red, green and gold decorations and the big Christmas tree with its tinsel and lights and baubles. Ada had got rid of all the old multi-coloured paper chains, glittery paper bells and mainly home-made tree decorations she had formerly used for the festive season.

'Harry, get Flo a Babycham and give Bob a drop of that good whiskey you bought,' Ada instructed her husband, basking in the compliment.

Young Davie Campbell had been left at home. He had been instructed that he could watch television until nine o'clock and then he was to go to bed. His older brother was to make sure he did as Graham wasn't going out that night because he had a very bad head cold and a sore throat, neither of which were very conducive to enjoying dancing the night away in the smoky atmosphere of a club. Jean and Dee had gone to the staff dance in the Cherry Tree Hotel.

'Isn't it great to be able to sit and relax in comfort for a bit?' Ada commented when everyone had a drink.

'It is but I think we deserve it after all the running around we have to do,' Flo replied. 'Remember what Christmases in Cobden Street were like, Ada? The whole family crowded together in that tiny kitchen listening to the carols on the radio? Now we're sitting in a comfortable, spacious room like this with a television, something nice to eat and drink and a bit of peace and quiet.'

'Oh, it's great to just relax, Flo. And with all the food we've prepared for tomorrow out in the kitchen where it should be,' Ada added, smiling at their good fortune.

'You'd think we were feeding an army with all the stuff she's bought,' Harry confided to Bob.

'Well, Frank is bringing our Margaret and his mam down for dinner and tea tomorrow so there won't be much left over,' Ada replied.

'The girls have been looking forward to this dance so much and I have to admit they both looked very smart. I'm sure it will be a real occasion for them but I hope they won't be too late. They'll have to get a taxi home. I told Dee under no circumstances were they to try to walk. There will be far too many drunks hanging around tonight.'

Ada nodded. 'And I want our Jean to give me a hand in the morning, there will be a lot to do.' She cast a look at the ceiling. 'And I expect meladdo up there will be up at the crack of dawn.'

Flo sipped her sweet, sparkling drink and smiled. 'I expect so, Ada. Still, Christmas is a special time for kids, that's what I always say. And this time next year we won't be getting those two lads to bed until all hours so we'd better make the most of this bit of time to ourselves.'

Harry refilled his wife's glass. 'There's a good variety

show on in a few minutes, will we watch that?' he asked, getting up to switch on the television set.

Dee and Jean handed their coats to the attendant in the cloakroom of the hotel and Jean looked around the festively decorated foyer in admiration.

'It's quite posh in here,' she whispered to Dee excitedly. 'Do you think this dress is all right? It's not too plain for somewhere like this?' She smoothed down the skirt of the plain, burgundy-coloured, sleeveless shift dress, thinking something a bit more glittery would have been more appropriate.

'It's fine. That necklace and earrings dress it up,' Dee replied, thinking that the colour suited her friend and the silver beads and drop earrings and the fancy silver slide holding Jean's hair in a French pleat at the back looked elegant. Dee was wearing a forest-green fine needlecord two-piece. The skirt was short and straight and the top, which came to just below her waist, had elbow-length sleeves and was scalloped around the neck and hemline. With it she wore a necklace that consisted of ten strands of pearlised beads and earrings that looked like clusters of pearl grapes. Both girls wore black patent-leather stiletto-heeled shoes and carried black satin clutch bags.

Jean was feeling a little apprehensive as they entered the large room that had been hired for the occasion. 'I've never been to a do this like before,' she commented. Everyone was very well dressed, she thought, glancing around as Dee led her over to a table where a young man and woman were seated.

'Neither have I, but just relax and enjoy yourself. No one is going to eat you!' Dee urged.

Jean looked at her friend in alarm. 'That's not your boss and his wife, is it?'

'No. It's Celia. We share an office,' Dee informed her and Jean was introduced as Dee's best friend and Celia introduced her husband, John.

Jean looked around. 'So, where is he? You said he'd be here,' she whispered to Dee.

Dee felt shyly excited. She had already caught sight of Billy Grainger sitting a couple of tables away with some of his colleagues. 'He's over there at that table with those four other lads, but don't go turning around and making it obvious,' she whispered back. 'I'll just have to wait and see if he asks me to dance.'

Celia smiled at her. 'I'm sure he will. He saw you arrive and he hasn't taken his eyes off you since.'

Soon they were both enjoying themselves and in the interval Jean won a large tin of Quality Street in the raffle.

Dee laughed. 'Your Peter will make short work of them.'

'Not if Mam has anything to do with it,' Jean replied before they both tucked into the fancy sandwiches, sausage rolls, vol-au-vents and mini pies that constituted the first course of the buffet.

When all the dishes had been cleared the band struck up and the dancing began again.

Jean nudged Dee. 'He's finally coming over. I think he's going to ask you up, Dee.'

Dee smiled, feeling excited and relieved. She'd started to think he wasn't really interested in her.

'He's quite good-looking, and he does look friendly,' Jean hissed.

'Would you care to dance?'

Dee looked up and smiled. 'I'd love to, thanks.'

'I'm Billy Grainger by the way. I work in the drawing office. I've seen you quite a few times.' In fact she'd caught his eye almost from the first week she'd worked there. He'd enquired who she was and since then he'd made a point of looking out for her in the staff canteen, but he'd still wasted half the evening trying to pluck up courage to ask her to dance. 'You're Mr Dawson's secretary.'

Dee smiled at him. 'I am. I'm Denise Campbell, but my family and friends call me Dee.'

'Will it be all right if I call you Dee?'

She laughed. 'Of course, providing I can call you Billy.'

'My mates have been skitting me all night for being a bit slow off the mark.'

'Really?' she asked. 'Why?'

'I've been trying to find the nerve to ask you up for ages,' he replied frankly.

She looked at him with mock horror. 'I'm not that intimidating, am I? I don't look like some sort of a dragon?'

'I think you look amazing, and that's the truth,' he replied honestly.

She smiled and felt quite at ease with him as they'd progressed around the floor.

'Do you live in Kirkby?' she asked.

He shook his head. 'No, out at Norris Green. It's quite a way to travel but I don't mind. It's a decent job and when I've qualified the pay will be good. Where do you live, Dee?'

'In Northwood. We were rehoused a couple of years ago. Before that we lived in Cobden Street in Everton. The houses were dreadful, very old and with no modern facilities.'

'I know. My family originally came from Everton,' he replied, thinking she was fortunate to live so close to work.

The dance finished and he saw her back to the table.

'Well, what did you think?' Jean asked, having just returned to her seat after dancing with John Ellerby.

'He's quite nice. He works in the drawing office. He lives out at Norris Green,' Dee replied, before taking a sip of her drink.

He asked her to dance twice more and by the end of the evening she'd decided that she really liked him and that she'd look out for him at work in future.

Jean had enjoyed herself too, she'd been asked up to dance just as often as Dee. She thought that Celia Ellerby and her husband were both very nice but she had been a bit uneasy and abashed when Dee had introduced her to Mr and Mrs Dawson, her boss and his wife, who had come over to see if they were all enjoying the evening.

They didn't have to pay for a taxi home as John Ellerby insisted on giving them a lift in his car, something they were both grateful for.

'I've got a feeling that Billy Grainger from the drawing office has his eye on you, Dee,' Celia informed her as they walked to the car park where the Austin A40 was.

'He certainly danced with you often enough,' Jean added.

Dee laughed. 'He's quite nice really.'

'He goes to night school, Dee, I know that for a fact,' Celia informed her, for she was aware of Dee's intention to learn French in the New Year.

'So, apart from seeing him at work, you might run into him after classes,' Jean added.

'Will you stop it, the pair of you?' Dee laughed. 'I really don't need you both playing matchmaker.'

Celia laughed too and then shivered as they reached the car. 'Hurry up, John, and unlock it before I freeze! Dee and Jean have their coats, I've only got this wool stole. But I bet he asks you out, Dee, and sooner rather than later,' she predicted.

After the holiday, when things had returned to normal and Jean and Dee had begun their evening classes, Jean started on an extensive search for a shop to rent. At the end of the month she found one in Walton Vale, which was the main road that ran from the Black Bull public house in Aintree through to the Windsor Castle pub at the bottom of Orrell Lane. The road was a popular shopping area, being lined on both sides with retail premises including a small branch of Woolworths and one of Boots the Chemist.

'It's no use having somewhere that's miles away from other shops. You need to be where there are a lot of people and this is a busy area and there are plenty of houses too, so lots of potential customers,' she explained to Dee as they got off the bus outside the church of the Blessed Sacrament and crossed over the road. She wanted Dee to see the premises she had found.

The shop Jean was going to rent was set between Ziegler's pork butcher's and Tyler's shoe shop.

'It's quite big,' Dee exclaimed, looking around as Jean unlocked the door and they went inside.

Jean was full of plans. 'I'm going to have the washbasins over there on that wall, the dryers on the wall opposite the window and the setting and combing-out area on the other wall. In that corner by the door I'm going to have a little reception desk. Through the back there are two more rooms. I'll use one as a stockroom and the other as a bit of a kitchen where we can make a cup of tea. Pauline says we should also get a manicurist in for the busy days as the big salons in town do. Girls these days like to have their nails done as well as their hair but I think I'll wait a bit and see how the business goes.'

Both Jean and Pauline had given in their notices. Pauline was going to oversee the rest of Jean's training and had been thrilled to be asked to join Jean in this venture, especially as Jean was giving her a rise. Mrs Nelson hadn't been a bit pleased about losing two good girls but had eventually wished Jean luck – grudgingly.

'What colours do you think you'll do it out in?' Dee asked, looking around the rather drab and dusty shop that had formerly sold paint and wallpaper.

'I've been thinking about that. I want something modern and sort of *striking*, not wishy-washy pastels. I quite like the idea of black and white with bright red towels and accessories to liven it all up.'

Dee nodded. She'd never seen her friend so enthusiastic. 'Will you get someone in to do it all for you, the decorating, I mean?'

'There's a firm called Littlemore and Wilson who specialise in shopfitting for hairdressers. I've already been in touch with them and someone is coming out to have a look at the place this morning. That's why I asked you to come here with me.'

'Will you advertise?' Dee asked.

Jean looked thoughtful. 'I might but I want to appeal to younger women so I'll have to think where it will be best to place adverts.'

'And you'll have to think of a name for the place. Something a bit different to "Sadie's Salon".'

Jean grimaced. 'You'd definitely want something a bit more up market than *that*! It sounds awful and everyone always called it just "Sadie's", which to my mind made it even worse.'

Dee had to agree. 'You want something a bit different. Something that sounds classy.'

Jean wrinkled her brow thoughtfully as she rubbed a finger up and down the dust-streaked glass of the shop window. She wanted her customers, or 'clients' as Pauline said they should be called, to look fantastic when they left her shop and feel as though it had been money well spent and hopefully come back and bring their friends and relations. That's how a business became successful. 'I'd like something with my name in it, you know like "Andre Bernard" or "Ellison Lee" but with Jean or Williams, but obviously not just plain "Jean Williams",' she confided, thinking of two of Liverpool's largest and most successful hairdressing salons.

Dee looked thoughtful; she could see her point. 'What about "Maison Jeanne"? Spell the "Jean" the French way, "J-e-a-n-n-e," and "Maison" means "house" but sounds much grander, and I don't suppose many people will know it just means house, unless they speak French,' she suggested.

Jean repeated it aloud and then smiled. 'I like the sound of that.'

Dee grinned at her. 'My French evening class is proving useful already.'

'I'll have it done in black and gold lettering across this window and I'll have it printed on my appointment cards.'

Before Dee could reply the shop door opened and a man in his forties, accompanied by a lad she judged to be about twenty, stepped inside.

'Miss Williams?' the older man asked.

'Are you from Littlemore and Wilson?' Jean enquired.

'We are. I'm Derek Wilson and this is Tony Littlemore. Mr Ernest Littlemore's son. He's learning the business.'

Tony Littlemore smiled at the two girls. Both were attractive but the small blonde girl appealed to his taste more. He wasn't very tall himself and tall girls always made him feel a bit uneasy. 'Which one of you is Miss Williams?' he asked.

Jean liked him. He had dark hair cut in a style like the Beatles and he wore a dark grey Italian-style suit. His dark brown eyes were full of intelligence. 'I am.' She held out her hand. 'Jean Williams. And this is my friend Dee Campbell.'

Both men shook hands. 'And is it to be a joint venture?' Mr Wilson asked, looking around.

Dee laughed. 'No. Jean is the hairdresser, I'm a secretary.'

'You are very young to have your own salon, if I might say so,' Mr Wilson remarked.

'I'm not out of my time yet but I'll be having a fully qualified hairdresser working with me and we will be taking on an apprentice and maybe a manicurist.'

Tony Littlemore nodded his approval. 'You should do well here, it's a busy area with plenty of other shops to attract customers and I didn't notice any other hairdressing salons near by.'

Mr Wilson got down to the business in hand. 'Right then, Miss Williams, have you anything particular in mind? As you know we are very experienced in this field.'

For the next half-hour Dee watched as her friend outlined her ideas and was then guided expertly through what appeared to be quite a complicated process of design and planning. All the positions of electrical sockets and lights were marked on the plan by Mr Wilson and Tony Littlemore suggested the positioning of shelving for storage in both the main salon and the stockroom. He thought Jean's ideas for the colour scheme were great and he produced catalogues of salon equipment, paint colour charts, lighting, flooring materials and accessories. The firm could supply and install everything that would be required, he assured her as Mr Wilson made notes in a large notebook.

'I'll leave everything with you and you can make your final decision, Miss Williams, and then when you contact us we'll put the orders in, but work can commence immediately on stripping out all this old stuff and sorting out the plumbing and electrics,' he assured her. 'Our team is very efficient.'

'That all sounds excellent.' Jean examined the business card he'd given her.

He smiled at her. 'So, I expect we will be seeing quite a lot of each other as I'll be in and out to oversee everything and no doubt you will want to see how the work is progressing.'

Jean smiled back, feeling a little flutter of excitement. He really was quite handsome and very charming. 'Oh, indeed I will.'

'Well, he certainly made an impression on you and I don't think it's all to do with fitting out the shop,' Dee said when they'd gone.

Jean's cheeks flushed pink. 'He is very nice.'

Dee laughed. 'And his dad is part owner of the business.'

Jean looked indignant. 'I wasn't thinking like that at all!'

'Will you go out with him, if he asks you?' Dee pressed.

'Of course. It's about time I got myself a feller. You have.'

'I've only been for a coffee after evening class twice with Billy Grainger, you can hardly say he's my "feller",' Dee replied, but she already knew that her feelings for Billy were verging on more than just friendship. They tried to see each other at work. If she was in the staff canteen at lunchtime he would come over and join her, and lately they'd tried to get out at the same time at the end of the day and he would walk her to the bus stop. She smiled to herself. Yes, she very much hoped that she could think of Billy as her 'special feller'.

Chapter Nine

———◆———

JEAN WAS KEPT VERY busy over the following weeks choosing colours, flooring, fittings and furnishings and work progressed quickly on transforming the drab former wallpaper shop into a light, bright and airy space. She saw a great deal of Tony Littlemore and she found that they got on very well together. They seemed to have similar interests and he was very enthusiastic about all her ideas and had even made some suggestions which she thought would improve the décor.

'Derek Wilson is a bit on the conservative side. He tends to stick to tried and tested designs instead of making an effort to be more innovative,' he confided to her as they watched the signwriter carefully painting the words 'Maison Jeanne' in gold lettering edged with black across the outside of the shop window.

Jean gestured with a hand around the half-finished

interior. 'I hope this will look very innovative when it's finished, and appealing to my prospective customers. I've always thought that people shouldn't have to traipse all the way into town for a good modern salon. It's far better to have one on your doorstep. I've been talking about the advertising with Pauline, my "senior stylist" as she calls herself, and we intend to offer a good discount for the first week on everything. Perms, tints, sets, trims and restyling.'

He nodded, his dark hair falling across his eyes. 'Are you putting an ad in the local rag?'

'Yes, and a notice on the shop door too.'

'You could get some flyers done giving all the details of the special introductory discounts plus your normal prices and ask the management at the Orrell Park Ballroom and at the Aintree Institute if they can be handed out to their customers,' he suggested.

'That's a great idea. You get a fairly young crowd at both places. And we are going to employ a manicurist. Pauline's got a friend who knows someone who will come in on Fridays and Saturdays and we're taking on Pauline's youngest sister, Bernice, as an apprentice.' She turned her attention to the small reception desk that was rapidly taking shape. 'What would you suggest I put on the top of it? A flower arrangement?'

He shook his head, making a comical face. 'It would make the place look a bit like a funeral parlour!'

Jean laughed. 'Oh, God forbid! What then? I don't want to leave it totally bare.'

'Maybe a tasteful art deco statue or a tall, slim and

111

very plain vase with just one or two long-stemmed red flowers. Any variety except roses, they would look just too tacky.'

'You really have got a lot of flair for a feller,' she replied with a note of admiration in her voice.

He shrugged. 'I wanted to go to art school but the old man wasn't having any of it.'

Jean was sympathetic. 'I suppose I was lucky. I managed to convince Mam that I'd *loathe* the civil service, which is where she wanted me to go. Still, you can use your artistic talents to an extent in this type of work.'

He smiled at her. 'But only if I get to work with people like you who have modern ideas.' He admired her greatly. Her ideas were go ahead and she was ambitious. She was also a pretty girl with a vivacious personality, just the type he liked.

She blushed at the compliment. 'Did you see the Beatles on the telly the other night on *Thank Your Lucky Stars*?'

He nodded enthusiastically. 'They were great! I've just bought their first LP. *Please Please Me*.' He looked at her seriously. 'Would you like to go out with me one night? We could go to a dance, that's if you won't be too worn out getting this place sorted out?'

'I'd like that,' Jean replied. She'd been hoping he would ask her. The more she saw of him the more she liked him. She felt they were alike. Ambitious, confident, looking forward to everything the future could offer – and he was very charming. Whenever she thought of him she felt a little tingle of excitement run through her.

'How about Saturday? The Swinging Blue Jeans are on at the Mardi Gras and I really enjoy dancing.'

She nodded, mentally making a note to splash out on a new dress for the occasion. 'Should I meet you in town? Kirkby's miles out of your way.' She'd already ascertained that he lived in Walton Park where there were some very big, affluent-looking houses and which was further on towards town.

He looked at her with mischief in his eyes. 'What about outside Lewis's?'

She looked at him with mock horror. 'Are you kidding? I'm not standing waiting for you underneath *that* statue!' she retorted, thinking of the large bronze of a naked man that stood above the main entrance to the department store, and which had given rise to the local popular but derogatory saying: 'Stood there like one of Lewis's'.

He grinned. 'All right, I was only joking. I'll see you at seven outside the Mardi.'

Dee's evening class was held on Thursday nights and she had arranged to meet Billy Grainger after it finished at nine o'clock as they'd done twice before. This time, however, she had made a special effort with her appearance, wanting to look her best.

'I don't know what you're dolling yourself up for. It's only night school,' Flo had remarked, but Dee had shrugged her mother's comments aside.

113

'You look great. Really cheerful. You brighten up a miserable night,' Billy greeted her, smiling and tucking her arm through his.

Dee smiled back up at him. He was younger than Graham but was as tall as her brother. He had thick wavy brown hair that defied all his attempts to comb it into the style adopted by so many lads who modelled themselves on the Beatles. His eyes were penny brown like her own and he was what her Mam called 'fresh-faced'. She thought he was quite handsome. He wore a grey shortie overcoat over dark grey trousers and a royal blue sweater. He was a good deal brighter than her brother and so far she'd found him honest, generous and fun to be with.

'Will we go and get a coffee? It wasn't exactly what you'd call warm in there,' he asked as they left the building together.

'Yes, please. I could do with something to warm me up.'

He laughed. 'Sometimes, Dee, you say things that a feller could take the wrong way. Now, if I wasn't a gentleman I'd reply that I've—'

She dug him playfully in the ribs. 'Don't you dare say what I think you're about to!'

He grimaced. 'Ouch! You've got sharp little elbows!'

They settled themselves at a table in the corner of the Rococo Coffee Bar and he ordered two coffees. There was a jukebox on the opposite side of the room that was playing Acker Bilk's 'Stranger on the Shore' and at the counter a waitress was busy at the steaming

Gaggia coffee machine as the place was quite busy with students who, like themselves, had come in for coffee and a chat.

'How is the French course going?' he asked, unwinding the scarf from around his neck.

'I'm enjoying it but it is getting a bit harder now. It's all verbs – *présent, futur, passé composé, passé simple*. Still, I suppose you have to get the basics right.'

He nodded. 'I often think the easiest way to learn a language would be to actually go and live in the country, mix with the people.'

Dee frowned. 'How could I do that? I'd have to get a job and as I'm far from proficient in French yet I'd never be able to manage, especially with shorthand.' Then she looked thoughtful. 'I suppose if I had a holiday there it would help. Jean and I would like to go abroad one day, we've always said how exciting it would be to travel. See how the rest of the world live.'

'How is she getting on with doing up her shop?' he asked as the coffees arrived.

'Great. It's going to look really trendy and I know she will make a success of it. It will be hard work so we'll have to put the holiday idea on hold for a while yet.' Dee spooned sugar into her frothy coffee. 'And she's got a date with Tony Littlemore, you remember I told you about him? She's delighted, she really likes him. They're going to the Mardi Gras on Saturday.'

He nodded. 'Do you fancy going there too? It's usually a good night and I've never taken you anywhere decent yet. Just for coffee after night school and we only have an hour – it's not a proper date, not a whole evening together. Unless you think Jean would get upset? She might think you're spying on her?'

Dee smiled at him. 'I'll mention it to her but I'm sure she won't mind at all. We could make up a foursome. She's meeting him outside at seven. We can get the bus into town together.'

He reached across and took her hand and squeezed it. 'I hope you won't want to go home together.'

Dee smiled again. 'I'm sure Jean would like to have a bit of time on her own with Tony and I . . . I'd like some time with you so . . .'

'So we'll play the "going home" bit by ear?' he suggested. Now he knew her better he was becoming very fond of her. In his eyes she was beautiful and had a warm, straightforward, gentle nature.

She nodded and finished her coffee.

Billy stood up. 'I'll walk you to the bus stop. The crowd from night school will have gone by now.'

Dee fastened her coat and collected her bag and her books together and they left, walking out into the dark, almost deserted street. Although they worked for the same firm Billy lived quite a distance away from her in the opposite direction.

Before they reached the bus stop he gently pulled her into a shop doorway and took her in his arms.

'Have I told you that you are the most gorgeous girl I've ever met? I thought it the very first time I saw you and I could hardly take my eyes off you at that dance.'

Dee felt her heart skip a beat and she blushed

with pleasure. 'Oh, Billy! I'm far from gorgeous,' she protested.

He lifted her chin with his forefinger and kissed her. 'I think you're underestimating yourself, Dee. Gorgeous, beautiful, stunning, I could go on and on. You're really special to me.'

Dee tightened her arms around his neck and kissed him back. She wished she could stay here all night in his arms. Reluctantly she at last drew away from him. 'You're very special to me too, Billy. I really mean that,' she whispered sincerely, wondering if she was falling in love.

Jean said she didn't mind at all about them making a foursome.

'If you'd sooner not, I'll understand. I mean it's the first time you've been out with him. I don't want to cramp your style or anything and Billy and Tony don't know each other.'

'Oh, don't talk daft! "Cramping my style"! As if, and the lads are bound to get on,' Jean had retorted. 'Now, what are you going to wear? I'm going into town on Saturday morning to look for something new, what about you?'

Dee had readily agreed; she had saved her wages since the holiday so she had a few pounds to spend.

She settled on one of the new trouser suits in pale blue crimplene. The top was a sort of tunic with wide bell-shaped sleeves and the trousers were flared at the bottom. It was trimmed with a dark blue and silver braid.

'That style looks fab on you but I'm just not tall enough to carry it off. If anything it makes me look even smaller,' Jean had said, looking at herself in the mirror of the changing room without much pleasure. The emerald-green trouser suit, similar in style to the one Dee had chosen, definitely did not suit her. 'I look like a leprechaun! All I need is the hat!'

'It's not *that* bad!' Dee protested.

'It is! The last thing I want is for Tony to think I look like something out of a pantomime! I'll take that fuchsia pink shift dress. I've got earrings that will match it and with black accessories it will look great.'

Dee smiled at her and passed her the pink dress and they both made their way to the cash desk.

Both Ada and Flo thought rather too much effort and expense was going into this evening out.

'It's only a dance, you'd think the pair of them were going to a Buckingham Palace garden party!' Ada commented to Flo as the two women sat in Ada's kitchen having a cup of tea after finishing the Saturday-morning shopping.

Flo nodded. 'Dee's had her hair in rollers ever since she got in from town and she's moaning that if it rains or is damp it will all be a waste of time as it will curl up again. She's got lovely curly hair, Ada. Don't we have to have ours permed to get it to curl like that?'

'They're never satisfied, Flo. Our Jean says she can't decide whether to put a rinse on hers to "brighten it up". God knows what for, she's dead lucky she's a natural blonde and doesn't have to have it bleached.

Still, I suppose she wants to make an impression on this lad.'

Flo nodded sagely. 'She wants to cultivate him, Ada. I mean his old man can't be short of a bob or two, not with being part-owner of the business.'

Ada looked at her friend closely. 'I don't think our Jean is thinking along those lines, Flo. And she's got a business herself, don't forget.'

'I wasn't implying she was a gold-digger, Ada. Anyway, I mean it's not as if either of them are courting steady, is it?'

'Not yet but who knows? Frank Woodward was our Margaret's first steady boyfriend. What about this Billy Grainger? Is Dee serious about him?'

'I don't know much about him at all. Dee said they live in Norris Green and that his mam's sister, who is a widow, lives with them. There are no brothers or sisters from what I can gather. I suppose a draughtsman is a good steady job; Bob seems to think so anyway.'

Ada nodded. 'Do you think they'll be bringing them home so we can give them the once-over?'

Flo shrugged and then frowned. Of course she wanted to see Dee happily married one day. 'We'll just have to wait and see. You know what the young ones are like these days, Ada. Fickle. The "romance" might not last long at all. Look at our Graham. He seems to have a different girl every other week.'

Chapter Ten

—◆—

THE TWO GIRLS ALIGHTED from the bus and hurried across the road and Dee felt a flutter of excitement as she caught sight of Billy waiting outside the main door of the dance hall. Her dark eyes lit up, her heart beat faster and she smiled. 'There's Billy. I hope he hasn't been waiting long.'

Jean was scanning the small group of people who were also obviously waiting for their partners. 'I can't see any sign of Tony.' She felt a little dart of apprehension. Surely he wouldn't stand her up? He'd been the one to suggest they meet here.

Billy joined them, taking Dee's hand. 'Right on time. I was a bit early myself.'

'You remember Jean from the dance at the Cherry Tree?'

Billy smiled at Jean. 'Of course I do and you both look fantastic.'

Dee was pleased she had made such an effort with her appearance but Jean shrugged. If Tony didn't turn up she would have to play the wallflower all night for Dee would insist she stayed with them, there would be no getting the bus back home. She checked her watch. 'He's late,' she said curtly.

'Give him a chance, it's not even ten past yet,' Dee urged. She could see Jean was getting upset.

'He might have missed the bus,' Billy added.

'He can get any number of buses,' Jean replied.

'It might have broken down, they do sometimes, usually when you're in a hurry. Or they might have changed drivers at Spellow Lane and you know how long that can take.' Billy was trying to put her mind at ease.

Jean looked unsure. She supposed he could be right. Maybe she was just too on edge.

To take her mind off Tony's unpunctuality Billy asked her about the refurbishment of the shop and when she hoped to have her grand opening but before she had finished telling him Dee spotted Tony dodging the traffic as he crossed the road.

'Here he is, you can stop worrying now,' she announced.

Jean smiled with relief. 'You'll get yourself killed darting in and out between cars like that.'

Tony grinned and gave an apologetic shrug. 'Sorry, Mum kept fussing about me not bringing a coat and so I missed two buses. Have you been here long?' He looked at Dee and Billy questioningly. He remembered Dee but he had no idea who the lad was.

'Not long. I hope you don't mind but Dee and Billy are joining us.'

'The more the merrier!' Tony replied light-heartedly although he was a bit disappointed that she had invited them. He'd wanted her to himself for the entire evening.

Billy extended his hand. 'Billy Grainger.'

Tony shook it. 'Tony. Tony Littlemore. Well, shall we go for a drink first? It doesn't really get going in there until about half eight.'

The two girls looked at each other. Even at nineteen they were too young to drink in a pub, you had to be twenty-one. In fact Tony was the only one who had reached the age of majority.

'Don't worry, you'll all pass for twenty-one and anyway half the time no one asks,' Tony reassured them as he took Jean's arm and steered her towards the pub on the corner. Billy and Dee followed.

It was quite crowded but Tony pushed through and found them seats at a table in the corner of the Lounge Bar.

'I'd say most of this lot are the same age as us,' Jean whispered to Dee as they took off their coats and sat down. She was feeling a bit nervous, hoping they didn't look under age.

'Act as if we go into pubs every week,' Dee whispered, looking around. 'It's quite smoky and there is definitely a strong smell of drink,' she added.

'What did you expect? They sell "drink",' Jean hissed, grinning.

Dee nodded, glancing around at the laughing and chattering young girls and lads who seemed to constitute a major section of the clientele.

'We haven't a hope in hell's chance of getting served, so I'll go up to the bar,' Tony stated.

'I'll come with you; you'll have a job getting through this crowd carrying four glasses and ten to one they won't have a tray. What's it to be Dee?' Billy asked.

'I'll have a Babycham, please.'

'A Cherry B for me, please,' Jean added.

'Any crisps or nuts?' Tony enquired, extracting a packet of Rothmans cigarettes from his jacket pocket and offering Billy one.

Billy shook his head. 'Thanks, but I don't.'

Tony shrugged good-naturedly and offered the packet to the girls. Nearly everyone else in the room was smoking. Dee shook her head but Jean accepted one and Tony lit it for her before he and Billy made their way to the bar.

'You don't smoke!' Dee hissed.

'There's a first time for everything,' Jean replied, trying not to cough. Her da had always smoked so she was more than used to the smell and the cloud of smoke.

'Don't blame me if you're sick,' Dee warned.

After a few tentative puffs Jean decided to let the cigarette burn down; she wasn't finding it a pleasant experience.

'Put it in the ashtray before the ash falls off and ruins your dress,' Dee advised.

As they waited at the bar Billy looked more closely at Tony. Far from concentrating on catching the eye of one of the barmen Tony was looking across into the smaller room at the other side of the pub, which was also crowded.

'Some nice-looking girls over there, Billy. If those two we've brought get fed up with us we'll know where to come,' he remarked, nudging Billy and winking.

'We'll just have to make sure "our two" don't get fed up with us then,' Billy replied light-heartedly, but he was thinking it was a bit of a strange thing for Tony Littlemore to say on what he knew was his first date with Jean.

The two lads returned with the drinks and four packets of Smith's crisps. Jean had stubbed the cigarette out in the ashtray and had vowed not to have another. She'd thought it would make her appear more sophisticated but it had made her feel a bit queasy and she certainly wasn't going to risk making a complete show of herself.

They stayed for an hour chatting and then Billy suggested they go along to the dance hall. The girls left their coats in the cloakroom and went to touch up their make-up in the Ladies.

'I'm glad I didn't let you talk me into that green trouser suit,' Jean remarked, looking askance at a small, dark-haired girl dressed in a bright red suit very similar to the one she had tried on. She glanced with satisfaction at her reflection in the mirror above the washbasin. The short, bright pink shift dress looked well and her earrings matched it perfectly. She applied another coat of Crushed Strawberry lipstick.

'I can see now what you meant,' Dee concurred as she smoothed down her dark hair and made sure her navy blue and silver earrings were securely clipped on. 'We'd better get going or the lads will think we've deserted them,' she added.

They all agreed it had been a great night. They'd hardly been off the dance floor and Jean had confided to Dee that she'd never seen anyone do the Twist as well as Tony. The couples around them had actually stopped to watch.

'What are we going to do about getting home? Has Tony mentioned it?' Dee asked as they went to retrieve their coats, having agreed to meet the lads in the foyer.

'He's insisting on taking me right to our front door and I think we'd all like a bit of privacy to say our goodnights.'

Dee nodded. 'Billy sort of implied the same thing but we can't let them miss the last bus. They'd have to walk miles. It's not fair for them to have to get a taxi home. They can't even share one, they live in different directions and it would cost an arm and a leg.'

Jean sighed as she nodded, thinking there were still disadvantages in living so far out of town. 'We'd better get a move on then.'

In the end they all decided to get the bus to the Pier Head and say their goodnights there. Then the girls could get the last bus to Kirkby and the two lads could go their separate ways. It wasn't really what Tony had wanted but he could see the sense in it.

'At least it's not as crowded as it is in the town centre,' Dee remarked as they walked across the open space of Man Island towards the waterfront where they hoped there would be very few people around.

'It's a damned sight colder and windier though,' Tony remarked as a few couples hurried past them to where the last ferry was waiting to leave for Birkenhead.

Dee and Billy walked on, leaving Jean and Tony huddled together in the lee of the wall of the floating roadway. The lights from the ferry and the landing stage were reflected in the dark ripples of the river as it lapped against the wooden stage.

Billy put his arm around her, drawing her closer. 'It's been a great night but I think I'd sooner have you all to myself in future. Is that being really selfish?'

Dee smiled up at him. 'No. I've enjoyed myself but I do see Jean nearly every day.'

'Is she really keen on Tony?' Billy asked, glancing back to where Jean was now enveloped in Tony's embrace.

'Yes. She's been dying for him to ask her out. Why?' She frowned, wondering why Billy had asked.

'I don't really know him but there's just something about him . . .'

'What? Did he say anything to annoy you?' she asked.

'No, nothing like that but he's a bit too glib, a bit too

much of a charmer.' He didn't want to tell her how often Tony Littlemore's glance had strayed away from Jean and had settled on other attractive girls, not just in the pub but at the dance too. Billy hadn't even looked at anyone else other than Dee all night.

'I suppose it could have something to do with his work. He has to be "charming" to all sorts of people.'

'You're probably right. He deals mainly with women whereas I work in a drawing office full of men. But let's not waste any more time on them. I'm going to have to wait five whole days before I have you to myself again so I'm going to make the most of this last bit of the night. And I'd like you to come and meet my parents. Would next Tuesday after night school be convenient?'

Dee felt a wave of excitement mingled with happiness surge through her – he must really be serious about her. 'Yes. Oh, that would be great, Billy.' He took her in his arms and sought her lips and all thoughts of Jean and Tony Littlemore fled from her mind.

Both girls were preoccupied as they sat on the bus after having waved a regretful farewell to the boys. Finally Jean spoke.

'Do you think you've found "Mr Right", as Mam always puts it?'

Dee nodded slowly. 'I think so. I just feel so happy and sort of "different" when I'm with Billy and the time seems to go really slowly when I'm not, even though I'm at work and there're plenty of things going on around me – if that makes any sense.'

Jean sighed. 'It does. I've never felt like this about

anyone before. I liked Tony from the moment I first met him. He said he hasn't been able to stop thinking about me and has called into the shop nearly every day, hoping to see me. I just hope he doesn't change his mind. I really, really like him, Dee, but he hasn't asked me out again. He said he'll see me at the shop on Monday morning.'

Dee smiled at her. 'That's a sort of date and I bet he will ask you out again. He won't change his mind. You two are just made for each other.'

Jean felt more confident. Dee was right. She would only have to wait until Monday to see him again. 'You know we really are lucky, Dee, we're both doing so well at work, we've both finally met lads we really like and we've had a great evening. What more could either of us ask for?'

Dee felt a little nervous when, on the following Tuesday, Billy escorted her up the front path of the house in Lorenzo Drive. She had told her parents she would be late home and Flo had raised her eyebrows and had remarked to Bob, after their daughter had left, that it looked as if Billy Grainger was serious about Dee.

'Don't worry, Dee. They'll like you, I promise,' Billy said confidently.

It was a similar style of house to their own, Dee thought as Billy ushered her into the living room.

'Mam, Dad, this is Dee,' Billy announced with pride.

Dee smiled shyly at the couple. Billy's mother was a small, plump woman with red-gold hair and blue eyes who immediately got to her feet, smiling.

'We're very pleased to meet you, Dee. He never stops talking about you, does he, Will?'

Will Grainger had also stood up and was extending his hand. He was not quite as tall as his son and his hair was grey and thinning on top but his smile was genuine. 'Pleased to meet you, Dee, and if I may say so our Billy's right. He said you were a "real smasher".'

Dee blushed. 'I wouldn't go so far as that, Mr Grainger.'

'Don't go embarrassing the girl, Will,' his wife chided before turning to a pale, thin woman who was sitting on the sofa. 'This is our Alice. My sister. She's a widow and lives with us.'

Dee smiled at the woman, thinking how unlike in appearance she was to Billy's mother. 'I'm pleased to meet you too.'

'Now, Dee, tell us how you're getting on with your French lessons? Alice and I think it's very brave of you to learn a foreign language. I don't think I could manage it at all,' Doreen Granger confided, trying to put the girl at ease. She liked her; she didn't seem to be at all forward or pushy.

As he walked her to the bus stop later Billy put his arm around her shoulder. 'I told you they'd like you.'

Dee smiled up at him. 'And I liked them. Your Aunt Alice is rather quiet though.'

He nodded. 'She is.'

'I suppose it can't be much fun for her being a widow. She must get lonely.'

Billy looked thoughtful. 'I've never really thought about that. But let's not waste time talking about them. Where will we go on Saturday night?'

Chapter Eleven

———❖———

A T LAST EVERYTHING WAS READY, Jean thought with rising excitement as she looked around the newly decorated and refurbished salon. Today was the day when Maison Jeanne would be open for business. She turned to Tony and her smile was radiant, lighting up her face.

'It looks absolutely great! Just like one of the really smart salons you see in all the modern magazines.'

He grinned back and put his arm around her. 'It certainly does. Well, our motto is "We aim to please" but I think we've excelled ourselves.'

A sense of achievement and satisfaction filled her as she glanced around checking that every little detail was just right. For the last two days both she and Pauline had worked hard: scrubbing and cleaning; polishing mirrors and light fittings; attaching the glossy advertising posters to the walls; folding towels and gowns and checking all the new stock in the little room at the back. Now the salon – *her salon* – looked so light and airy, the white walls making it appear larger than it actually was.

Her small reception desk was black and placed beside her new appointments book was a tall, slender, plain glass vase in which she had artistically arranged three long-stemmed, artificial scarlet gladioli of varying heights. Also on the top of the desk was a clear perspex box that held a supply of her business and appointment cards and beneath it on a shelf she had placed her style book and a pile of new women's magazines. She gave a little nod and her eyes sparkled. Yes, everything was just perfect.

She checked her watch. It was ten minutes to nine and they were due to open the door at nine o'clock sharp. Dee was coming in to be her first customer and Flo had promised to follow her. She had also asked her mother and Margaret to come along a bit later in the morning. Margaret had been delighted at the prospect of a free hairdo and Jean wanted the shop to appear busy, which she hoped would encourage people to come in and make appointments. The last thing she wanted was for herself, Pauline and young Bernice to be standing around doing nothing: that wouldn't create a good impression to anyone calling in or glancing through the window.

She had taken a large bundle of the flyers she'd had printed up to the Orrell Park Ballroom and Pauline had taken another bundle to the Aintree Institute, and she'd paid what she considered to be an extortionate amount of money for a half-page advertisement in the *Walton Times*, which Tony had assured her had a wide circulation. She had commented to him that she sincerely hoped the expense was going to be worth it and he'd replied that there was a considerable amount of truth in the saying you had to 'speculate to accumulate'. They had spent a lot of time together these last few weeks. He'd taken her out on quite a few evenings and she'd begun to realise that she was falling in love with him. Gradually her world had begun to revolve around him and on the infrequent days when she didn't see him she felt as though something vital was missing from her life. She relied on his judgement and they seemed to work so well together. They had so much in common, she thought, their hopes and ambitions were the same, they enjoyed going out, they liked the same music and they liked to dance. And he'd told her that he thought she was the most attractive, bubbly, confident and forward-looking girl he'd ever met. In fact he'd admitted that he'd met quite a few, but that hadn't bothered her because he'd said she was the only one for him and lads had to sow a few wild oats, after all.

Pauline was rechecking the supply of the new scarlet and black towels and was impressing upon her sister Bernice that the black ones were to be used specifically for tints. All three girls wore black 'shortie' overalls piped with scarlet around the collar and cuffs and with the words 'Maison Jeanne' embroidered in red across the top pocket.

Tony bent and kissed Jean on the cheek. 'I'd best be

off now, but I'll be back later and I'll bring a bottle of bubbly to celebrate your first day in business. Good luck!'

Jean laughed and pressed her hands to her cheeks. 'My first day in business! Doesn't that sound wonderful?'

Pauline smiled at her. 'And I bet they flock in. There isn't a decent salon for miles. I've checked. Those I've seen seem to be on the lines of Sadie's. Here's Dee,' she announced.

Dee opened the door and looked around admiringly. 'This looks fantastic! Mam said she will be here by about half past nine.'

Jean smiled at her. 'Good. I'll just turn the sign on the door around to "Open". Bernice will take your coat.'

Dee smiled at the girl as she took off her coat. 'Isn't it all exciting?'

Bernice nodded a little shyly. 'It's my first day in my first job.'

Pauline handed her sister a red nylon gown and a thick fluffy scarlet towel and smiled at Dee. 'It's all right, Dee, she's been practising so she won't drown you – hopefully. Use a back-wash bowl, Bernice, it's easier and that way Dee won't end up looking like a panda and with mascara all down her cheeks.'

'Are you going to set it or is Jean?' Dee asked as she was led towards the washbasin.

'You'll have the benefit of my experience today, Dee.'

Dee smiled at Jean who was sitting behind the reception desk, the appointment book open in front of her. 'It's a big day for her in more ways than one,' she confided to Pauline. 'She's taking Tony home to meet the family.'

'He's coming back later and he's bringing a bottle of champagne to celebrate our first day,' Jean informed her friend.

Dee grinned at her. 'Is that wise? I mean to take him home reeking of drink.'

'He won't!' Jean protested. 'After we've all had a glass there won't be very much left.'

As Dee leaned back to have her hair washed she sighed. She knew that Ada had already informed her mother of Tony Littlemore's impending visit. Ada had given the house a spring clean and had bought flowers and even some new dishes for the occasion, including a milk jug and sugar basin and a new teapot. She'd said she wasn't going to have him thinking they didn't live as well as his own parents did even though they didn't have a big fancy house in Walton Park. Harry had strict instructions that he wasn't to stay in the pub all afternoon and that he would have to wear a jacket and tie. Ada wasn't having him sitting there in his shirt sleeves and slippers. Dee thought she was taking things a bit too far, as did Jean, but Ada was adamant.

As Bernice shampooed her hair Dee was fully aware that now Flo would start asking why she hadn't brought Billy home yet. It wasn't that she had deliberately avoided the decision, the opportunity just hadn't arisen, but she'd get no peace now until she did. They were going to a dance tonight which was being held in the hall of a nearby Catholic church and which was referred to, somewhat irreverently, as 'the holy hop'. It never finished late so maybe she'd ask him in just for a few minutes. That way he wouldn't miss his bus home and it would satisfy her parents, particularly her mother, and her mam wouldn't have much advance warning so there could be no opportunity to go to the extremes that Ada was indulging in. It could be brief and informal, unlike Tony's impending visit, which she knew that Jean was now viewing with some trepidation.

To everyone's profound relief the shop had been busy all day. Some people called in to make appointments, some called in to see did they actually need an appointment or could they wait. All were welcomed, as were Flo, Ada and Margaret, who in her advanced state of pregnancy said a new hairdo would cheer her up no end for she felt and looked like a baby elephant.

'Indeed you do not!' Ada protested. 'You look positively blooming, doesn't she, Flo?'

Flo nodded her agreement as, with her hair duly set on small rollers and covered with a hairnet, she was settled under one of the hairdryers with a magazine.

Ada had taken this opportunity to have a perm, seeing as how Jean was bringing 'the boyfriend', as Ada called Tony, home that evening. 'But nothing too tight or frizzy,' she had instructed Jean, who had raised her eyes to the ceiling.

'It will *not* be tight or frizzy, Mam! I'm using the

most expensive lotion I have,' she had replied firmly, wishing her mother wasn't quite so outspoken. After all, Ada wasn't paying for it.

Pauline had suggested that Margaret's hair be cut shorter and given a special rinse to bring out the highlights. Margaret had looked a little doubtful.

'Frank likes it long and I don't want the colour changing.'

'It won't alter the colour that much and a shorter length will suit you. You did say you wanted a change,' Pauline had persisted and so Margaret had agreed and had been delighted with the result.

'You'll need to have it trimmed every six weeks or so,' Pauline had informed her.

Margaret had nodded slowly. 'I suppose after I've had the baby I can get Ma-in-law to mind it for an hour.'

'That's not much to ask and just because you'll be a mother that's no excuse to let yourself go,' Jean had added.

After the last satisfied customer had left and they had tidied up Jean was checking her appointments when Tony arrived, clutching a bunch of flowers and a bottle of Asti Spumante.

'How did it go?' he asked, giving her a peck on the cheek. He was confident she'd have done well.

'Just great. We've been kept busy all day and although the early part of the week is a bit slack I've plenty of appointments for Friday and Saturday. I was thinking of putting a sign in the window saying "No

Appointment necessary for Monday or Tuesday". We're closed on Wednesdays.'

'Why not make Monday and Tuesday pensioners' days? Give them a special rate. Save having an empty shop,' he suggested.

Jean glanced at Pauline, who nodded her approval. 'Good idea. I often wondered why Sadie Nelson didn't do that. Sometimes we were bored rigid on Mondays.'

Tony opened the bottle of sparkling wine with a flourish and Bernice went to fetch four cups as they had no glasses. When they all had a cup Tony raised his and touched the cup to Jean's. 'Here's to the success of Maison Jeanne and its gorgeous proprietor.'

They all laughed and cheered and Jean beamed happily at Tony as he poured out the remaining wine.

'Bernice, don't gulp it down as if it was lemonade! You're not used to drinking, it will go straight to your head and I'm not carrying you home,' Pauline admonished her sister before turning to Jean. 'You get your coat on and put the day's takings in your bag and get off home. We'll lock up.'

'Thanks,' Jean replied and then she grimaced. 'Mam's probably got everyone into a right state by now.'

When they finally arrived in Buttermere Close Jean was feeling excitement at the prospect of telling them all about her successful day mingled with trepidation about the reception in store for Tony.

'Here we are, Mam!' she called as they hung their coats up in the hall.

Ada appeared from the kitchen, a broad smile on her face. She was wearing the dress she had bought for Christmas covered by a clean, fancy apron and her hair had been brushed into soft waves and curls. 'So, you must be Tony?'

'That's me all right, Mrs Williams. These are for you.' He handed over the flowers.

Ada thanked him, thinking he had good manners at least and that he was a handsome enough boy. 'The tea won't be long now. Jean, take the lad into the living room and introduce him to your da,' she instructed.

Jean had intended to go upstairs and get changed but she did as she was bid. She gave an amused little smile as she saw her father sitting bolt upright on the sofa and wearing a shirt and tie and his best jacket.

'Dad, this is Tony Littlemore.'

Harry got to his feet, looking a little awkward, and held out his hand. 'Nice to meet you, lad. Sit down.'

Tony shook his hand and sat down, looking around the comfortable room.

'I'll just nip up and get changed out of this overall,' Jean said, smiling at them both.

'Well, how did it all go then? Today I mean, in the shop,' Harry asked, feeling a bit awkward at being left alone with the lad.

'Very well, so Jean said. They were busy all day and have lots of appointments for next week. She'll make a go of it, Mr Williams, you'll see. It's a wise investment, she won't let you down. She's a really great girl and I'm very . . . er . . . fond of her.'

Harry nodded, wondering what to say next. Should he offer the lad a drink or would Ada frown on that? He could certainly do with one himself.

'That's a smart-looking television set,' Tony remarked, sensing the older man's discomfort.

Seizing on his words Harry got to his feet. 'I'll switch it on, we might get the football scores. See how the "Mighty Blues" got on today.'

'Great. I'm an Everton supporter and I take it you are too?'

'Too right.' Harry grinned, switching on the set and feeling more relaxed. At least they had something in common and any lad who supported Everton Football Club was more than welcome in this house.

The evening went far better than Jean could have hoped. Her mam had served up a home-made steak and kidney pie which was delicious and the new china looked lovely. Ada had refrained from asking too many probing questions and had only glared at her husband once when he'd remarked how much fuss there had been over this visit. Tony seemed to get on very well with her da and even young Peter behaved himself and didn't ask any embarrassing questions, such as were they going to get married?

When Tony finally bade them all goodnight, thanking Harry for a pleasant evening and Ada for a memorable meal, Harry had told him he was welcome to come any time.

In the hall he took Jean in his arms. 'I think it's been a very successful day, don't you?'

Jean reached up and kissed him. 'I certainly do. You got on well with them. At first I was a bit worried Mam would sort of interrogate you or fuss around interminably or that Da would drag you down to the pub.'

He laughed. 'They're very easy to get on with. I just hope you'll find my parents as hospitable.'

Jean frowned, wondering what he meant. 'You mean . . . ?'

He nuzzled her neck. 'Well, it's only right that you meet them, isn't it? I mean now we're going steady and if I'm going to start saving up for a ring . . .'

Jean drew away and looked up at him, her eyes shining. 'You . . . you mean . . . ?'

'You know I love you and we get on so well together . . .' It hadn't been a hard decision to come to. He did love her, she was by far the best girl he'd ever been out with and they had a great future together. They'd both be successful in business, they'd buy a house, there would be no shortage of money, and they would enjoy life together.

'You're my "soul mate", Tony, and I love you too. I don't want anyone else. I'll *never* want anyone else,' Jean replied. She meant every word and she was so full of happiness that she felt a little dizzy.

He kissed her passionately and she told herself that she had never been happier in her entire life than she was at this very moment. She would remember this day all her life. The first day of her business venture and the day he had told her he wanted to marry her.

*

Next morning, after a virtually sleepless night, Jean couldn't wait to go and see Dee to tell her all her news. She found Dee in the living room half-heartedly leafing through the Sunday paper. On seeing her friend Dee got to her feet; she could see Jean was bursting to tell her something important.

'Let's go for a walk. It's not a bad morning and we'll get no peace here. I'm fed up listening to Mam bawling up the stairs to our Graham, trying to make him get up. She's gone on and on to Da about the time that lad, as she calls him, comes in.'

Jean nodded and Dee got her coat, scarf, gloves and a tam-o'-shanter hat.

'Won't be long, Mam!' she called to Flo who was in the kitchen.

As she closed the front gate behind them she linked arms with Jean. 'I can see you're bursting to tell me something. How did everything go yesterday? Start at the beginning.'

'Oh, I'll come to all that later! Tony . . . Tony and I are going to get engaged!'

Dee stopped dead and stared at her in astonishment. 'When was that decided?'

'Last night when he was leaving our house. Oh, Dee, I've hardly had a wink of sleep I'm that thrilled.'

'I don't wonder. But . . . but you *are* sure, Jean? You haven't been going out with him for long and you're still very young.'

Jean nodded emphatically. 'I love him and he loves

me and we get on so well together, we have so much in common. We hardly ever disagree, you know that.'

It was Dee's turn to nod her agreement. They did seem like the perfect couple and yet they *hadn't* really known each other for very long and Jean was still not twenty. She remembered Jean's comments about Margaret getting married so young but she didn't remind her friend. She smiled. 'So, when is the happy day?'

'We haven't even thought about that yet. He's going to take me home to meet his parents and then he's going to save up for the ring. I suppose we'll set a date but we'll both have to save up first.'

Dee was relieved. At least they were not going to rush into it. It sounded as if it would be a couple of years yet before Jean walked up the aisle with Tony Littlemore. 'I'm really happy for you, Jean. You're my closest friend and I just want to see you happy and successful.'

Jean squeezed her arm and smiled. 'I know, Dee.'

'Have you told your mam yet?' Dee asked as they walked on.

Jean shook her head. 'God, no! I don't intend to tell her until I get the ring. I couldn't stand all the fuss and palaver, so don't say a word to anyone. Especially not your mam.'

'I won't. I promise. Now, start at the beginning and tell me all about how your first day in business went.'

Jean was a bit overawed by the size of the Littlemores' house in Walton Park. It was four storeys high and there were five steps leading up to the front door. 'Don't you all feel a bit sort of lost in a house this size?' she asked as Tony ushered her into the wide hallway.

He grinned at her. 'No. I suppose you get used to the space.'

He took her coat and hung it up on the ornate hallstand and she noted the large floral arrangement on a chest of drawers on the opposite wall, above which hung a gilt-framed mirror. It was all very grand for just a hallway, she thought.

The room she was ushered into was even bigger and very light from the two double sash windows that went almost from floor to ceiling.

'So, this is Jean? You are very welcome, do sit down.' Tony's father greeted her kindly, shaking her hand and drawing her towards the long brocade-covered sofa on which his wife sat.

Jean liked him immediately but she wasn't too sure about the woman who was sitting staring at her with what looked like a forced smile on her face. Tony's mother was slim, fair and very fashionably dressed in what was obviously an expensive knitted two-piece in shades of green. There were pearls around her neck and small pearl studs in her ears.

'Do sit down, dear. Tony has told us so much about you. You are very fortunate to have your own business at such a young age. Your father had a stroke of good luck, I believe. On a horse race or something?'

Inwardly Jean cringed. The tone in which this last

had been uttered had held a definite note of disdain. 'The Irish Sweepstake.'

'Really? How fascinating. Would you like some tea, Jean?' Mrs Littlemore offered.

Jean nodded her thanks.

'Ernest, would you ring for Mary to bring the tea, please?'

Tony's father smiled fondly at her. 'Of course, Mavis.'

As Tony's father crossed to press the bell beside the fireplace Jean looked at Tony in horror. He'd never said anything about them having a flaming maid!

He grinned and squeezed her hand. 'Don't worry, she only comes in on special occasions,' he whispered reassuringly.

Jean relaxed a little, thinking that at least his mother viewed her visit as a special occasion even though it was quite obvious the woman was going out of her way to impress upon her the fact that they had a far grander home and lifestyle than her family had. She decided then that she didn't really like Mavis Littlemore and her airs and graces. Mentally she shrugged; at least she liked Tony's father. There was no side to him at all. And she was going to marry Tony, not his mother.

Part III

Part III

Chapter Twelve

<hr>

1964

J EAN LOCKED THE DOOR of the shop, bade goodnight
to Pauline and Bernice and began to walk to the bus
stop. It was a pleasant enough April evening but they
had been very busy and she was tired. She fervently
hoped that Margaret would have taken her small son,
Francis, home by the time she herself got home. She
was very fond of her nephew but her sister had taken to
bringing the child to see his grandparents on a
Saturday afternoon and even Ada had to admit he was
a handful.

When she got home she found her mother on her
knees on the kitchen floor, floor cloth in hand and no
sign of a meal in preparation. 'What in the name of
God are you doing, Mam?'

'What does it look like?' Ada replied irritably.

'There's so much Ribena been spilled on this floor that your feet would stick to it.'

Jean sighed heavily, put her bag on the table and took off her light raincoat. 'Honestly, Mam, you'd think our Margaret would watch what he's doing. You can bet your life she doesn't let him make such a mess in her kitchen. I'll put the kettle on.'

Ada silently agreed with her as she got to her feet. 'And all I've heard from your da since he got in is moans and complaints about the price of beer and fags and he certainly spends enough on both. I keep telling him the bit we have saved from his big win won't last for ever.'

Jean filled the kettle and spooned the tea into the teapot. 'He's not still going on about the budget. He's beginning to sound like a cracked record. "Two shillings and a penny for a pint! Four and eleven for a packet of fags! It's daylight robbery!"' Jean mimicked. 'Well, he should cut down on both like Tony has.'

Ada didn't hold out much hope of that and said so. 'Is Tony coming for his tea tonight?' she added. They had been engaged for a year now and he often came for meals. She had wondered more than once did he never get a decent meal at home? Oh, Mavis Littlemore was full of airs and graces and always dressed to the nines but she didn't think she spent much time slaving over a hot stove. She'd been delighted when Jean had announced that she and Tony were getting engaged. She liked the lad although she knew he came from a more privileged background than her daughter, a fact that had been borne out when they had all been invited up to the house in Walton Park for tea. She'd liked his father Ernest, a down-to-earth man with good manners and a sense of humour. She hadn't been too sure about his mother though, and by the end of the visit she had decided that Mavis Littlemore was a bit of a snob who didn't think Jean was good enough for her son. Still, he'd bought Jean a beautiful ring and they were saving up for the deposit on a house.

Both she and Harry worried about them getting into so much debt and having a mortgage around their necks like a millstone for the next twenty-five years. There were some rooms above Jean's shop which they could have rented but Jean had said firmly that she wasn't going to live so close to work and Tony had said property was a good investment. She hoped he was right. He was still working for his father and Maison Jeanne had gone from strength to strength. Jean was nearly twenty-one and was as good a hairdresser now as Pauline; their 'clients', as Jean called them, came from a wide area and were very loyal. Young Bernice was doing well too and they had a manicurist who came in on Fridays and Saturdays. She and Flo had marvelled at the money young women spent on having their nails painted. It was a sign of the times, Flo had said; with girls now earning between ten and twelve pounds a week they didn't know how fortunate they were and could afford to be wasting money on manicures. Dee had her hair and nails done every week, something Flo would never have dreamed of doing.

'Have the pair of you decided on a date for the wedding yet?' Ada asked as she sipped her tea.

Jean didn't answer at once. They were thinking of getting married towards the end of the year but once she announced this her mother would start fussing. 'We want to find a house first, Mam.'

Ada nodded. 'Well, you know you have to book things, like the church and somewhere for the reception, and you can't just walk into a shop and buy a wedding dress, you have to order it or have one made by a dressmaker. And you'll have to give both Margaret and Dee fair notice if they're going to be matron of honour and bridesmaid respectively.'

'I know all that, Mam. Now, I'm going up to have a bath. I'm aching all over. Tony will be here about half past six and we're going to the local hop. Graham and his group are playing there and while they're not exactly the Rolling Stones, they're not bad. And it's reasonably cheap and we haven't been out for ages.'

'You get yourself all dolled up and go out and have a bit of fun while you can, you deserve it. You both work hard. We're going to watch *Steptoe and Son*. It's one of your da's favourite programmes.'

Jean had a hot bath which helped to relieve the aches and pains of a long day on her feet. Then she painted her nails with a pale varnish. It was pointless having her nails done by a professional as her hands were always in water, so she just kept her nails short and neat. She selected an apple-green cotton shift dress from the wardrobe. Dee often wore the trouser suits that were now in fashion but Jean still felt she wasn't tall enough or slim enough to carry them off successfully. The shift style and the Empire line that was also fashionable hid a multitude of sins and gave the illusion of height and slenderness. She had gone to an exhibition earlier in the year where the emphasis had been on the short styles created by Vidal Sassoon and had taken the plunge and had her hair cut. That hadn't pleased her mam at all but Tony loved it – and so did Dee, although as yet she hadn't been able to persuade her friend to have her thick dark hair cut in a similar style, mainly because of a comment by Pauline that it was a style that worked best on straight hair.

It was true that she and Tony hadn't been out for over a month now, they were saving very hard. Tonight they were meeting up with Dee and Billy. Dee would be twenty-one in two weeks' time and a party had been planned for the occasion; at the do Dee and Billy were going to announce their engagement. Dee had told her in strict confidence about their plans and she had been delighted for her friend. She liked Billy. He was considerate, generous, amusing and principled. Oh, he didn't go in much for things like flowers and compliments the way Tony did but she knew he really loved Dee and her friend idolised him. For herself, she loved the way Tony was always surprising her with flowers and chocolates. He made her feel so special and so happy.

Tony duly arrived and they ate their evening meal together.

'Your mam really is a great cook, Jean!' Tony stated, his mouth full of cottage pie.

Jean grinned at him. 'Didn't your mam teach you not to speak with your mouth full?'

He nodded. 'But she never cooks anything like this,' he informed her after swallowing the mouthful of meat and potato. 'I hope when we're married you'll cook all my favourites.'

'After a day on my feet in the shop I don't intend to spend my entire evening cooking. Anyway, what's wrong with you learning to cook? All the top chefs seem to be men.'

He looked thoughtful. 'I might just do that. Your mam could give me lessons.'

Jean stood up as he finished. 'I'll just wash these few dishes, Mam's had a hard enough day with our Margaret and little Francis, then we'd better get off.'

Dee and Billy were standing outside the hall chatting amiably. 'Sorry we're a bit late,' Jean apologised.

Dee smiled. 'That's all right, we didn't mind waiting.'

'But let's not stand here all night! I can hear your Graham's lot going full belt inside,' Tony said, grinning. 'We've come out to enjoy ourselves.'

They all did have a good time and Jean remarked to Dee that Graham's group had certainly improved. They sounded quite professional now. They finished the evening by getting fish and chips, which they ate on the way back to Buttermere Close, as Dee had invited Jean and Tony back.

'They always taste much better out of newspaper but Mum would have ten fits if she saw me,' Tony said, wiping his greasy fingers on his handkerchief.

Jean looked knowingly at Dee, who grinned back. She knew what Jean thought of her future mother-in-law. She herself got on very well with Billy's mam and da and even his Aunt Alice who was a bit of a misery.

'Will your parents both still be up?' Billy asked as they all went up the front path of Dee's house.

'Of course. Our Davie will be in bed though and Graham won't be home for a while yet. It seems to take them ages to pack all their stuff up,' Dee replied as she opened the front door and they all went inside.

Bob and Flo were sitting watching the end of the late news and Flo looked a little surprised to see that Jean and Tony were with her daughter and Billy. Both she and Bob liked Billy a great deal and they had been delighted when it became obvious that this romance was destined to last. They wanted Dee to be happy, to have a good marriage and a secure future and they agreed that Billy Grainger seemed to be the right person for her.

'Is this some sort of deputation?' Bob asked jovially.

'Sort of. I asked Jean and Tony to come in with us because . . .' Dee smiled at Billy. 'We went and bought an engagement ring this afternoon. We're going to be married.'

Billy looked a little sheepish. 'I hope you don't mind, Mr Campbell? I know I really should have asked your permission but . . .'

Bob was on his feet, beaming at them both and shaking Billy's hand vigorously while Flo uttered a cry of delight and threw her arms around Dee.

Jean gave a little mock shriek of surprise 'Dee Campbell, you dark horse! You never said a single word all night!'

Tony put his arm around Jean and they both looked on, smiling.

'No need to apologise, Billy. All this "permission" stuff is a bit old-fashioned nowadays. We're delighted, aren't we, Flo?'

Flo's cheeks were pink with pleasure. 'That we are. Oh, you make a lovely couple! Get everyone a drink, Bob. This is something to celebrate. Put the ring on her finger, Billy,' she urged and Billy duly slipped the single diamond surrounded by sapphires on the third finger of Dee's hand.

'Oh, it's gorgeous, Dee! I know you'll both be so happy!' Jean cried, examining the ring.

Dee looked up at Billy, her eyes shining. 'We will, won't we Billy?'

'The happiest couple in the world,' Billy replied. He'd never felt so proud or happy. Dee meant the world to him. He loved her deeply and wanted to give her the best of everything. She was the girl he wanted to spend the rest of his life with. He'd never had any doubts at all about that.

Bob duly handed round a celebratory drink to everyone. He'd always liked Billy. They'd got on well from the moment Dee had first brought the lad home.

He was a good, steady boy with a decent job and he'd take good care of Dee. 'Here's to the happy couple. To both happy couples.' He beamed at the four young people.

Dee laughed as she sat holding Billy's hand tightly. 'We're going to announce it officially at my birthday party but don't start asking us if we've set a date yet, Mam.' She was positive that she wanted to spend the rest of her life with him and she'd never felt so happy or so elated.

'You'd better tell your mam and da before that, Billy. It wouldn't be right to tell us and not them,' Flo said.

'I know, Mrs Campbell. Dee's coming for tea tomorrow so we'll tell them then, but they'll be as delighted as you are. It should even bring a smile to my Aunt Alice's face.'

'Poor soul, being a widow all these years,' Flo added.

'Just how long has her husband been dead?' Jean asked. She was curious as Dee said the woman was always mournful-looking and never had much to say for herself.

'He was killed in the war,' Billy replied as Bob refilled everyone's glasses.

'Was he in the Army?' Jean asked, sipping the sweet sherry, which she wasn't exactly fond of.

Billy nodded. 'He was with Monty in North Africa. Mam said the night they came to tell Aunt Alice that Walter Dobson had been killed in action was one of the worst days in her life. Aunt Alice never really got over it.'

They all shook their heads at the tragedy but Bob felt as though a dagger had been thrust into his chest. He felt icily cold and his hands began to tremble. It couldn't be! It just *couldn't* be! Alice Dobson was Billy's *aunt*! He could see her as she'd been all those years ago. Dark-haired and pretty, her blue eyes dancing, her soft lips slightly parted. Dear God, how often had he regretted that mad, wartime affair, how guilty he'd felt all these years and how desperately hard he'd tried to keep it a secret and now ... now ... ! A terrible suspicion was taking hold of him: would it all come out and shatter everyone's happiness? There was only one thing he could do: go and see her and beg her not to say a word about it. But would she listen? Was she still bitter at the way he'd ended that mad fling when the guilt had finally made him see sense? He just prayed that she wasn't, prayed that she had mellowed with the years.

Chapter Thirteen

———◆———

IT HAD BEEN THE WORST weekend of Bob's life. It had taken every ounce of strength and self-control to remain outwardly his usual self. Fear and guilt were tearing him apart. He'd hardly slept, going over and over in his mind the times he had spent with Alice. He hadn't known her before that night when he'd been patrolling his area. He had been rejected for active service because at the medical they'd found a heart murmur, something that he'd never suspected he had nor had bothered him since, so he'd become an Air Raid Patrol warden. He could vividly remember knocking on her door after he'd spotted a chink of light showing from an upstairs window. She'd come to the door wearing a pale blue dressing gown, her dark hair falling loose around her shoulders, and he'd thought how lovely she looked. He'd started to tell her about the light when the siren had sounded.

'For God's sake, go and get dressed and get to the shelter!' he'd urged her. She'd begged him to wait, she was on her own and she was terrified, she'd told him, her husband was serving overseas. He'd waited and then escorted her to the shelter. As the bombs had begun to fall, he'd been caught up in the mayhem of the raid, but when the all-clear had sounded he'd gone to find her. Why he'd done so he never knew. He'd seen her home and had fallen under the spell of those luminous blue eyes. He had been infatuated with her, unable to keep away. It wasn't love, it never had been, but almost every night he'd gone to see her. With Walter Dobson away in North Africa she was lonely and nervous but he'd also deduced from things she said that the marriage wasn't very happy. His own marriage was no bed of roses either. The war was playing havoc with Flo's nerves. She was tense and irritable and impatient with him, and having to spend hours queuing for food each day with Graham as a fractious baby in the pram didn't help. There were times when he hadn't wanted to go home and listen to all her complaints. Now he wished he'd never set eyes on Alice Dobson. The memory of that affair had haunted him down the years.

On Monday morning, with a feeling of utter dread, he left for work as usual but he got off the bus at Fazakerley Terminus and changed for a bus that would take him to Norris Green. When he got off at Broadway he bought a copy of the *Daily Post* and walked down Utting Avenue. He'd obtained the address from

Dee and now he lingered on the corner of Lorenzo Drive pretending to be engrossed in the newspaper until at last he saw a woman leaving number fourteen. He fervently hoped it was Alice's sister and not Alice herself for he had no excuse to ask to see Alice. He would be a complete stranger to her sister.

When the woman was out of sight he walked slowly towards the house, his stomach churning with every step. Bracing himself, he knocked on the front door.

He barely recognised the woman who opened it as the Alice he'd known. She was pale, thin and dressed in a drab-looking skirt and blouse covered by a grey cardigan. Her hair was no longer dark, thick and glossy. It was greying and pulled back into a bun. Her eyes seemed to have faded to a light blue-grey and lines of worry and discontent were etched deeply on her face.

'Alice? Alice Dobson?' He could barely get the words out.

She nodded. 'Are you the new insurance man?' Her tone was sharp.

'No. No . . . I'm Bob, Bob Campbell and I have to speak to you. Can I come in?'

Her eyebrows shot up in surprise and her hand went to her throat but mistrust filled her eyes. She'd never expected to see him again. She'd never wanted to. He'd put on weight and his hair was greying. 'What . . . what the hell do you want? How did you find me?'

'Alice, please! Can I come in? I can't talk to you on the doorstep,' he pleaded.

Reluctantly she opened the door wider and he

stepped into the hall. She closed the door behind him. 'Have your say and then go! Our Doreen won't be long and I don't want her to see *you* here.'

'Alice I've come to beg you not to say a thing about what happened between us . . . during the war.'

Her eyes narrowed and she clutched the cardigan closer to her. 'Why?'

'Because Dee is my daughter and she and Billy have just got engaged and if . . . if anything ever . . . came out . . . Don't you see, Alice, it would ruin everything,' he begged. 'You wouldn't want everything to . . . to blow up in their faces.'

She stared at him, unable to keep the shock from her expression. 'Dee is your *daughter*?'

He nodded. 'I know I didn't treat you very well back then, Alice—'

'You didn't!' she interrupted angrily. 'You left me to face . . . things alone.'

'It was wartime, Alice! We didn't know if we would survive from day to day. It was madness, I know, but that doesn't change the fact that it happened.'

'It shouldn't have!' she snapped back. She held his gaze. 'You'd better come into the kitchen,' she said flatly. She turned and went down the hall and into the kitchen. Bob followed her apprehensively.

She sat down clasping her hands tightly together, her eyes fixed on the floor. 'This . . . this isn't going to be easy but . . . but you'll have to know now. After you stopped coming round to see me, after you dropped me and all that . . . madness was finally over, I found I was pregnant. I . . . I knew it wasn't Walter's – it couldn't have been – and then he was killed. I was in such a state . . . the shock . . .' She was struggling with the words and the memories. She'd tried to obliterate them from her mind for so long. 'I didn't know where to turn but in the end I had to tell Doreen.'

'Why didn't you tell me!' Bob cried. The blood was pounding in his head. He couldn't believe this.

She looked up at him with venom in her eyes. 'You'd made it very clear that you didn't care about me so I wanted nothing more to do with you! I *hated* you! I still hate you, you ruined my life! Doreen and Will took me in. I was so distraught with . . . with everything but I wouldn't say whose it was. Both she and Will were good to me. She looked after me and I had the child and they adopted him. I called him William – Billy – after Will Grainger. And from that day I've been beholden to them for a roof over my head, for their silence that's given me the "respectability" of being a childless war widow.' She gave a bitter laugh. 'So, now you know.'

Bob couldn't speak, a terrible, dark fear washed over him and he felt dizzy. He clutched at the edge of the table to steady himself.

Alice looked at him coldly.

Bob was shaking his head in disbelief at the enormity of the disaster that was looming in his mind. 'But Dee and . . . and Billy . . . they . . .' He couldn't go on. He couldn't frame the words, face the possibility.

'I never knew you'd had more children. I never even

suspected that Dee was your daughter. Why should I? Campbell is a common enough name.'

Bob could only shake his head in mute misery and shock.

He was icily cold and his heart was thumping in his chest.

She jumped to her feet. 'They can't be engaged! They're brother and sister!' she said. A wave of intense fury surged through her. 'All these years I blamed myself. I told myself the pain of having to watch Billy grow up and never know I was his mother was my punishment for the sins I committed with you. But it's nothing compared to what you've done. It's all your fault, Bob Campbell! You deserted me and went back to your wife and you had Dee! You've ruined my life, our Billy's and now Dee's! I hope you're satisfied – and I hope when you die you rot in hell for it. Get out! Go back and tell them what you've done. I hope she throws you out and that Dee never speaks to you again! Get out, get out ... you ... selfish, cheating swine!'

Bob stumbled from the room and out of the house, feeling as if he were indeed about to die. Her words hammered in his head; he felt sick and dizzy and he was finding it hard to get his breath. He dragged himself slowly back towards the bus stop. She was right. It was all his fault. A tide of guilt and anguish engulfed him and he leaned against the wall of a shop, fighting for breath. How was he going to tell them? What was he going to say to them: Flo and Dee and Graham and

Davie? And what would this terrible news do to Dee? He felt the cold sweat trickle down his face.

A passer-by stopped. ''Ere, mate, are you all right? Yer look terrible!'

'Don't . . . don't feel good. Can you get me to the bus stop?' Bob pleaded.

The man looked perturbed. 'I think it's an ambulance yer need, mate, not a bus,' he urged.

Bob shook his head. He'd be all right if he could just get home. He'd lie down and this would pass. It was shock, pure and simple. 'Please, please . . . just the bus to Fazakerley.'

'Where do yer live?'

'Kirkby.' Bob's breath was coming a little easier.

'Christ! Yer'll never get that far. Look, I'll come with yer. I'm a steward on the *Laconia* and I don't sail until tomorrow. Give me yer arm, take it slow now.'

Leaning heavily on the man's arm Bob slowly made his way to the bus stop.

As the journey progressed Bob felt stronger although his mind was still in a daze and his heart was still thumping in his chest. He learned that his Good Samaritan's name was Tommy Doyle and he'd been going into Liverpool to sort out a 'bit of business' but it could wait. Bob was only half listening; he felt profoundly grateful for the man's company and compassion and the fact that he didn't ask too many questions.

After what seemed like hours to Bob they finally reached Buttermere Close and Tommy Doyle knocked on the front door, having said it would probably give

Flo a terrible shock to suddenly see her husband and a complete stranger appear in the hallway if Bob used his key.

'Bob! Dear God! What's the matter?' Flo cried as she took in her husband's ashen face.

'It's all right, luv. He took a bad turn so I brought him home. I think he'd best see a doctor though.'

Flo ushered them both in. 'That was very good of you, Mr . . . ?'

'Doyle. Tommy Doyle. I'd get him straight to bed, luv.'

Flo nodded. She'd never seen Bob look so ill and he seemed to have aged too. 'Will you help me get him upstairs, please?' She was very worried.

Between them they got him upstairs and while Flo got Bob into bed Tommy Doyle went down to put the kettle on. The poor woman looked almost as bad as her husband and to his mind didn't look as if she could cope.

'Here, sit yourself down and have this cup of tea. I can see it's been a bit of a shock for yer, like,' Tommy Doyle instructed.

Flo nodded and sank down on a kitchen chair.

'Do yer have a phone?' he asked.

'No. No, but there's a phone box on the corner.'

'Is there anyone – a neighbour – who can come and sit with yer while I go and phone for the doctor?'

'Yes. Yes, Ada Williams at number six. I'll get you the doctor's number and I can't thank you enough, Mr Doyle.'

'Well, I couldn't just leave the poor feller, now could I? Mind you, I did say it was an ambulance he needed not a bus but he wouldn't have it. Thankfully we were near the bus stop. I'll go along and get this Ada Williams.'

Ada soon came bustling into the kitchen, concern written all over her face. 'What's happened to him, Flo? That feller who's gone to phone the doctor said he took a turn.'

Flo bit her lip. 'I don't know, Ada, but he looks terrible. Thank God that kind Mr Doyle went out of his way to help.'

'Was he all right going out to work?' Ada had never known Bob Campbell to be ill.

Flo nodded, still looking anxious. 'Same as usual although he's been a bit sort of quiet since Saturday night.'

'Well, maybe he's just been doing too much and after all we none of us are getting any younger, Flo.'

Flo sipped the strong, sweet tea. She hoped Ada was right but she'd have to make sure Bob took things easier in future. 'I'll go up and sit with him, Ada. Until the doctor comes.'

'Aye, luv, you do that,' Ada urged.

A few minutes later Tommy Doyle reappeared. 'Doc's on his way, luv. He'll sort everything out. Well, I'd better get going now. Things ter do, people ter see.'

Ada got to her feet. 'She . . . we can't thank you enough. God bless you for the kind, caring man you are. At least let me give you your bus fares?'

'Wouldn't hear of it, luv! If yer can't do someone a good turn in their hour of need then it's a poor show, that's what I say. Good luck to yer both.'

Once upstairs Flo had sat down beside the bed, biting her lip anxiously. Bob didn't look at all well. His skin had a greyish tinge and he was finding it hard to breathe. 'The doctor will be here soon now, luv.' She took his hand.

'I . . . I'm sorry . . . Flo.' The words came slowly.

'Don't try to speak, Bob. Just try and rest now.' Oh, how she wished the doctor would hurry. What was keeping him?

Bob tried again although the pain in his chest was terrible. 'I . . . It's you I really love, Flo and . . . and Dee! I'm so sorry . . . sorry about . . . Dee.'

'Hush! All you're doing is making yourself worse, luv. Don't try to say another word. I know you love me and the kids. Hush now,' she urged, almost frantic with worry.

At least he seemed to have taken notice of her, she thought as he closed his eyes.

Ada had poured in the washing-up liquid and filled the sink with hot water and had started to wash up when she heard Flo's screams. The cup she was in the act of placing on the draining board slipped from her hand and smashed on the floor but she didn't give it a single thought as she cried out sharply and dashed for the stairs. When she reached the bedroom it was to find Flo on her knees beside the bed, crying hysterically and shaking her husband.

'Flo! Flo, luv! What's wrong?'

'Bob! Bob! Oh, God, Ada! He . . . he's not breathing!'

With a hand that shook visibly Ada reached out and took his wrist, feeling for a pulse. There was none. Bob Campbell was dead.

Despite her own shock Ada had managed to get a distraught Flo downstairs and when Dr Fairfax arrived it was she who told him what had happened. He'd gone upstairs and had then returned to the kitchen to confirm what both women already knew. Bob Campbell had most probably died of a heart attack, he'd told them, but he wouldn't know for certain until there had been a post-mortem and then probably an inquest. He would set things in motion. He'd given Flo a sedative and asked Ada about the rest of the family. Ada said she would get in touch with Graham and Dee's works and ask them to send them home. She would also phone the school and ask them to send Davie home.

'I think it best, Mrs Williams, if you just say there has been an emergency at home. Don't give any details, not over the phone,' he advised.

Ada had nodded. 'I . . . I'll tell them when they get home, doctor. She's not in any fit state to do it, God help her.'

He'd nodded sympathetically and taken his leave.

Ada sat down at the table, her head in her hands. She wasn't looking forward to having to impart this terrible news. She couldn't take it in herself. It was beyond belief. He'd left the house that morning, fit and well, and now just a few hours later he was dead! She'd known him for so long and he'd been a great friend. He'd always been such a steady, reliable man. A good husband and father. He'd come through all the trauma and horror of war and the terrible May Blitz and just when they'd got a decent house and life was good, this had to happen. She'd miss him terribly, as would Harry. What was poor Flo going to do now? she wondered sadly.

Chapter Fourteen

———◆———

A S SHE SAT ON THE bus Dee was confused and worried. Stephanie Black, the welfare officer, had come up to the office to give her Ada's message. Just what had happened at home that constituted this 'emergency'? Was it her Da, she wondered, could something have happened to him? Or was it Mam? Could she have been taken ill or fallen or had some kind of accident for Ada to ring up and summon her home? Or maybe it was Davie, he always seemed to be in some scrape or other, but no, in that case Mam would have phoned herself. All the way home she fretted and worried, wishing Ada had given some clue as to what had happened.

When she rushed into the living room it was to find her mother sitting on the sofa looking as though she was half asleep and Davie, with his head buried on her shoulder, sobbing.

'Oh, Mam! What's happened? Are you all right? Are you ill? Did you fall?' she cried, her voice shrill with worry.

Ada got to her feet wearily. Telling Dee the terrible news was going to be harder than it had been telling Davie. Dee had been the apple of her da's eye.

'It's not your mam. Oh, Dee, luv! It's terrible . . . terrible! I hate to have to tell you this but . . . but it's your da. Some feller brought him home from work – he'd had a bad turn – and . . . and then before the doctor could get here he had a heart attack and . . . died.' Ada wiped her eyes with her apron.

Dee shook her head in total disbelief. No! No! Da couldn't be *dead*! He'd kissed her on the cheek before he'd left for work only a few hours ago and now . . . now Ada was telling her that she'd never see him again, that he'd gone from her life . . . all their lives . . . for ever! The realisation hit her like a physical blow.

'No! No, not Da! He . . . he can't be . . . dead!' She flung herself into Ada's arms, sobbing as though her heart would break.

'Hush. Hush now, luv. At least it was quick.' Ada tried to calm her, knowing how utterly pointless it was. Shock, disbelief and searing grief were what they were all suffering and soon Graham would be home and she would have to find the strength to repeat it all again. Her heart was so heavy and aching for them all.

Dee didn't remember much about the rest of that awful afternoon. She just couldn't take it in that her da was dead. She'd loved him so much, relied on him, always turned to him for advice. She and Graham had clung together as the undertakers had arrived. Ada had told her that the doctor had given Flo something to calm her, which was why she looked dazed and as if she was half asleep. Davie had stopped sobbing but he was very bewildered. Ada wondered if it had it really sunk in, and he was also obviously frightened by the grief of his older brother and sister and his mother's confused, half-conscious state. As soon as young Peter Williams arrived home from school she sent the two lads down to her own house, hoping the company of his friend might help Davie.

Dee felt as if she were in a dream, or rather a sort of waking nightmare. There seemed to be people in and out of the house all the time: the undertakers, the neighbours, the minister from the church, who had called to offer his condolences even though they were infrequent church-goers. Then at last Jean arrived and she clung to her friend, sobbing brokenly.

Jean herself was shocked and upset by the news. She'd known Bob Campbell all her life and she'd liked him enormously.

'It's awful, Jean! I just can't believe I'll never see him again!'

'Neither can I, Dee. Oh, what a thing to happen and he was such a lovely man!'

Dee raised a tear-stained face, her eyes red and swollen. 'He wasn't ill. He didn't complain about anything, he went off to work this morning the same as usual and now . . .' She broke down again and Jean was completely at a loss to what to say or do to comfort her. She felt utterly helpless.

'Has anyone had anything to eat today?' she asked when Dee had calmed down a little.

Dee shook her head. 'I couldn't force anything past my lips, I . . . I'd be sick.'

'You have to eat – all of you! Mam must have told you that,' Jean urged.

'She made some toast earlier but none of us could touch it.'

Jean sighed. 'I phoned Tony from the shop as soon as I heard and asked him to get in touch with Billy. I told him to tell Billy what's happened and ask him to come over as soon as he possibly can.' She hoped that he wouldn't be long and that he might be able to bring some comfort to Dee.

Dee was calmer when Billy arrived, looking very concerned. They were all still sitting in the darkened living room for, according to custom, Ada had closed the curtains, shutting out the bright, sunny April evening. Dee immediately went to him and he took her in his arms.

'Dee, I'm so, so sorry! It's a tragedy. A terrible tragedy.'

'Jean, you can give me a hand to get poor Flo to bed. She's like the walking dead herself, poor soul, with what the doctor gave her. Maybe after a night's rest she'll be a bit more her usual self tomorrow although I doubt it. And just when things were going so well for her. Her nerves have been so much better this last year.' Ada was worried for them all. She had decided to keep Davie overnight for Peter seemed to have been able to calm the lad. Flo would definitely be better off in bed rather than sitting slumped on the sofa and Dee and Billy deserved a bit of privacy. Graham was up in his room and he'd begged not to be disturbed. He just wanted some time on his own, he'd told her.

Billy eased Dee down on to the sofa and held her tightly. 'Do you want me to stay overnight? I don't mind. I told Mam I probably would.' His mother had been genuinely upset for Dee and, inexplicably, his Aunt Alice seemed to have been very shocked by the news. In fact she'd gone very pale and had had to sit down.

'No. Thank you, Billy, I'll be all right.'

'Shall I let them know you won't be going into work this week?'

She nodded. Even in this state of shock and grief and confusion she realised that there were things that had to be done, arrangements to be made, and she wondered how both she and her mother were going to cope. What kind of effect would this have on her mother's nerves?

After Billy, Ada and Jean had gone Graham came downstairs. His eyes were red and he looked drawn and utterly miserable. He sat down beside Dee.

'What are we going to do now, Dee? We all relied on him so much. We all took him for granted.'

'I don't know,' she replied tiredly. She felt drained.

'Do you think Mam will be able to cope with it all? I mean, you know, with her nerves?'

175

Dee shook her head. 'I don't know that either.'

He sighed deeply. 'I suppose I'll have to try to take his place. I mean look after all the things he did. The finances and things like that.'

She felt sorry for him. He was trying so hard. 'We'll both have to help Mam with everything now. We'll manage. We'll get through these next days and weeks – somehow.'

They did indeed muddle through as best they could with the help of Ada and Harry Williams and their family. Dee was so grateful for the comfort and support both Billy and Jean gave her. The post-mortem results were just what they expected: a massive heart attack. There was no need for an inquest and the funeral was arranged. They were all dreading it but Dee most of all because her mother seemed incapable of making any kind of effort to do *anything* at all. She was sunk in apathy. It was Dee and Ada who managed the day-to-day chores and sorted out suitable mourning clothes. They chose the hymns for the church service, ordered the flowers and put the obituary in the paper.

'I just couldn't stand having everyone back here for something to eat afterwards,' Dee confided to Ada after they'd got back from the florist's.

Ada understood, but she looked doubtful. 'It will be expected, Dee. I know the neighbours have clubbed together for a wreath.'

Dee rubbed her aching temples and tried to concentrate. 'That was good of them, but do you think they will understand how hard a day it's going to be for us?'

Ada nodded slowly. She would try her best to explain that Flo was so stunned that she didn't know what day of the week it was and the others were so young and their grief so raw. 'There will be just us then, and Tony.'

'Billy said his parents were going to come to the church service but that they wouldn't impose on us by coming back to the house,' Dee informed her.

'That's good of them. What about the aunt?' Ada asked.

Dee shook her head. 'No, she's not coming.'

Ada sighed. 'Probably bring back too many memories of when she buried her own husband, poor soul.'

She got to her feet to make a pot of tea before she made out the list of groceries they would need. There would still be ten people to feed when they returned from the cemetery.

The morning of Bob Campbell's funeral was bright and sunny with barely a cloud in the sky. Spring flowers were blooming in gardens and under hedges and birds swooped and twittered in the branches of trees where green buds were unfurling. It was all wrong, Dee thought miserably. The skies should be dull and grey, with no sunlight sparkling off windows. How could the day be so full of brightness and the sounds and scents of spring when she felt so utterly bereft? Graham was supporting their mother who was calm. Too calm, a state induced by tablets. The black coat and hat Flo wore had taken every scrap of colour from her face and she looked pale and tired and seemed to have aged ten years. Dee herself clung tightly to Billy's arm for support, her other arm around the shoulders of Davie who was fighting down the sobs.

Ada and Harry followed them, Harry pensive and serious for once, Ada dabbing at reddened eyes. They had both lost an old and trusted friend. Jean walked behind them with Tony and Peter. Margaret had been told in no uncertain terms by her grieving and harassed mother that if she was going to come she must come alone and not bring little Francis who would undoubtedly disrupt things and cause more upset. Margaret had taken umbrage at this slight on her son and cross words had passed between her and Ada, the upshot of which was that she was absent. Jean doubted that Dee would even notice that she wasn't there.

After the service they were all driven to the cemetery and Dee found it almost impossible not to break down completely as the coffin that contained her beloved father's body was lowered into the grave. She buried her face in Billy's shoulder and sobbed while he held her tightly, wishing he could do or say something that would alleviate her grief. Her twenty-first birthday had been totally forgotten and so had their engagement. She wore her ring and he'd seen Ada glance at it but she'd said nothing. He hoped that now the funeral was over poor Dee could try to pick up the pieces of her life. He'd be by her side to help her every step of the way.

Chapter Fifteen

———◆———

ALICE LOOKED AT HERSELF in the dressing-table mirror. There was no colour at all in her face, even her lips appeared bloodless. Was it any wonder? she thought dully. She had been totally shocked when she'd heard he had died of a heart attack. She'd been furious with him for the situation he'd created but she hadn't wished him dead. She was aware now that it had been that visit and what she had said to him that had shocked him so much that it had killed him. He'd looked like death when he'd left but she hadn't cared.

She dropped her head into her hands. Oh, what had she done? What must she do now? With him dead and buried she was the only one who knew who Billy's natural father was and that now Billy could no longer go on seeing Dee. At times, as she tossed and turned during the night when sleep eluded her, she was tempted to say nothing. What harm could it do?

No one would ever know that they were brother and sister – *half*-brother and -sister. Then reason and her conscience would prevail. It would be neither right nor fair to put Billy in that position or leave Dee in the dark. What if by some malign quirk of fate it came out. When she died she would have to face her Maker and hadn't she enough sins on her soul already? This terrible situation that now faced her was of her own making. She had thought that she had more than paid for her adulterous affair with Bob Campbell but now it appeared she hadn't even begun to suffer. Guilt, remorse, anguish and heartbreak would be her lot for the rest of her life.

At last she got up, straightening her thin shoulders. She would have to tell her sister. She would have to start a chain of misery which would encircle them all and because of it she would be reviled by everyone who was involved. Bitterly she wished now that she had broken the news to him in a gentler way. That she had not yelled at him that it was all his fault and used those vicious, vituperative, vindictive words. Now she was going to have to bear the full brunt of everyone's anger and disgust alone.

Doreen Grainger was clearing away the breakfast dishes in the kitchen but she looked up as Alice came into the room. She frowned with concern. She was aware that there was something troubling her sister; Alice'd been quieter than normal and she'd heard her pacing the floor during the night.

'You look terrible. You need a decent night's sleep,

Alice. I heard you up again last night. What's wrong? There's something worrying you.'

Alice sat down at the table. She couldn't meet her sister's eyes. 'I have to tell you this, Doreen. It . . . it's going to break so many hearts but I can't keep quiet about it any longer. Bob Campbell came here the morning before he . . . he died.' She twisted her hands together helplessly.

Doreen nodded slowly. She had wondered why Alice had been so shocked when they'd heard the news. She hadn't thought her sister had known him. 'What did he come here for? Was there a message for Billy?'

'No, but it was about Billy,' Alice answered, her hands were now shaking.

Doreen waited, and a feeling of dread began to creep over her.

'He'd come to beg me not to say anything about the affair we had . . . during the Blitz.'

Doreen caught her breath. After all these years was Alice now revealing to her who the boy's father was, something she had always stubbornly refused to do? 'And?' It was a whisper.

Alice nodded miserably. 'I had to tell him about . . . Billy. I wish to God I'd never set eyes on him all those years ago, Doreen, I mean that!'

Doreen was shaking her head, her eyes wide with disbelief. All the colour had drained from her face.

'I had to tell him, Doreen, because . . . because, oh, dear God! Dee . . . Dee is his daughter.'

The full realisation of what Alice was saying dawned

on Doreen. 'You mean ... you mean that Billy and Dee ... ?'

Again Alice nodded miserably.

Doreen was on her feet, her eyes blazing. 'For the love of God, Alice! Why didn't you say something when he first brought Dee home? Why did you let it get to this stage? They're engaged! Oh, sweet Jesus! Do you realise what this means? Do you realise what this will do to them both?'

'I didn't know! I swear to God, I didn't know! Campbell is a common enough name. He went out of my life and I wanted it that way. I didn't realise he had had two more children. Do you think if I'd have known Dee was his daughter I'd have kept quiet?' Alice's guilt and sorrow overwhelmed her and she broke down, sobs racking her thin body.

Doreen fought down her shock and anger. She'd thought it had been best for herself and Will to adopt Billy and thus save her sister from disgrace. She'd known she could never have children and she'd desperately wanted one. She and Will had given him a good home and a chance in life, something Alice on her own could never have done. Now it seemed as though her sister's sin of adultery was coming home to roost. Billy would have to know the truth and so would Dee and the rest of her family. Oh, dear God! What a mess! What a bloody mess! she thought.

She put her arm around her weeping sister. 'What's done is done, Alice. We can't change it no matter how much we long to. I'll have to tell Will and then we'll decide how and when we're going to tell Billy and Dee.'

It was something she wished with all her heart they didn't have to do. It would break her heart to see Billy's reaction. She'd loved the boy from the moment he'd been born and Will idolised him too – he was their life. They'd liked Dee, too, as soon as they'd met her and had been looking forward to welcoming her as their daughter. They had seemed such a close and loving couple. And no wonder! she thought bitterly. 'And it will tear that whole family apart. After the shock of Bob Campbell's death they are going to have to face . . . *this*.'

Alice sobbed harder. 'I wish I was dead! I told him I hoped he'd rot in hell but I deserve the same fate. All the lives I've destroyed, Doreen! No one will ever forgive me and I'll never forgive myself!'

Sadly Doreen nodded. Alice was right. A brief wartime fling and a generation later everyone would experience the terrible repercussions.

When Will Grainger came home from work it was to news that shocked him to the core. Alice was in her room, still crying, and after his wife had told him the whole sorry story he had put his head in his hands and wept. Doreen had put her arms around him until he finally calmed down.

'They are both going to have to be told, Will. And as soon as possible. It's not something that we can in all conscience keep from them.'

'Is Dee coming tonight?'

Doreen nodded miserably.

'Then we'll tell them tonight and . . . and afterwards I'll go home with Dee. That poor woman will have to be told and Dee isn't going to be in any fit state to tell her.' He felt desolate. The more he thought about it the worse it got. Dee had been the apple of her father's eye and now added to the grief she was suffering would be the bitter knowledge that his infidelity and betrayal was the cause of the terrible heartbreak she would be suffering. That they would all be suffering.

When Billy and Dee came in after night school they were both surprised to find Will and Doreen in such a sombre mood. Billy was even more puzzled when his father told them both to sit down for there was something important he had to tell them. They sat side by side on the sofa and listened in stunned and disbelieving silence as Will, briefly and as gently as he could, told them about Alice and Bob Campbell. When he'd finished Billy stood up, running his hands through his hair, trying to assimilate everything.

'You mean Aunt Alice is my mother? And . . . and . . .'

Will caught him by the shoulders. 'Billy, I wish to God this wasn't true!'

Billy turned and look down at Dee, who was sitting bolt upright, her eyes wide with shock, her hands over her mouth, her face the colour of parchment. He loved Dee with all his heart and soul; he'd never wanted anyone else. They'd been going to get married but now they had no future! All those years ago . . . Aunt Alice his *mother* and . . . and Bob Campbell his *father*! A rage, the like of which he'd never experienced before, boiled in him. 'Let me go, Da! You lied to me! You all lied to me! And she's the worst, a lying, cheating whore!' He tried to shake off Will's grip but the man he'd always thought of as his father held him in a grip like a vice.

'No, lad! Raging at her won't change things! And I know you don't want to hear this right now, but she's paid for it. She's suffered and she'll go on suffering. We're still your mother and father, we brought you up, we love you! Oh, God! I'm so sorry, Billy!'

Billy was shaking; his breath was coming in racking sobs as he clung to Will. 'I . . . I'm glad *he's* dead because I'd have killed him with my bare hands for this!'

Dee had watched all this in terror and now she screamed, holding her arms out to him. 'Billy! Billy!'

Doreen immediately went to her and took her in her arms. 'Dee, we'd hoped you'd be so happy, we loved you as our own! But, my love, it's over! It has to be! You can never see each other again. My heart is breaking in two, luv. I swear to God it is! Oh, may He give us all the strength to get through this,' Doreen cried, the tears streaming down her cheeks.

Dee looked at her as if she were a stranger. Her world, already shaken by the loss of her father, was crashing to bits around her. Billy, the only boy she had ever loved and whom she'd thought she would spend the rest of her life with, was the son of her father and

Alice Dobson. He had been cruelly snatched away from her. Her father, whom she had also loved so much, had betrayed her in a way she had never thought possible. She was shaking and crying as she clung to Doreen.

When Dee was calmer Will wearily put on his jacket. This terrible night wasn't over yet. 'I'll take you home, luv. Someone has got to tell your mam. You can have a few minutes with Billy before you go.'

They clung silently to each other. Dee was still sobbing brokenly and tears were now falling slowly down Billy's cheeks. She was too devastated, too utterly broken-hearted to speak and Billy couldn't find any words at all. What *was* there to say? he thought bitterly. Despite everything he loved her but now he would have to watch her walk out of his life for ever.

At last Will and Doreen came and gently separated them, Will helping Dee on with her coat and Doreen putting her arms around Billy, who was still weeping quietly. She knew there would be some very difficult days ahead with Billy but she prayed that in time he would get over the terrible anguish he was now suffering.

Dee let Will Grainger lead her from the room. She couldn't look at Billy or even utter a single word to him. The bright dream of their future together lay broken and dead, killed by his natural mother and her father. She forced herself not to think of her da; if she did she would go mad.

On the bus it was as if her mind was a void. She could concentrate on nothing. Most of the time she didn't even know where she was. She held tightly to Will Grainger's arm, fearing if she let go she would fall and go on falling into . . . what? From time to time he asked her if she was all right and she nodded but all she wanted to do was find somewhere, some haven where she could lie down and close her eyes and her mind. Shut out everything that had happened. She didn't want to have to see the horror on her mam's face or hear her hysterical screams and recriminations. She couldn't bring herself to worry or care how Mam would cope with it all. She was too tired, too shocked and sick, too heartsore.

When they arrived home she ignored her mother's astonished look and the questions that rose to Flo's lips. Without a word she went straight up the stairs to her room and closed the door. Not bothering to get undressed she fell on her bed and covered her head with the pillows. The terrible sense of loss, of disgust at her father's betrayal, and of grief she had never known could be so profound or overwhelming was tearing her apart.

Flo took the news as Will Grainger had expected. First disbelief, then fury, and then horror as she realised Dee and Billy could never see each other again. Will was at his wits' end and had no idea what to do. He couldn't leave the woman in this state and yet he had no desire to remain here. He had to get back home. The Lord alone knew what was going on there. If Billy lost control and decided to confront Alice, Doreen wouldn't be able to stop him.

Wakened by the sound of his mother's angry outburst and hearing Dee sobbing in her room, Davie came down and peered sheepishly around the door.

'I'm Will Grainger. Billy's father. She . . . she's had some bad news. Is there anyone – a friend – who could come and sit with her?' he asked.

'Is Dee all right?' Davie asked.

'She's upset too.'

'I'll go and get Jean and Mrs Williams.' Davie didn't know what it was that had upset his mam and Dee or why Billy's da had brought Dee home. Since his da had died so suddenly everything had changed. His world had been turned upside down and he didn't feel he could cope with whatever had happened now. By the look of things it was something else bad.

Will was relieved. 'Aye, lad. Tell them that no one has died but that it's a disaster just the same.'

Chapter Sixteen

———◆———

NEITHER JEAN NOR ADA could believe it. They had hastily followed Davie upon being summoned, despite the fact that it was now late at night.

'What the hell has gone wrong now?' Ada had muttered as she pulled a coat around her shoulders. Jean dragged on a jacket and they started after Davie who was already halfway down the front path.

Will Grainger had repeated the terrible story while Flo paced the room crying and interrupting with angry tirades. When he'd finished, Ada, who felt she'd been physically struck, pushed a stunned Jean towards the hall.

'Go on up to her, luv, and see what you can do.'

Jean found Dee lying face down on her bed, her face in the pillow, her shoulders shaking. She sat down beside her friend and reached out for her. 'Dee, it's me, Jean. I've just heard. Oh! I don't know what to say to you.'

Dee slowly turned over and sat up and at the sight of her red, swollen eyes and blotchy face Jean put her arms around her. 'It's terrible, Dee! I can hardly believe it.'

'I've lost him, Jean, and I love him so much and now . . . now that's wrong. He . . . he's my half-brother and I can never see him again!'

Jean was desperately trying to find words that would help but what was there she could say? All she could do was nod. Poor, poor Dee. She did love him so very much.

'Why? Why did it have to happen, Jean? Why did Da never tell anyone about himself and Alice and Billy? He must have suspected, why did he never say anything?' she pleaded brokenly.

'Dee, he didn't know. You heard what Mr Grainger said.'

'My da! How could he have done something like that? It . . . it's *horrible*! It's *disgusting*! The whole thing is *revolting*!'

Jean had to agree with her. Bob Campbell was the last person on earth she would have suspected of carrying on like that. 'I suppose . . . things like that happened. It's just a terrible twist of fate that you had to fall in love with Billy. It just wasn't meant to be, Dee.' That all sounded so ineffectual, so utterly pathetic, she thought desperately.

Dee collapsed in sobs again. Her head was pounding and she felt totally drained. 'What am I going to do now, Jean? How am I going to go on? I can't think of my life without Billy. I . . . I just feel as if I want to die!'

'Oh, please don't say things like that, Dee! You've got the rest of your life ahead of you,' Jean cried, frightened by the despair in her friend's voice.

'What kind of a life will it be without Billy? We had such plans, you know we did.'

Jean stroked Dee's thick curly hair, feeling so helpless. 'I know you did but try not to think about it all now. You're shocked and you've cried yourself into exhaustion, do you think you could try and sleep? I'll stay here with you, I promise.'

Dee thought she would never sleep peacefully ever again but she was exhausted. The force of her emotions had drained her. 'I'll try, Jean.'

Thankful that her friend was calmer, Jean helped Dee undress and then pulled the quilt over her. 'I'll sit here on the end of the bed. Try and sleep,' she urged. She would stay until her mam came up and then she'd phone Pauline first thing in the morning to tell her she wouldn't be in until lunchtime. In the morning Dee might be able to look at the whole situation in a different light but she would need help and support and judging by the sounds coming from downstairs she wouldn't get either from her mam. Oh, in time she prayed Dee would get over it all. There would be deep scars but maybe one day she'd find someone else and be happy, although she doubted Dee would ever forgive her father. In Dee's place she knew she never would. In some ways it was better that he had died.

*

Ada was having almost as difficult a time with Flo. She had sent young Davie back up to bed, telling him not to worry, there had been a terrible row between Dee and Billy and the engagement was off. She knew Flo wouldn't have wanted the lad to know the truth, he was too young. Graham was still out and Ada knew it would fall to her to tell him what had happened when he finally arrived home.

'How could he do such a thing to me, Ada? I've never looked at another man, you know that! And you know what times were like then, and there I was with our Graham a baby, at my wits' end – my nerves in tatters with all the bombing and the queuing and the hardships. How could he go to *that* one and ... and ... ?' Flo was beside herself with hurt, shame and rage.

Ada shook her head. They'd known each other for so long and she had never, ever suspected that Bob Campbell could have been unfaithful to Flo. There had never been a whisper or a hint of anything like this; he was the most respectable, quiet, steady man she'd known. He'd lived for his family and he'd had the patience of Job with Flo and her nerves. Now she knew why.

'It was wartime, Flo, luv. It went on all the time. The fellers were away, women were lonely. You remember that one who lived at the bottom of Cobden Street? When her husband was wounded in North Africa and was sent home he found her with two kids that weren't his. And I bet she wasn't the only one in this city either. Oh, I'm not trying to make excuses for him, but times back then just weren't *normal*.'

Flo flung off Ada's comforting arm. 'And then . . . then he came back to me! After being with that whore! That *tart*! He came back to our bed! I've never felt so hurt, Ada, so humiliated, so disgusted! I swear to God, I'll never, never forgive him!'

'No one can blame you, Flo. It was a terrible betrayal.'

'Oh, if I'd have known, or even suspected, Ada . . .' Flo raged.

'Would you really have wanted to know, luv? And if you had, what would you have done? Thrown him out? How would you have managed then with three kids to bring up on your own?'

Flo ignored her. She was too wounded and full of rancour to think about that. 'And why did he never mention anything when our Dee first brought the lad home?' She was shaking with fury.

'He didn't know. If he had done you think he would have kept quiet? Didn't Will Grainger say he only found out when he went to see that Alice, the day he died?'

Flo uttered a harsh cry. 'And now we know what brought on the heart attack! He knew he'd been found out. He couldn't face the consequences of what he'd done. That's what killed him, Ada. And there's me heartbroken about it. Out of my mind with shock and grief. And poor Dee too. Oh, what he's done to that girl is criminal!'

Ada almost dragged her to the sofa and forced her to sit down. If she carried on like this then Ada was afraid that she too would have a heart attack. She didn't know which was worse: Flo in a dazed, sedative-induced state or almost bursting with the terrible fury that now drove her.

'Flo, sit down and try to calm yourself a bit. It is a devastating shock for you all, but particularly for Dee. No one loved or trusted their da more than she did and she loves that lad too. She's going to need a lot of comforting and support in the future and she's going to need it to come from *you*. You know we'll do whatever we can to help and our Jean is up there with her now, but it's her mam she's going to need.'

Flo dashed away her tears with the back of her hand. 'Oh, the shame of it all, Ada!'

Ada misunderstood her. 'No one but us need ever know. If anyone remarks about your Dee and Billy tell them they broke it off.'

'I didn't mean that kind of shame, although now you mention it . . . No, I mean the pity of it all. What will our Graham and young Davie think of their da now?' Her voice became harsh and strident again. 'Better they know the truth about him. The hypocritical, lying, cheating, selfish . . .'

'Ah, Flo! Try not to dwell on all that. You're going to make yourself ill. I know you're as mad as hell and I don't blame you. I would be too but they're all going to need you. You're going to have to be the steady one now. You'll have to help them overcome it all. Their security has been snatched away from them. It was bad enough them losing their da like that but now to find out that he wasn't all he seemed, and that Dee and Billy are . . . Well, it's a terrible thing for them to have to get used to.'

Flo wondered if she could ever be calm again. Her security had been snatched away too. All the happy memories of her marriage, the birth of her children, the family days out at New Brighton, Dee winning a scholarship, passing her exams, the delight in this new house, Dee's engagement, all were now tainted. And what about poor Billy? What kind of life would he now have? Having to live under the same roof as the woman he'd always believed was his aunt, the woman who had robbed him of the love of his life – Dee.

Ada patted her arm. 'Time is a great healer, Flo. I know that's not what you want to hear right now but it will get better, easier to cope with. And Dee is still very young and kids are resilient. Give it time, Flo. Just give it time.'

Flo nodded slowly. A great heaviness seemed to have descended on her.

'I'll make us a nice cup of tea. Have you any of those tablets the doctor left? They'll make you sleep.'

'No. I finished them and anyway, Ada, they really don't help. They just block out . . . things . . . feelings, for a short time. Then everything comes rushing back at you.'

Maybe it was for the best, Ada thought. You couldn't spend your life on tablets. There were things that had to be faced squarely no matter how painful. She sighed heavily as she got to her feet. There'd been no such thing as tranquillisers or anti-depressants during the war. They'd had to face the strain and terror of that with the aid of strong tea and an aspirin, if they were lucky enough to have both. If not, they'd coped without.

She left after Graham got home. Flo was composed enough to tell the lad herself what had happened and Ada felt weary and heartsore for them all. She had gone up to fetch Jean and found her sitting on Dee's bed, dozing fitfully. Dee was asleep, utterly exhausted.

'How is everything, Mam?' Jean whispered, taking in her mother's troubled frown and the lines of exhaustion around her eyes.

'Well, she's stopped ranting and raving and cursing him to high heaven but she's terribly upset. I've never seen her like that in all the years I've known her. I thought she'd have gone to pieces. I never expected such . . . such utter *fury*. How is Dee taking it?'

'The way you'd expect, Mam. She's devastated. Her world has fallen apart. She truly loves Billy. I don't know how she's going to come to terms with it all. I promised I'd come round in the morning. I'm not going into the salon until lunchtime. Pauline and Bernice will manage and Dee's going to need someone to be with her.'

'I told Flo I'd be back first thing too. As soon as I've got your da off to work and our Peter to school.' Ada leaned on her daughter's arm as they walked slowly home. 'Oh, there are dark days ahead for them, Jean, and my heart goes out to them all. God help them.'

Part IV

Chapter Seventeen

———◆———

THE ATMOSPHERE IN THE house was still terrible, even after three months, Dee thought as she left for work that warm July morning. Even at this hour the sun was hot on her back. It promised to be very hot later on. When she thought about it, and she tried desperately hard not to, she wondered just how she had got through those first awful weeks. There had been times when she thought she was going to lose all reason. Times when the pain and despair that filled her heart was so bad she could scarcely bear it. Times when she had cried day and night. She hadn't been able to go to work for almost two weeks.

Jean had been so good through it all. Almost every evening and on her days off she had come and sat with her. Listened patiently as she'd repeated the same things over and over again and asked questions to which there was no answer. Jean had tried to comfort her and instil in her some hope for the future. In those first dreadful days and nights she hadn't really cared how her mother and brothers were coping, she'd been completely overwhelmed by her own emotions. Gradually, however, as time had gone on she'd realised that Flo had changed. There didn't seem to be any pity or softness left in her. Nor was there any sign of the nerves that used to afflict her. It was as if what had happened and the way she had assimilated it had totally altered her nature. Her mother had become hard and bitter. She was quieter; she never smiled. Every photograph of her father had been destroyed. His name was never to be mentioned. Flo had tried to bury all the hurt and humiliation deep inside herself but it showed on her face and in her manner.

Graham had become withdrawn at first, refusing to speak to anyone about it, although she did remember him coming into her room and telling her he was so sorry for her and for Billy. Next he'd taken to going to the pub on his way home from work and staying out even later at weekends. Then the rows had started. Rows in which her mother irrationally heaped all their father's failings upon her brother's head. The fact that Graham looked very like his father didn't help, nor did the fact that he refused to place the blame entirely on Bob's shoulders. Often slurring his words Graham would shout back that if he'd been married to Flo he would have found an Alice Dobson too. She'd obviously driven him to it. Then her mam would yell that he was going to turn out just the same. A cheat, a liar, a bloody hypocrite. It was terrible and at first Dee had tried to intervene but it had been useless and lately she'd given up. Graham spent less and less time in the house and her mother never had a good word to say about her eldest son. Davie spent most of his time at Ada's house and he'd confided to her that at least the Williamses were a normal family. Their house wasn't like a lunatic asylum with his mam and Graham at each other's throats.

Her own life felt empty and pointless now. There were times when she felt utterly lost, times when she felt as angry as her mother at her father's betrayal and times when she felt weighed down by the sadness of his loss, and that of Billy. The future was a void and something she wouldn't let herself contemplate. She dragged herself to work each day, thankful that at least there she could forget her unhappiness, but evenings and weekends were becoming unbearable.

She stood waiting for her bus beneath the branches of a large elm by the side of the road that gave some shade. She was neat and tidy but she didn't have the same interest in her appearance as she once had. There seemed little point. Her pale pink cotton dress was fashionable, as were her sandals, and she carried a small handbag made of woven straw with a cane handle, decorated with a bunch of artificial cherries. Jean had virtually dragged her into town a couple of weeks ago, saying she must make an effort to look stylish, even if it was only for work, and she'd bought the bag and sandals then. She had some savings but she gave more to her mother now for her keep. She didn't mind, she had little interest in new clothes or going out. She knew her mother worried about their financial situation, a fact that also featured prominently in the rows. It was another accusation that was hurled at her brother: the amount of money he wasted on drink and cigarettes.

Celia had been very kind to her. Of course she hadn't told her the full story, just that she and Billy had split up and that coming so soon after her Da's death it had upset her terribly. It was Celia who told her that Billy had left. She'd heard that to everyone's surprise he had joined the Merchant Navy. Dee had felt some relief at this. She'd been terrified of bumping into him at work. She could understand his desire to get away from home too. It must have become unbearable for him.

At lunchtimes, as the weather was so fine, Celia often insisted they go for a walk and gradually Dee had begun to confide in her about how things were at home. Celia was a good listener and Dee felt grateful that she neither made comments nor offered advice on how to deal with her mother and older brother.

When she arrived in the office Celia looked up from the newspaper she was browsing through and smiled. They were always in the office fifteen minutes before they were officially due to start work.

'It's going to be another scorcher. There's a cup of tea for you on your desk. I brought one for us both from the canteen on my way in.'

Dee put her bag in the bottom drawer of her desk. 'Thanks. Anything interesting in that?'

Celia shrugged. 'I was just browsing. Seeing if there were any interesting offers for holidays. We're having a bit of a disagreement about where to go. I want to go to Spain on one of those package tours; because we have to have the "factory fortnight" everywhere is so crowded and all the kids are off school. I told you what it was like in Torquay last year – kids everywhere! John says we can't afford to be going abroad but it's not as expensive as it used to be. Have you any plans?'

Dee shook her head. 'I hadn't really thought about holidays.'

Celia looked concerned. 'Wouldn't you be better going somewhere for at least a week rather than being at home all day with your mother?'

Dee definitely didn't want to spend two weeks stuck at home all day. She knew Jean couldn't take time off from the salon, she was too busy, nor could she ask her to go away on holiday when she was saving up.

'I suppose I'd better start thinking of going somewhere then.'

Celia sipped her tea and looked thoughtful. 'There's something here that might interest you.'

'What?' Dee asked.

Celia peered closely at the paper. 'Ireland. It's not too far. You can go by ferry or there are flights from Liverpool. It says here: "Looking for a peaceful holiday away from the crowds? Bed, breakfast and evening meal in an historic house on the Grand Canal in the rural Irish countryside. Fresh air, good food, country walks and convivial company. Outside the county town of Tullamore, which has shops, cinemas and a rail link to Dublin. Apply for rates and vacancies to Mrs Mulcahey, The Canal House, Rahan." Well, does that sound interesting?' Celia passed her the paper.

Dee scanned the advertisement closely. She had never been on a holiday alone before. She had never been outside the country either.

'You could write and see if you can find out more. You need a break and some peace and quiet and that sounds just the place,' Celia urged.

'I'll think about it, Celia. I'll copy down the details.'

Celia nodded and got to her feet, checking her watch. 'Right. I'll get rid of these cups and then we'd both better look as if we're here to work and not to sit around reading the paper. I've got the minutes of yesterday's production meeting to transcribe before ten o'clock.'

Dee decided to ask Jean's advice about a holiday in Ireland. After she'd helped her mother wash up the tea dishes she went to see her friend. As usual there was no sign of Graham and she had had to listen to Flo's acid comments on another ruined meal.

Jean was getting ready to go out. She and Tony were going to look at a house in Moss Lane which was fairly near the salon and which she hoped they would both like and be able to afford. She hadn't told Dee much about their house-hunting, not wanting to upset her.

'Seeing Tony tonight?' Dee asked as Jean brushed

her short hair into place and then clipped on the black and white plastic hoop earrings that matched her white piqué dress trimmed with black braid.

'We're going to look at a house.' She gave an apologetic little smile.

'Jean, you don't have to keep thinking you're upsetting me.'

'I know, but it would be really hurtful of me to keep going on and on about houses and . . . things.'

Dee sat on the edge of the bed. 'I'm thinking of going away on holiday. Celia suggested it. You know we have to have the last week in July and the first in August – the "factory fortnight" – and if I don't go somewhere I'll be stuck at home all day with Mam.'

Jean nodded. She was fully aware of the situation in Dee's home. Her mam had even managed to persuade her da to have a serious talk to Graham about his drinking. Like the pot talking to the kettle, she'd thought, and unsurprisingly it hadn't done any good. 'I think it's a good idea but will you mind going on your own?' They'd always planned to go on a holiday but it just hadn't worked out.

'No, I don't think so. I've got the advertisement here. Celia cut it out for me.' She passed the clipping over to Jean who scanned it quickly.

'Ireland! Doesn't it always rain there?'

'It can't rain all the time. What do you think?'

'It sounds lovely and peaceful and maybe that's what you need. Time on your own, somewhere quiet, away from . . .' She bit her lip.

'All the memories and familiar places and things?' Dee said quietly. Maybe it was exactly what she needed. 'I'll write to this Mrs Mulcahey and see what she says.'

'Ask her how far it is to the town. You might be bored to death after a day or so. You might feel like a bit of the "convivial company" she mentions.'

Dee folded up the clipping and put it back in her bag. 'I'll let you know what she says. Good luck with the house.'

She wrote as soon as she got home and made up her mind to call in to the post office tomorrow to post it. It was 3 July today and she hoped Mrs Mulcahey wouldn't be fully booked. She did need a break and a change of scenery.

Tony was waiting rather impatiently at the top of Orrell Lane, the estate agent's details in his hand.

'Sorry I'm a bit late. Dee called in.'

Tony frowned. Of course he was terribly sorry for what had happened to Dee, it was really dreadful, and he hadn't begrudged the time Jean had spent comforting her friend, but they couldn't put their lives on hold for ever. It just wasn't fair on either of them, especially himself. He wasn't as close to Dee as Jean was.

'What did she want?' he asked as they walked up the tree-lined road.

'She's thinking of going to Ireland for a holiday. I told her I thought it was a great idea. It will do her good to get away, especially from her mam.'

Tony looked more cheerful. It was a good idea and

it meant that Jean could spend more time with him; they could really start to make plans without the shadow of Dee's unhappiness hanging over everything. 'You're right. Now, I think it's the second of the next pair of semis.'

'It looks very nice,' Jean commented. 'It's a quiet area and yet it's near to the shops, close enough to the salon for me to walk to work, and there's the ballroom and the Carlton picture house in walking distance too.'

Half an hour later they emerged smiling. It was exactly what they wanted and at the right price.

Tony was full of enthusiasm. 'I'll go into the estate agent's first thing in the morning and tell them we've agreed with the owners to take it. Then we'll have to go and see about getting a mortgage and then we can start to make plans for the wedding.'

'I'll have to tell Mam and you know what that means? Fuss, fuss, fuss!' She sighed. 'After we've put down the deposit we won't have much left over for furniture but never mind. As long as we've just got the basics we can manage. We'll get things as we go along.'

'Dad's promised to buy us a suite for the lounge as a wedding present and we should get something fairly decent from Aunt Maud, his sister. Maybe a cooker or a fridge, she's not short of money and I'm her only nephew.'

'If Mam and Da give us money we can get some bedroom furniture and we should get pots and pans and dishes and sheets for wedding presents,' Jean added happily.

Tony laughed. 'Yes, probably three tea sets and dozens of Pyrex casserole dishes. Do you think we should make one of those "wedding lists"?'

Jean looked doubtful. It was a new idea but it did save people buying the same things. 'It would help to stop duplicates but I can just hear some of the comments from my side of the family. I'll ask Mam what she thinks.'

'Will we go for a drink to celebrate and discuss what church to have the ceremony in, where we'll have the reception and who we'll have to invite?'

'Why not? It's a gorgeous evening so we might as well make the most of it.'

Tony tucked her arm through his and looked delighted with himself. 'Mr and Mrs Littlemore. Successful business people and property owners. We'll show everyone that our generation is really going up in the world. We don't have to settle for our parents' ideas about life and its expectations.'

Jean smiled up at him, pride and love and excitement shining in her eyes. They'd both worked hard and saved for this day. Only one thing nagged at her. How was all this going to affect Dee? And how could she possibly ask her friend to be her bridesmaid now?

Chapter Eighteen

——◆——

JEAN TOLD ADA THEIR plans the following evening. Tony had phoned her at the salon to tell her that their offer had been formally accepted and that he was calling into the building society where their savings were lodged to see about a mortgage.

'Are you really sure about this, Jean? Being in debt like that for all those years?' Ada was concerned.

'Of course I'm sure. We've worked everything out. With what Tony and I earn we can more than afford the repayments and it won't be "dead" money as it would be if we rented. One day we'll own it.'

Ada was still doubtful. 'And what happens when there is only Tony's wage coming in? If you have children you won't be able to work and kids cost money. I know our Margaret is always moaning that she doesn't have the money to spend on herself the way she used to.'

Jean was not going to be put off by her mother's pessimistic outlook. 'We'll cross that bridge when we come to it. We've agreed that we're not going to start a family for at least two years, maybe longer. That will give us time to get all the things we want for the house. Oh, it's really lovely, Mam. When all the paperwork has gone through I'll take you to see it.'

Ada could see she was getting nowhere with her warnings so she changed the subject. 'So, have you set a definite date then?'

Jean nodded. 'October the twenty-first. It's a Wednesday.'

'Wednesday! What's the matter with a Saturday?' Ada demanded.

Jean sighed. Sometimes her mam was hard work. 'Because Saturday is my busiest day. I can't leave Pauline and Bernice to do everything, not on a Saturday.'

'But everyone else will have to take a day off work and lose a day's pay into the bargain,' Ada reminded her.

'I can't help that and it will also be easier and cheaper to have it midweek,' Jean stated.

At least Ada could see the sense in this. If they wanted to have the reception somewhere popular it would no doubt be booked up already. 'So, which church is it to be?'

Jean frowned, thinking of her conversation with Tony on this subject. 'Tony says his mam will want it to be at St Mary's, Walton-on-the-Hill. It's their parish church, apparently.'

'And since when has Mavis Littlemore been calling the shots? It's *your* wedding, not hers,' Ada demanded, thinking Tony's mother had far too much to say in matters that should be settled by Tony and Jean. She was delighted that Jean was getting married and thinking of her daughter's big day was filling her with excitement. She had no intention of letting Mavis Littlemore put a damper on that excitement.

Jean nodded. She had said something along similar lines to Tony. 'I told him that but he said we should humour her. It will be worth it in the long run. She won't go fussing too much about other things. It's that big church at the top of Rice Lane.'

'I know,' Ada replied sharply.

'It's got lovely grounds for the photos. Tony says it's very high church. They have statues and a lady chapel and confessional boxes and incense like they do in the Catholic Church.'

Ada sniffed. 'Trust that one to be high church! What about the reception? Don't forget your Da is going to be paying for all this.'

'Tony said his father will chip in. These days it's not the bride's father who has to pay for everything and you have to agree they've got more money than we have. And I'm going to buy my own dress. I can afford it.'

Ada was mollified. She'd had visions of Mavis Littlemore demanding the best of everything and Harry having to pay for it. 'So?' she pressed.

'We were thinking of either Reece's Restaurant or the Stork Hotel in town.'

'Thank God for that. I thought that one might be expecting the Adelphi!' Ada said, thinking of Liverpool's grandest hotel. 'Then there are cars and flowers.'

Jean got up. 'I think we'd better start making lists, Mam. We'll have to make a guest list too and then at some stage you and Mrs Littlemore will have to get together to sort out table plans and outfits.'

Ada nodded, although she wasn't looking forward to that.

Jean sat down with a pen and a pad, her forehead creased in a frown.

'Mam, I don't know what to do about Dee. Before . . . before all the trouble I'd asked her to be my bridesmaid and she said she'd be delighted but . . . but now? How is she going to feel seeing me so happy on my big day? It will be unbearable for her, she'll be thinking of herself and Billy.'

Ada sighed. 'I know. That poor girl has a lot to put up with these days. I've tried to talk to Flo but I just can't seem to get through to her. If she'd only sit down and have a good talk to Graham: he's just using the drink as a crutch and I'm sure it would help. All that rowing and fighting isn't doing anyone any good and poor Dee is stuck in the middle.'

'What should I do, Mam?' Jean pressed.

Ada looked thoughtful. 'Well, you can't ignore the whole thing. Ask her if she still wants to be bridesmaid. Tell her it's fine if she doesn't, that you understand perfectly but that the offer is still open if she feels up to it.'

Jean nodded slowly. 'It's not going to be easy.'

'Of course it isn't. These days there doesn't seem to be an easy way to deal with that family at all. Right, start with the cars. How many will we need?'

Jean had finished early the following day for she had had to accompany Tony to the building society. To their relief they had got the mortgage they wanted but not without some prevarication. She had hoped they might get something higher than just the two and a half times Tony's salary, then they would have been able to buy some of the things they needed for the house, but she had been surprised to hear that they wouldn't take her earnings into consideration.

'I'm afraid it's not something we do, Miss Williams. We assume that at some stage you will be having a family and therefore will cease to work. Neither do we take overtime into consideration – it's not guaranteed – although in Mr Littlemore's case it's not relevant.'

'But I have my own business. I employ staff and even if there comes a time when I'm not working there myself I will still have an income from the salon,' she had informed the manager.

He'd smiled ruefully. 'We do have to protect our money, Miss Williams.'

'Honestly! So much for "equality"!' she'd said to Tony as they'd left.

'It's just the way they work. Never mind, we got what we needed. We can go ahead with everything now,' he'd replied with satisfaction before heading off on what he'd told Jean was 'just another boring business appointment'.

She called in to see Dee on her way home. Flo was in the kitchen peeling potatoes and she knew that Davie would be with her brother in their house, probably watching television or poring over their albums of football stickers.

'Is Dee in yet, Mrs Campbell?'

'You're early home from work. Did you close up?' Flo asked.

Jean sighed inwardly. 'No. Tony and I had to go to see about a mortgage for the house we're buying.'

'Isn't it well for some?' Flo retorted.

Jean looked uneasy, not knowing what to say.

'She's upstairs getting changed. Go on up but don't be upsetting her with talk of houses. She doesn't need reminding about the plans she had,' Flo warned. It just didn't seem fair that everything was going so well for Jean. She cursed Bob Campbell again, something she seemed to do at least a dozen times a day.

'Dee's my closest friend, you know that, and I wouldn't say or do anything to upset her,' Jean replied curtly before walking into the hall.

Dee was sitting on the little stool in front of the dressing table reading a letter.

'Is that the reply from that place in Ireland?' Jean asked, sitting down on the edge of Dee's bed. The window was wide open to let in the air but the room was still hot and stuffy.

'Yes. It came in the post at lunchtime.'

'So, what does she say?' Jean pressed.

'She has a vacancy for the weeks I asked for and her terms are very reasonable. She's sent a picture of the place.' Dee passed Jean a small photo.

'It looks nice. Sort of quaint,' Jean commented. It was a white two-storeyed house with a dark green front door and to the side two large green gates. It seemed to be situated on a rise and you could just see the waters of the canal in front of it.

'She says it was built in 1806 for the Canal Agent,' Dee read from the letter. 'She says it's very comfortably furnished with a washbasin in each of the guest rooms and a bathroom on the landing. The meals are taken in the dining room and there is a separate lounge for the guests.'

Jean passed the snapshot back. 'So, will you go?' She felt that this was just what Dee needed. She hated to see her friend in so much pain. 'I really think you should, Dee.'

Dee nodded. 'Yes. I'm going to write back tonight and send the deposit. Then I'll see about flights. I don't fancy the ferry journey and I've never flown before, it will be a new experience. Then all I have to do is tell Mam.' She grimaced.

Jean didn't envy her. You could barely get a civil word out of Flo Campbell these days. 'Surely she won't begrudge you a holiday?'

Dee shrugged. 'I don't much care if she does.' All Dee wanted was to get away from the atmosphere at home and perhaps find some peace and solace.

'We always used to talk about us travelling, remember? Now you are going to and on a plane.'

Dee smiled at her. 'It's not exactly the same as going to somewhere like Spain or Italy. It's not *that* far away.'

'It's further than I've been. Dee, I called in to talk to you about . . . something,' Jean finished hesitantly.

Dee looked at her steadily. She knew Jean tried to avoid any talk of weddings to spare her feelings. 'What?'

Jean took a deep breath. 'We've set a date for the wedding. We're buying that house we went to see in Moss Lane. That's why I finished early. I went with Tony to the building society about the mortgage.'

Dee nodded slowly. 'I'm really glad, Jean. I mean that.' She did.

'So, I . . . I don't want to upset you, Dee, but about being my bridesmaid? If you can't face it, it's all right, honestly it is. I know it will be an ordeal for you and I don't want to make you even more unhappy.'

Again Dee nodded. It *would* be an ordeal to see Jean so radiantly happy in her wedding dress, walking down the aisle on her father's arm to marry the man she loved. It would bring back all the plans she and Billy had had and yet Jean was her closest friend and she had been so supportive.

'Can I think about it, Jean? I don't want to mess you around but . . .'

'Of course you can. There's no rush.' Jean was relieved. At least Dee hadn't refused point blank.

'It wouldn't be fair to say yes and then back out but

I won't keep you hanging on for weeks. I'll have plenty of time to think about . . . things when I'm on holiday so I'll let you know when I get back. Is that all right?'

'Of course and if you feel you can't, I'll still have our Margaret as matron of honour. I never wanted half a dozen bridesmaids, that starts to look like a May procession rather than a wedding.' Jean stood up. 'I'll leave you to reply to Mrs Mulcahey and I'll send Davie up home for his tea.'

When she'd gone Dee read the letter again and sighed. There were so many things she needed to think about and to face; she just hoped that a holiday in the peaceful Irish countryside would help.

'Well, did you get the mortgage?' Ada asked when Jean walked into the kitchen.

'We did, Mam, so we can go ahead and start booking things. I called in to see Dee and Mrs Campbell wanted to know had I closed up early.'

Ada looked up from her task of setting the table. 'What did you say?'

'I told her we'd been to the building society. She made some comment but I just ignored her. I asked Dee.'

'And what did she say?' Ada knew that in happier times she and Flo would have been discussing the plans for Jean's forthcoming wedding in great detail but now . . . now any mention of it would be like a red rag to a bull as far as Flo was concerned.

'She wants to think about it. She's going to tell me one way or another after she's been on this holiday.'

'So she has decided to go then?'

'Yes.'

'I hope it helps her, Jean, I really do. She'll make herself ill the way she's going on and Flo's attitude doesn't help. Dee has got the whole of her life ahead of her. She's going to have to try to put everything behind her and start again. Flo's not making life any easier for any of them. I can understand that she's still upset and annoyed herself but she should try to get over it for the sake of them all. If I've told Flo that once I've told her a dozen times!'

Chapter Nineteen

———◆———

DEE FELT A LITTLE nervous as she sat in the small lounge area at Liverpool airport just over three weeks later. Out on the tarmac apron she could see two planes. The sun was glinting off their propellers and she didn't think they looked very big at all. Still, there was no going back now, her case had already gone through. She turned the boarding pass over in her hands. It had been very easy to make the arrangements. Jean had suggested she go to Ron Booth's Travel Agency on Longmoor Lane and they had done everything. They'd booked the plane tickets, the train ticket to Tullamore, even the transport to the airport. Then all she'd had to do was inform her mother.

She frowned as she thought of Flo's reaction. As she'd expected there had been a row, although she had tried her best to avoid it. Her mother had accused her of wasting money they could ill afford, reminding her that she had to manage now on a widow's pension, and of thinking solely of herself. She had tried to explain that it was only for a couple of weeks, that she had never had a proper holiday and she needed a break and some peace and quiet. That had been totally the wrong thing to say.

'And when have I had a "proper" holiday? When will I get a break from all this? And what about my peace and quiet? No one ever considers what *I* need,' Flo had retorted.

'Mam, I'm sorry but I just can't face . . . things. I need time by myself.'

'That's all I ever hear these days. Me, me, me! You're as selfish as your brother. The pair of you only ever think of yourselves.'

That had been so unfair, she'd thought angrily. 'That's not true, Mam, and you know it. Well, I'm going! And that's all there is to it. I'm twenty-one so I can please myself!' Her outburst hadn't improved the atmosphere one bit.

There was no more time for deliberations as her flight was called and Dee joined the other passengers and walked out to board the plane. She looked upwards, feeling both apprehensive and excited. What would it feel like to be up there? Would she feel a long way from home?

The take-off had been a bit scary, she thought, but she soon settled down and found it not uncomfortable. It was even less bumpy than a bus or train, she mused. She seemed hardly to have settled down to look at the magazine she had bought before the plane began its descent. After they had landed and she had collected her case she followed the signs to the arrivals hall. She quickly picked out a man who was holding a large piece of cardboard with the word 'Campbell' written on it.

'I'm Dee Campbell, are you my taxi driver?' she asked the middle-aged man who smiled back broadly at her.

'Ah, that's me all right. Give that case over to me. You're for Heuston Station, isn't that the way of it?'

She nodded and followed him out to the taxi.

'Well now, are you here to visit the relations?' he asked as they left the airport and turned on to the road for the city.

'No. I've come on holiday. I've never been to Ireland before,' she answered, looking around at the fields that surrounded them.

'Won't you have the time of your life then? Are you off to Galway or is it Cork or Kerry? Sure, the scenery down there is grand.'

'I'm going to Tullamore in County Offaly,' she replied.

He looked at her askance. 'Mother of God! What's a fine-looking young one like yourself going to bury herself down there in the bogs with the culchies for?'

She couldn't help but smile. 'For some peace and quiet.'

'Sure, you'll have that in plenty down there, so you will,' he replied a little scathingly.

It seemed quite a long way Dee thought but soon

the outskirts of the city started to appear. She was surprised that there seemed to be very little traffic on the streets compared to Liverpool and remarked upon the fact.

'Well now, don't go expecting things to be like they are in Liverpool. Compared to England this is a poor country. And down there in the bogs haven't they only just got the electricity installed.'

'Oh, I didn't mean to sound as if I was complaining. I hope I haven't offended you.'

He grinned at her. 'Ah, no offence taken at all.'

He dropped her off at the station and she made enquiries as to which platform her train would leave from. She also ascertained that it would take an hour and a half to get to Tullamore. It seemed quite a long journey but then she remembered what the taxi driver had said. She shouldn't expect things to be as they were at home and she'd come for a change of scenery and lifestyle.

She settled herself into her seat and brought the magazine out again but as the train pulled out of the station and left the city suburbs behind she began to take more of an interest in the countryside. If she was really honest with herself she had to admit to feeling a little anxious and apprehensive. She was a city girl, what if she didn't like this place? Would it be too quiet? She was going to be there for two whole weeks and the taxi driver's comments hadn't helped. Well, it was too late now to do anything about it, she told herself firmly.

When she alighted from the train at Tullamore station the station master kindly summoned a taxi. She gave the driver the address and he seemed to know exactly where they were going. From the little she had glimpsed of the small town it looked pleasant enough, if a little quiet and sleepy.

Gradually the roads became narrower and twisting, and then they were in a very narrow lane flanked either side by high hedges beyond which were fields in which cattle grazed. It must be at least seven or eight miles from town, she thought as they turned left and came up on to the path that ran beside the canal itself. On the opposite bank they passed two single-storeyed cottages and as they rounded a slight bend she could see ahead of them a small stone humpbacked bridge that spanned the canal. On the right-hand bank beside the bridge was a long, low house and on the left-hand side the white two-storeyed house Mrs Mulcahey had sent a snapshot of.

As they drew up outside the big green gates to the side of the house a plump, middle-aged woman came out to greet them, smiling broadly.

'Ah, there you are now. It's Miss Campbell, isn't it?'

Dee shook her hand. 'Yes. I'm Dee Campbell.'

'Come on inside with you, 'tis a desperate long journey you've had. I've a fresh pot of tea made and some buttered brack. Come on in with you too, John.'

Dee was ushered into a large kitchen followed by the taxi driver.

'Can I put my case in my room first, please?' Dee asked. She felt hot and grubby after the journey and really wanted to wash her face and hands.

Mrs Mulcahey indicated that the taxi driver sit down at the table and took Dee's case. Dee followed her through a small room that was obviously her landlady's sitting room into another room furnished in a more formal style, obviously the sitting room for the guests. She wondered how many guests there were staying at the moment and asked.

'There's just yourself and Mr Perry. He's over from Kent for the fishing, so he is. He comes every year. Nice quiet old gentleman.' Mrs Mulcahey was puffing a little as they climbed the stairs. 'I've put you in the front bedroom here, right next to the bathroom. There's a grand view out over the lock.'

Dee looked around and smiled. It was a lovely room. The walls had been painted in a pale lemon which made it appear bright and larger than it actually was. Lemon and white striped curtains framed the small sash window. There was a single bed with a pine headboard and a lemon, white and green quilt. There was a small dressing table and a single wardrobe and in one corner a washbasin, complete with soap dish and soap. A white towel was folded neatly on the end of the bed.

'It's lovely!' she exclaimed, smiling.

'Come on down when you're ready and I'll show you the dining room and tell you what time meals are.'

Dee took off her light linen jacket and hung it up in the wardrobe. She washed her hands and face and then she went to the low window and knelt down to look out. It was indeed an old house, she thought, for the walls were very thick. Below her the waters of the canal were calm, reflecting the blue sky and the tall reeds that lined the bank and which swayed gently in the breeze. She had a clear view of the house opposite now and from this angle she could see that it also was two-storeyed but it had been built in such a way that from the road it looked like a cottage. It too was painted white but the door and the window frames were bright scarlet. On the other side of the bridge she could see the two huge wooden levers that opened and closed the lock gates. The grass verge on the side of the lock was neatly trimmed and from the two arms of an old-fashioned cast-iron lamp-post hung baskets of trailing blue lobelia and red, purple and white busy Lizzies. Beside the picket fence that separated the lock from the road, a couple of rose bushes were in full bloom adding bright splashes of colour. An old iron ploughshare that had been painted black had been placed decoratively beside a wrought-iron post from which hung a sign with the words 'Clarkes' Lock' painted in red lettering. Fields, hedgerows and trees stretched for miles on the other side of the canal and in the distance she could see bright splashes of yellow furze. It was a pretty spot, she thought, and very quiet and peaceful. The only sound she could hear was that of the water trickling through the lock gates and the twittering of the swallows as they dived and swooped over the water or as they perched on the new electricity cables. She'd been foolish to have doubts about the place. It was lovely and was just what she needed; she felt more relaxed already.

Jean was finding that there didn't seem to be enough hours in the day for everything she needed to do. They had been to see the priest – as Tony assured her he was called – at St Mary's to arrange the church service and she had been very impressed and a little overawed by the beautiful interior of the church with its magnificent stained-glass windows. The only times she had been to church the interior had been much plainer, less imposing. Father Adrian had been very helpful, noting all her details, informing them of when the banns would be called and suggesting suitable hymns.

She had had an argument with her mother over the guest list after she had announced that she was thinking of not having any children under the age of ten at the reception.

Ada had been outraged. 'You can't do that! You'll upset no end of people including your own sister! You know how she carried on over Bob Campbell's funeral. She didn't speak to me for three weeks.'

'But, Mam, it will be bedlam. None of them will behave properly, they'll start running around, shouting, fighting and getting under people's feet, and can you just imagine what Tony's mother will have to say?'

'I don't care what she has to say, Jean. You can't go upsetting people like that. How can you not want your own little nephew at your wedding? Now, let's hear no more about it.' Ada had firmly quashed the idea and the invitations had duly been sent out.

Then she and Ada had gone to the Stork Hotel in

Queen's Square to book the reception. It was a fairly small hotel but select and comfortable and central. They had chosen the menu and had accepted the banqueting manager's advice on the wine to be served with the meal and the choice of a sparkling wine for the toasts. The cars had been booked and Jean had started to look around at wedding dresses. She wished she had Dee to go with her to choose this, the most important outfit she would ever wear, but sadly she knew it was impossible. If she had been planning this wedding six or seven months ago, before Bob Campbell's terrible secret had been revealed, Dee would have been with her, she thought sadly. She didn't look at bridesmaids' dresses even though Margaret was beginning to ask just what she had in mind. She would do that when Dee had given her her answer.

For herself she wanted something simple, she told Ada. She was too small to carry off anything very fancy with layers of petticoats; she had no intention of looking like a meringue. It would be long but probably straight or Empire line with long sleeves and a plain neckline, but with a short train.

'You're being very precise,' Ada had commented, wondering if Jean was going to be equally 'precise' in the matter of what she, her mother, was to wear.

'I know but I want to look really sensational and I have to take the time of year into consideration too,' Jean had replied, thinking back to the white lace dress her sister had worn and the lemon lace that she'd shivered in.

'I think you might be better off having one made. That way you will get exactly what you want. Ask around your clients, someone is bound to know of a good dressmaker,' Ada had advised, having no desire to spend hours and hours trailing around the shops in Liverpool.

Jean had taken her mother's advice and was duly given the name, address and phone number of a Mrs Travis who lived in Edgeley Gardens and who specialised in wedding dresses and had an excellent reputation.

Ada and Pauline had gone with her to see the woman, who had been very businesslike, noting down Jean's requirements and then producing a number of patterns. Jean chose the one that really appealed to her the most and Mrs Travis took her measurements and wrote them down in a small notebook.

'Now, what kind of material would you like?' the dressmaker asked.

'I had thought of a heavy satin. Something that would be warm,' Jean had confided.

'Duchesse satin would be nice, it doesn't have that very shiny look and it's stiffer. It's quite a plain style you've chosen but I could embroider the cuffs and the neckline with seed pearls and crystal beads.'

'That sounds gorgeous,' Pauline had enthused.

'And for your head-dress?'

Jean had looked thoughtful and Mrs Travis had produced a book of pictures cut from magazines. It reminded Jean of her own style book.

'A satin bandeau embroidered like the dress would look well, and a short veil.' An appropriate picture was selected and Jean had to agree it would set the dress off to perfection.

When they'd left Jean felt as though she'd made a good choice and was quite relieved that it wasn't going to cost as much as she'd expected. She had made a note of the date and time of her first fitting.

'Well, that's another thing we can cross off the list,' Ada had remarked as they'd walked towards the bus stop. 'As soon as you know what Dee is going to do you'll have to think about their dresses. You might be as well to let Mrs Travis make them. She appears to be very efficient and her prices aren't too bad.'

Jean had to agree. She just hoped Dee was giving some serious thought to the matter.

Chapter Twenty

————◆————

DEE HAD INDEED BEEN thinking about her friend's
wedding that morning as she'd stood leaning on
one of the huge wooden levers gazing down into the
still, dark water of the lock. In the time she'd been here
she had thought about quite a lot of things that pre-
viously she'd pushed from her mind: Billy, her family
and what the future held. It must be the tranquillity of
the place, she'd reasoned. There were few distractions
so there was time to ponder. The weather was holding
well, something that her landlady informed her wasn't
always the case here even in summer, and she'd taken
to going for long walks down the country lanes or up
through the fields. The few people she did see on her
walks all waved or stopped to pass the time of day and
she thought how friendly everyone seemed to be.

Mrs Mulcahey was a very pleasant woman and after
a few conversations with her young guest was astute

enough to realise that the girl was troubled and had obviously come to get away from problems at home.

'You look as though you could do with feeding up a bit, Dee,' she'd remarked as she put a large plate of thick gammon slices, carrots and floury potatoes in front of Dee.

Dee had smiled at her. 'We've had a lot of ... sadness and upset at home lately and I suppose I have lost a bit of weight,' she'd replied.

Mrs Mulcahey hadn't pressed her as to the nature of this 'sadness and upset' but she'd hoped some time away from it all would bring the colour back to the girl's cheeks. She liked her. She was quiet and polite.

The food was plain but wholesome and plentiful and after hours spent in the open air Dee did regain her healthy appetite. She'd even begun to sleep better too, lulled by the soothing sound of the trickling water in the lock that could be heard through the open window.

On her first evening Mrs Mulcahey had informed her that if she was going to Mass tomorrow it would be held at ten o'clock at the church in Killina, which was quite a distance to walk but she was welcome to go with them in the little van. Dee had thanked her but replied that she wasn't of the Catholic faith, she was a Protestant. Her landlady had raised an eyebrow and nodded.

'There's a service in the big church in town, but not in the little local chapel. Not this week anyway. Himself beyond in the Lock House will have more information and no doubt he'll find it of great interest that you're of the same persuasion as himself,' Mrs Mulcahey had remarked but before Dee had had time to ask her about this statement she'd bustled out to make a pot of tea.

Mr Perry was a middle-aged man who was polite but who didn't talk a great deal and so mealtimes were quiet affairs. She didn't see him at all during the day, he seemed to spend his time fishing down the canal at a place called 'the wides'.

She'd seen the lock-keeper quite a few times; he always seemed to be out near the lock, and he always waved to her. He looked to be in his early thirties and was of medium height with fair hair. She'd stood and watched him on the first Sunday morning as he'd operated the huge wooden gates to allow a boat to negotiate the lock, thinking it was such a simple yet ingenious system, and when the narrowboat was clear and the gates were closed once more he'd come across to speak to her.

'You'll be one of Mrs Mulcahey's guests?'

She'd smiled politely. 'Yes. I'm here for a holiday. I'm from Liverpool.'

'Sure, this place must seem very quiet to you after a city. I'm Niall Clarke, by the way.'

'Denise – Dee – Campbell.' Her gaze had gone to the painted sign. 'The lock is called after your family?'

He'd smiled and she'd thought he was quite a good-looking young man. His skin was tanned by the weather, which seemed to darken the blue of his eyes. 'That's not the *official* name. It's the Thirtieth Lock but we've been lock-keepers here for seven generations. Since the canal was first built, in fact, so everyone calls it "Clarkes' Lock".'

'Did you never want to do anything else?' she'd asked.

He'd shaken his head. 'I never really thought about anything else. It's a grand life.'

'You keep it very neat and tidy and the flowers are lovely,' she'd replied.

'Thanks, I do my best. Are you off for a walk?'

She'd nodded. 'It's so quiet and peaceful here. No traffic noise, just birdsong and last night the sound of the water in the lock sent me straight off to sleep.' She'd laughed a little self-consciously, wondering if that sounded foolish.

'There'd be times in the winter months when it would keep you awake, so it would. After heavy rain I open most of the racks and then it thunders through.'

'I suppose it's a very different place in winter,' she'd mused.

'It is so. It can be a bit grim at times but you get used to it. 'Tis rather strange for someone like yourself to come on a holiday alone, if you don't mind me saying so. I take it you're not here for the fishing?'

She'd pulled a face. 'No. I really can't see the point of it. Mr Perry seems to spend hours and hours trying to catch a fish and then when he does he throws it back in.'

He'd grinned but she was aware that he was waiting for her to enlighten him as to why she was on her own.

'I wanted to get away from home for a while and my best friend couldn't spare the time from her business to come with me. I have a lot of things to try to sort out in my mind.'

He'd nodded. 'It's a grand place for that. Well, I'd best get on. There won't be another boat through until early evening and I have to go into town to the depot. Enjoy your day.'

As she'd walked up the fields towards the bog she'd wondered what it must be like to have spent your entire life in this place. A place where your family's roots stretched back for centuries. It would certainly give you a sense of identity, security and purpose.

She had seen Niall Clarke each morning and he'd always stopped to chat to her. She found him easy to talk to and he took a delight in pointing things out to her: the moorhens, the heron that stood like a statue on the bank and the bright flash of turquoise that was a kingfisher, none of which she had ever seen before. One morning he'd given her a working demonstration of how the lock gates were opened and had laughed good-naturedly at her attempts to copy him. Twice he had walked with her down towards the next lock.

'I'm going that way,' he'd replied when she had said she didn't want to keep him from his work. 'They have fine canals in England so I hear,' he'd remarked.

'The only one I've seen is the Leeds to Liverpool canal and it's certainly not like this one. It's dirty and smelly and people chuck rubbish into it. You wouldn't believe the stuff that's in there and in summer if it's very hot the kids *swim* in it, would you believe,' she'd informed him, grimacing.

'Isn't that dangerous? We have notices up here: "No swimming".'

She'd nodded. 'It is. There have been accidents; people have drowned. You'd think they'd have the sense to go to the public baths if they want to swim.'

'Do you swim, Dee?' he'd asked.

'Just about. Can you?'

He'd shaken his head and smiled wryly.

She'd been surprised. 'I would have thought that living beside the canal you would have learned as a child.'

'I learned all kinds of things but never how to swim. Ah, sure if you keep your wits about you and know the dangers it's fine.' He changed the subject. 'There must be parts of the canals over there that are like this; they don't all go through towns and cities, surely.'

Dee frowned, trying to remember the geography of the English midlands. 'I've heard of the Shropshire Union Canal and I suppose those canals that go through the country areas must be pretty, I don't know. This is the first time I've ever stayed in the country,' she informed him.

'Do you think you could get used to it?' he'd asked.

She'd looked up at him, a little bemused. 'I don't know. The way I've been feeling lately I think I could. I certainly don't miss the noise and the crowds.'

They had almost reached the Cornalaur Lock which Mrs Mulcahey always referred to as the 'far lock'.

He'd smiled at her. 'I'm calling in here to see Himself. I'll see you again tomorrow, Dee.'

'I'll be out walking again, Niall, weather permitting,' she'd replied as he'd crossed the narrow stone bridge and she'd walked on.

She sighed, watching the sunlight playing on the ripples of dark water, like flecks of gold on a background of black velvet. She had been here now for ten days. Could she find the strength to be Jean's bridesmaid? Could she put on a brave face and smile at the sight of her friend's happiness or would it be just too much to bear? Was it too soon? Her sense of loss was still great. She still loved Billy, she still thought of him and wondered where he was, what he was doing and if he still loved her. The wound was very raw. The destruction of all their hopes, dreams and plans would be forcefully thrust into her mind on Jean's wedding day. And once Jean was married to Tony she knew she wouldn't see as much of her. Jean would have a new life and she wouldn't be living just a few yards down the road.

She plucked the head from a stem of cow parsley, let it drop down on to the surface of the water and watched it slowly float away. And what did the future hold for her? She didn't want to go out to dances; she didn't want to look for someone to replace him. No one ever could, she was sure of that. Would she ever get over losing him? And then there was the situation at home. She wondered if her mother would ever change. In time would she be able to try to forget how she had been betrayed, even if she could never forgive? Or would the bitterness continue to grow with the years? Would first Graham and then Davie leave to find somewhere else to live? Would she be left to contend with her mother alone? She watched a swallow, its wings the colour of the midnight sky, swooping and darting acrobatically beneath the bridge as it chased the flying insects. Even in such a short space of time she'd found a measure of peace and solace here. It would be hard to go back to the tense atmosphere at home where almost everything that was mentioned was fraught with the possibility of an argument. It was like walking on eggshells and it took a toll on everyone's nerves.

'Are you not walking today?' Niall Clarke's voice broke into her thoughts. She'd not heard him come across the grass verge.

She frowned. 'I was trying to sort out a problem in my mind.'

'And have you found the answer?' he asked. He could see something was troubling her.

She shook her head. 'No, not yet. But I have to before I go back. Is there a boat due?' she asked to change the subject.

'Not for another two hours.'

She was intrigued. 'How do you know when they are due? Does someone telephone you to let you know?'

'No. There's no phone here yet. Sure, I know what time they leave Dublin and, coming the other way, Shannon Harbour, and I know how long the journey takes them. They're as regular as clockwork.' It was obvious she wasn't going to enlighten him as to what she had been thinking about. He'd been watching her closely from the opposite bank. She was an attractive girl, early twenties he guessed, and he liked her. She was well spoken without too much of an accent although even if she hadn't informed him she was from Liverpool, he would have guessed. He wondered what kind of a family she came from and was there anyone special in her life? He'd like to get to know her better.

'I was wondering if you would like to go into town one evening? That film *Cleopatra* is on at the Grand Central Cinema. Have you seen it already? We're a bit behind the times down here.'

She was surprised. 'I . . . I didn't get to see it actually.' She didn't know what to say. It would seem churlish to refuse and yet . . .

'What about tomorrow?' he pressed.

'Yes. Tomorrow would be . . . just fine.' She was still hesitant. 'How will we get there?'

'I've the motorbike, if you don't mind getting a bit blown about?'

She smiled. 'I'll put a scarf over my hair.'

He smiled back at her. 'I'll come over for you about half past seven then.'

Mrs Mulcahey was very interested to hear about this outing when Dee told her about it at dinner that evening. 'Sure, I've seen you chatting to him now and then. He must have taken a fancy to you. He's never asked any of my other guests out and I've had a few young ones in the past.'

'It's just a trip to the cinema, nothing that could be called serious.'

Her landlady had sniffed. 'Not at the moment but I'm after thinking he's on the lookout for a wife. Isn't he alone over there and if he never marries he'll be the last lock-keeper with the name of Clarke.'

Dee was puzzled. 'But surely there are plenty of local girls he could choose from?'

'There are but none suitable. The Clarkes are Protestant, always have been.'

Dee thought about it. In certain areas of Liverpool there had always been religious bigotry but it was gradually dying out and she hadn't been brought up to be overly religious. Here, the two religions obviously didn't mix or intermarry. Still, she was only going to the cinema with him and she certainly hadn't given him any cause to think it would go any further. She couldn't contemplate anything like that. Probably her landlady was just speculating because he had asked her out. After all, she was sure he didn't know what religion she was.

She enjoyed the film. The place wasn't like one of the huge cinemas such as the Odeon or the Gaumont in Liverpool; it was much smaller and had a far more intimate feel to it. Afterwards, they walked through the town and up to the canal at the Kilbeggan Bridge.

'The canal isn't as pretty here in town,' she commented.

'True enough. 'Tis because it *is* going through the

239

town. The distillery where they make Tullamore Dew and the grain warehouses are just down there,' he informed her. 'How many days have you left here now?'

'Three, then I have to go back up to Dublin to the airport.'

He nodded, seeming preoccupied, and they walked on for a few minutes.

Dee felt a little uncomfortable and decided to break the silence. 'Elizabeth Taylor's very beautiful, isn't she? After that film came out everyone was copying her make-up and hairstyle. My friend is a hairdresser and she said she'd never been asked to do so many dark tints in her life before.'

'Wasn't there a great fuss and bother over it too? Didn't she divorce the husband and marry Richard Burton?'

'Oh, they all live such a different life to the rest of us mere mortals,' Dee replied. She wondered if she should bring up the subject of her landlady's speculation just to see how he would react. 'And speaking of marriages, Mrs Mulcahey was hinting that you might be looking for a wife.'

He looked amused. 'Was she indeed?'

'Apparently, according to her, you don't have a great choice.'

He became serious. 'I don't. This is predominantly a Catholic country and most of the Protestant girls are already married or are still at school.' He looked down at her. 'I know you are a Protestant.'

That surprised her. 'How? Did she tell you? Or was it because you didn't see me going off to Mass in my Sunday best?'

They'd reached the edge of the town and there was a stone bench beside the path and he sat down. Dee sat beside him. Dusk was falling rapidly and a few bats flitted between the trees on the canal bank.

'She made a point of telling me.' He paused. It was a beautiful balmy summer evening, which was something of a rarity and had the effect of making him feel less reserved in his manner. He looked across to the opposite bank where the buildings seemed to be gradually fading into the warm indigo darkness. 'I like you very much, Dee, that's why I asked you out tonight and I was going to ask if you would consider writing to me after you go home? I don't know very much about you or you me – yet. That way we could get to know each other better.'

She looked perplexed. 'Do you want to get to know me better?'

'I do and I was after hoping that you'd like to know me better too. Will you write to me, Dee?'

'I . . . I don't know, Niall,' she answered truthfully.

'Is there someone special back there?' he asked.

She decided to tell him. 'There was someone, we were engaged, but then something . . . something terrible happened and we were forced to break up. I can never see him again. He joined the Merchant Navy and I don't even know where he is now.'

'I'm sorry, Dee. I didn't realise.' he said quietly.

She managed to smile. 'I felt I owed you an explanation.'

He nodded, staring down at his hands. How could he explain to her that he needed to get married and have children or there would be no one to carry on after him and that that was important to him? He'd made a promise to his grandfather and his father that he would not let the Clarke name die out. There was no one of his own religion he could marry and he really did like her but how would all this sound to her, a modern city-bred girl who could have no inkling of how much this meant to him? A girl who had been prepared to marry for love and who had obviously been badly hurt? The idea of marrying for the continuation of a name, a way of life, would seem very odd and old-fashioned to her. He decided he wouldn't tell her his thoughts, not yet. Maybe it would be easier in a letter. 'I really would like you to write to me,' he pressed.

At last she nodded. 'I will write to you, Niall. I promise.'

Chapter Twenty-One

———◆———

SHE DIDN'T SEE HIM again until just before the taxi came to take her to the station. She was thanking Mrs Mulcahey for a pleasant stay when he walked into the yard.

'Here's Himself come to say goodbye,' Mrs Mulcahey said with a wink before she turned and went back inside.

'I've written the address for you, Dee. You haven't changed your mind?' he asked a little bashfully.

She took the piece of paper from him. 'No, I haven't changed my mind.'

He smiled at her. He could only hope she was being truthful and he wished her stay had been longer. 'Have you enjoyed your time here?'

'Yes, indeed. It is a very peaceful place and I feel much better. Easier in my mind.'

He took her hand. 'Then maybe you'll come back one day?'

'I might,' she replied as the taxi swung into the yard and Mrs Mulcahey reappeared.

'Ah, here's John now. Well, Dee, safe journey and God bless you. It's been a pleasure to have known you.'

'Thank you for everything, Mrs Mulcahey. I've really enjoyed myself. Goodbye, Niall,' she replied, getting into the car.

They both stood and waved as the taxi pulled out on to the road and she waved back, feeling a tinge of sadness at leaving. She had enjoyed being here. She felt much calmer now and in a better frame of mind to face the future. She felt she could even possibly cope with her mother's outbursts with more tolerance. She put the paper with Niall's address on it into her bag. She would write to him. She wouldn't break a promise.

It was an uneventful trip home and when she arrived back in Buttermere Close it was to find her mother bringing in a line of washing.

'I'm home, Mam,' she announced, putting her case on the floor and her handbag on the table.

'I can see that. Well, did you get all the peace and quiet you wanted?' Flo asked bluntly.

She nodded. 'I did.'

'There's very little of that around here now, what with Ada continually fussing about with some problem or other to do with the wedding arrangements. I'm just

244

warning you so you won't go getting upset.' Flo's mouth was set in a thin, hard line of disapproval.

Dee sighed. It was almost as if she had never been away. 'I'm not going to get upset, Mam. I've made up my mind about that and I am going to be Jean's bridesmaid. I owe it to her, she's my dearest friend and she's stood by me through everything and I won't do anything to spoil her day.'

Flo looked at her closely. Was she starting to get over it? Well, Dee might be but hell would freeze over before she herself did. 'Suit yourself but I still think it will be too much of an ordeal for you.'

Jean was delighted and relieved when Dee told her. She hugged her tightly. 'Oh, I'm just so pleased, Dee! I would have felt as though something was really missing if you hadn't been able to go through with it. I promise I won't go on and on endlessly about all the arrangements.' She grimaced. 'Mam is quite capable of doing that. She's driving me mad and so is the future ma-in-law but we won't go into all that. Now, tell me all about your holiday? You certainly look better for it.' She was indeed relieved to see that Dee had more colour in her cheeks and that there was a greater lightness in her manner. She fervently hoped that this holiday had been the start of her friend's recovery from the despair and depression that she had suffered these past months.

True to her word Jean kept all the trivia of the wedding plans from Dee and she'd instructed her mother firmly that she was not to be going down to Flo by the minutes discussing them either. There was to be no mention of the argument between Ada and Mavis Littlemore over the colour and style of their outfits, or the argument between herself and Margaret over her proposed choice of burgundy velvet. Her sister had vociferously declared that it would make her look like a staid, middle-aged matron and would drain the colour from her complexion entirely. Jean had replied, just as vociferously, that the style was young and very modern, the material was far more suitable to the time of the year than the lemon lace she had been forced to wear as Margaret's bridesmaid and her sister should be grateful that she was thinking of her welfare and comfort. There had been another argument between them over little Francis. Margaret had wanted him to be a pageboy, complete with silk shirt and tartan kilt, but Jean had flatly refused, saying he was far too young. Ada had had to intervene over that matter. Jean often wished she could talk to Dee about such things but she told herself it was enough that her friend had agreed to be bridesmaid.

Dee had written to Niall Clarke, telling him a little about herself and her background and that she had indeed resolved one of the problems that had been troubling her, whether or not she could be strong enough to be bridesmaid to her best friend bearing in mind the break-up of her own engagement. She had received a reply almost immediately. He had been impressed with her strength of character, he wrote, it must have been a difficult decision. He was also interested in hearing about her job, she must find that both interesting and demanding. He had finished by begging her to continue writing and she had.

Flo had commented on the correspondence. 'I see you've got yourself a penfriend.'

'It was just someone I met and I promised to write to him,' Dee had answered without really thinking too deeply about her words.

'Oh, so it's a fellow then, is it?' Flo's tone had been curt.

Dee could have bitten her tongue. 'Mam, it's exactly as you said. He's a penfriend. He is the lock-keeper, he lives in the house opposite to the one I stayed in. We chatted a couple of times, that's all.' She wasn't going to mention the fact that she'd gone to the cinema with him.

Flo had nodded. She supposed it might prove to be a diversion for Dee.

The weeks were flying by or so it seemed to Jean. She was busy at work and there were a million and one things that took up the rest of the time. Tony seemed to be more interested in the plans he had for decorating the house, and he often went out with clients of an evening, she thought irritably, rather than helping her negotiate what was fast becoming the minefield of table plans – exacerbated by relations who still had not yet replied to the invitations – and the growing hostility between her mother and future mother-in-law. He'd insisted they both go up to the house to talk to the decorators who, although they worked for the family business during the day, had been persuaded to decorate the lounge, hall, kitchen and one of the bedrooms in the house in Moss Lane in the evenings. She had a fitting for her wedding dress that evening, she'd told him.

'Well, surely that won't take all night? And the dressmaker only lives around the corner to the house. Can't you call in when you've finished there?' he'd replied irritably, thinking she seemed to be placing more emphasis on how she would look on the day than their future home.

'I'll have Mam with me and you know what she's like. She'll go sticking her oar in about the colours we've chosen and then next time she's speaking to your mam she'll take a delight in telling her that she was there when we decided on the colour schemes and you know what will happen then!'

'Oh, honestly, Jean! They're like a pair of kids.' He was infuriated by their inability to get on with each other.

She'd sighed heavily. 'I know but we'll not change them.'

He'd been annoyed and looked petulant. 'I'll be glad when the wedding is over and we can get on with our lives without all this interference. I'm sorry now that we didn't just go off to Brougham Terrace to the register office. Just you, me and our two witnesses. I hardly ever see you and when I do you're always too preoccupied with this damned wedding to give much thought to me.' He meant it. The whole thing was escalating and causing far too many problems. He hardly saw Jean alone and when he did she was tense and there was always something worrying her. It wasn't what he had envisaged and he thought she should be more forceful with both his mother and her own.

She'd been upset. 'Don't say that, Tony! It's supposed to be the happiest day of our lives. And when it's all over we'll have all the time in the world together.'

What he needed was a good night out, he'd mused. It seemed ages since he'd really enjoyed himself. Maybe he'd go out on the town next week and forget about all this palaver over the wedding. He deserved some convivial company to cheer him up.

Dee had begun to look forward to Niall's letters; she now knew far more about him and his way of life, which, as she tried to cope with the atmosphere at home, seemed more and more idyllic. It was a quiet routine in a rural setting; the people in Offaly lacked many of the conveniences of a modern city but there was no tension, no sense of urgency, they seemed to have time for each other. However, she was genuinely surprised when two weeks before Jean's wedding he wrote and explained his position to her.

Dear Dee,
Many thanks for your last letter, I really do enjoy hearing all your news. You can see the change in the season here now. The leaves are turning and the

rushes on the bank are dry and dead-looking. When I was last speaking to her, Mrs Mulcahey asked to be remembered to you and she hopes that you might come over again next summer. I have to say, Dee, it's my hope too. I feel that I know you well enough now to tell you what has been on my mind for these last weeks. You remember I was telling you about the position I'm in – being a Protestant in a Catholic country? I hope you won't think me a crass, insensitive 'culchie' when I tell you that I made a promise to both my father and my grandfather that I would not let the name 'Clarke' die out. It was a promise given freely and with sincerity. I like you very much, Dee. Indeed I'm thinking that I have fallen in love with you and would like to marry you. I know you are not in love with me, I know you've been badly hurt and it takes time to get over such feelings, but I beg you not to dismiss my proposal out of hand. You seemed to find the time you spent here enjoyable, restful and peaceful and I can offer you a good life away from all your unhappy memories. I suppose you would call it a 'marriage of convenience' and I realise how strange and old-fashioned that must seem to a modern girl like yourself but I beg you to consider it. Take as much time as you need to come to a decision, I won't press you and I will resign myself to your decision. I pray to God that I haven't shocked or upset you. 'Tis the last thing I want to do.

Yours affectionately
Niall

Dee reread the slightly stiff and formally worded letter many times. At first she had dismissed it completely. They barely knew each other and it *was* a terribly old-fashioned thing to do, like something you read about in books, something that happened a century ago. However, after a week she had begun to think about it – to think about him. He had been totally honest with her, she told herself. She had liked him, he'd seemed quiet and genuine and she had enjoyed the time she had spent there, but was she looking at it through rose-tinted glasses? It had been a holiday and an escape from her life here. And she didn't love him. How could she marry someone she didn't love? She knew what it was like to be in love but did he? Had he really fallen in love with her? They had only spent a short time together each day and he'd taken her out once but that was all. She really didn't think she could ever consider a marriage of convenience. In the end she told herself she would have to reply one way or another, but she would leave it until after Jean's wedding. She would get over that ordeal first, and then maybe she could think about her future in a more positive way. There was no use trying to think about it now.

To everyone's relief Jean's big day finally arrived. The night before, Dee stood in her bedroom gazing at her reflection in the long mirror on the inside of the wardrobe door. The long burgundy velvet Empire-style dress with its tight sleeves suited her. It was plain except for a large bow that sat under the bust line. The head-dress consisted of a wide burgundy bandeau embroidered with pearls and Jean had put her hair up into large loose curls and had instructed her to try not to flatten it too much. The satin pumps had been dyed to match the dress and she wore pearl earrings and a single strand of imitation pearls. The bouquets were to be of cream and burgundy roses. Jean had chosen well, she thought. It was stylish, elegant and warm, as, undoubtedly, the bride's dress would be too. She had been to a fitting with her friend but she hadn't seen Jean's finished dress.

Now that the time had almost arrived she prayed she would be able to get through it with a smile on her face. She *wouldn't* think about him, she vowed. She would concentrate on seeing that Jean's day was perfect. In the morning her time would be taken up with seeing that her mother looked smart and that Davie looked presentable. Then she would go up to Jean's so Pauline could repair any damage a night's sleep had done to her hairstyle and make sure that Ada didn't upset Jean with her incessant fussing. For the rest of the day she would make sure she was surrounded by people so there would be no time to dwell on the past. She closed the wardrobe door and began to take off the wedding finery. That was all very well, she thought, but she had the long hours of the night to get through first.

She didn't sleep well. No matter how hard she tried the memories kept coming back. She did her best not to toss and turn for to do so would mean the ruination of her hairstyle but it was difficult and so when she got up she had a slight headache and there were dark smudges under her eyes. She sat on the edge of the bed and took a deep breath. This was Jean's day, she told herself firmly, and she wasn't going to be utterly selfish and do anything to spoil it. A deeper shade of foundation would conceal the signs of fatigue and she'd take a couple of aspirins for the headache.

'You look tired. Are you sure you're going to be all right?' Flo remarked when Dee came downstairs.

'I'll be just fine, Mam. If I look tired it's because I was so bothered about not ruining my hair that I didn't sleep well.'

Flo poured her a cup of tea. 'I said it was a ridiculous idea! You'd have been better off having it done fresh this morning.'

Dee sighed. 'Pauline will have enough to do with Jean and her mam.'

Flo sniffed. 'Ada didn't make all this fuss when their Margaret got married. She had her hair done the day before and anyway the hat will flatten it. It's this attitude she's taking towards Tony's mother. All this one-upmanship. I don't know what's got into her.'

Dee had to agree. 'I'll get the breakfast, Mam. Then I'll help you get ready and make sure our Davie gets a proper wash. You know what he can be like.' She didn't mention Graham. She wasn't sure he would even turn up although she knew he had been invited. For the last month he had stayed out every weekend, only returning home on a Sunday night and despite her mother's demands to know where he'd been they had learned nothing.

'You'd think that at nearly sixteen that lad would take more of an interest in his appearance,' Flo replied cuttingly.

Dee swallowed two tablets with the remains of her tea, hoping they would help. No matter how hard she had tried to be firm with herself she was still dreading the hours ahead.

Davie appeared looking half asleep, his hair tousled and holding an envelope. 'Post. It's for you, Dee,' he mumbled.

'Thanks. You'd better get a move on and for heaven's sake make sure you're clean and tidy. Don't have Mam getting upset or annoyed before we even get to the church.'

Without bothering to reply he helped himself to a piece of toast and wandered out of the kitchen.

Dee sighed and opened the letter. It was from Niall and it was very brief, little more than a note. *Hoping everything goes well for you today. I'll be thinking of you. Niall.*

She smiled. It was thoughtful of him to remember. And somehow she did get through it all with a smile on her face although when Jean, radiant with love and happiness and looking petite and elegant in what had turned out to be a quite stunning dress, promised to love, honour and obey her husband until death, she had to fight hard to keep the tears at bay. She forced herself to keep her eyes and her mind on Father Adrian as he continued with the ceremony. Behind her she could hear Ada sniffing and Margaret tutting under her breath. Then they were all walking back down the aisle as the organ thundered out and the assembled relations and friends smiled at them and the photographer waited to usher them into position for the photographs.

When she joined Margaret, Ada and Harry in the car that was to take them to the hotel she breathed a sigh of relief that the first part of the ordeal was over. The rest of the day couldn't be nearly as stressful.

'You'd better powder your nose, Mam. All that dabbing your eyes has left your face blotchy,' Margaret instructed, arranging the folds of her dress so that it wouldn't get creased. There certainly hadn't been so much fuss over her wedding day, she thought irritably.

'Oh, I got all emotional. She looked such a picture,' Ada replied, scrutinising her face in the mirror of her powder compact.

'She did. Just like a bride in one of those wedding magazines,' Dee agreed.

Ada dusted her nose and cheeks liberally with powder and then patted her hat with satisfaction. 'Everything went just perfectly. Even *that one* couldn't find fault.'

Margaret raised her eyes skywards. 'Oh, don't start, Mam! Let's all just enjoy ourselves and never mind what Tony's mother says or thinks. Frank and I don't get out much these days so we intend to make the most of the occasion.'

'Seeing how much it's all costing me, I'll certainly drink to that,' Harry replied cheerfully.

'Just as long as you don't go overdoing it,' Ada warned.

The meal was delicious and the service was excellent, Dee thought as she concentrated on engaging Tony's best man in conversation – something he was thankful for as he was getting a bit nervous about his speech, he confided to her. Her own resolve had faltered when in the hotel foyer Jean had given her a quick hug and said, 'Thanks, Dee. You've really made my day even more special.'

After the meal people went into the lounge to sit and chat while the room was cleared for the evening's festivities. Dee set off for the Ladies to touch up her make-up but on her way she caught Davie and Peter Williams lurking in the corridor, a pint glass of beer in each of their hands.

'Who said the pair of you could have that?' she demanded.

Peter grinned at her. 'My da but he said don't let your mam see you, that's why we're out here.'

'Well, don't go getting any more. Your mam will kill you if you get drunk and disgrace yourself, Peter, and the same goes for you, Davie. I haven't forgotten the carry-on of the pair of you at Margaret's wedding,' she warned.

'Mam's already had two glasses of wine and a glass of that fizzy stuff,' Davie informed her.

'Mam is well able to take care of herself. Did Graham say anything to you about turning up?' she asked. There had been no sign of him so far.

Davie shrugged. 'He said he might call in later in the evening.'

Dee bit her lip. The last thing they needed was her brother turning up drunk. She'd try and have a word with Jean's da and ask him to keep his eye out for her brother and thereby, hopefully, avoid any trouble should Graham be the worse for wear.

Everyone was getting on famously. There were gales of laughter coming from the table where Ada's sisters and their families were sitting; Harry and a few of his nephews were joking about events and misdemeanours from their past; Ernest Littlemore and his brother were circulating amongst the guests; and the lively music the band were playing had encouraged many people to dance. Graham did arrive after the evening buffet had been served and to her astonishment not only was he sober but he'd brought a girl with him.

'How's it been, sis?' he asked, his gaze sweeping the room.

'Not too bad for me and it's been everything Jean hoped for,' Dee answered.

He grinned at her and she felt a wave of relief wash over her. He was just like his old self. He turned to the girl beside him and grinned. 'This is Susie. We've been seeing each other for a couple of months.'

Dee smiled at the girl. She was probably the same age as herself and was very stylishly dressed in a vivid turquoise shift dress with a short skirt and three-quarter-length sleeves edged with a frill. Her hair was deep auburn and fell around her shoulders in tight curls and her eyes were the colour of amber. 'Nice to meet you, Susie. I'm Dee.'

Susie smiled back a little shyly. 'I wasn't sure if it would be all right for me to come.'

'The invitation did say "and guest",' Dee replied, 'and Jean will be delighted to meet you. Why don't you take Susie over and introduce her to the new Mrs Littlemore?' she urged Graham. So they had been seeing each other for a couple of months? Maybe Susie was just the person to get her brother back on the straight and narrow. She fervently hoped so.

Flo had had far too much to drink but she'd told Ada that for once she was going to enjoy herself so that was her excuse. In the church she'd thought that Dee was coping well but she hadn't been able to stop herself from thinking that her daughter should have had a wedding like this and a lovely house of her own like Jean and Tony had and a wonderful future to look forward to – if her father hadn't betrayed them all and ruined everything. She, too, could have looked as smart as Ada did in that deep rose-pink silk moiré dress and jacket and chocolate-brown fine straw hat with matching shoes and bag. Bob had earned far more than Harry Williams did. Of course they hadn't won the Irish Sweepstake but they could still have given Dee and Billy a decent wedding. Billy. She could never think of the lad without the black bitterness bubbling up inside her. When she thought of him she always thought of *her*, that tart – Alice Dobson! When the service was over she had determined to put it all out of her mind and enjoy the rare chance of a lovely meal in an hotel. So she had had two glasses of wine with the meal and a glass of 'bubbly' for the toasts and then Harry had insisted she have a large gin and tonic. She had felt a little light-headed after that but as the evening had worn on she had recklessly accepted another two from Ernest Littlemore.

Now her gaze had settled on her eldest son, who had finally put in an appearance and seemed to have a girl hanging on to his arm: a red-headed girl in a very flashy-coloured dress. A dress so short that if she bent over everyone would certainly be able to see what colour her knickers were. Anger welled up in her. How dare he come in at this hour and bring that *trollop* with him! After the way he'd been carrying on lately! He was going out of his way to humiliate her, just the way his father had done. Well, she wasn't going to stand for it. She got up and weaved her way unsteadily towards the little group that consisted of Jean and Tony and Dee and *those two*. They were all laughing at something Graham had said.

She caught her son's arm and pulled him around to face her. 'How dare you! How dare you!' she yelled at him.

Shocked, Dee tried to pull her mother away. 'Mam! Mam, please don't start an argument. Don't make a scene,' she begged.

Flo barely heard her. There was only one thing on her mind. 'I'm not having him coming in here drunk and with a trollop like that hanging on his arm. He's not humiliating me!' Flo's voice rose until she was screeching like a harpy. 'He's just like his father! I've told you that time and again, Dee. Don't go trying to defend him. If it hadn't been for your father you could have had a wedding like this! This could have been your day, yours and Billy's. You could have had a happy future together if it hadn't been for that bloody lying, cheating, adulterous . . .'

Dee stood rooted to the spot, her hands pressed against her cheeks, her eyes wide with shock and horror. Jean was on the verge of tears and Tony's eyes were blazing with anger. Poor Susie looked as if she was going to faint but it was Graham who grabbed his mother and shook her hard, fury and humiliation sweeping through him.

'Shut up! Shut up, Mam! I'm not drunk but you certainly are! You're a disgrace and I'm sick to death of you! What's done is done and Da's dead and you ranting and raving about him all the time isn't helping Dee at all! You're ruining Jean's day and I'm not having you insult Susie like this.'

He shoved her away from him and Flo began to cry noisy hysterical sobs. The whole room had gone quiet and even the band had stopped playing.

Ada rushed over. 'For the love of God, Flo! What's got into you?' she demanded furiously, having caught the look of disgust on Mavis Littlemore's face.

'Too much gin, I'd say,' Tony said grimly.

'She's drunk. Get her out of here before she ruins the whole evening,' Graham snapped before turning to Jean who was almost as white as her dress. 'I'm sorry, Jean. Really I am. We should never have come.

I should have known what her reaction would be. I'm taking Susie home and tell your mam to tell *her* when she sobers up that I've finished with her for good. I never want to see her again. Da made a terrible mistake but she'll never change and I'm sick of listening to her carrying on about it.'

Jean could only nod as she clung tightly to Tony's arm. Her da and her uncle Hughie were helping Ada to get a now half-collapsed Flo out of the room. Thankfully the band had started up again and people were making stilted conversation. She looked around for Dee but there was no sign of her friend.

As Graham had turned to apologise to Jean, Dee had fled. She'd run from the room, tears pouring down her cheeks, and she hadn't stopped until she'd reached the front door of the hotel. Out in the street she'd taken a few steps and had then leaned against the wall of an adjacent building. Oh, how could Mam have done that! She'd been like a hysterical banshee screaming all that abuse and dragging up the very thing she had been fighting all day to put out of her mind. It was just too much to bear! She'd disgraced them all in front of everyone, and ruined Jean's day and her own with all that hatred and vindictiveness that she just wouldn't let go of. Now she had driven Graham away too. She began to sob harder. Mam would never forgive or forget and she wasn't going to let her forget either. Every time her father's behaviour was mentioned she would be forced to remember Billy.

A crowd of girls and lads passed her, all half drunk

and singing noisily and their raucous voices only added to her misery, but she couldn't go back in there, she just *couldn't*. Not even for Jean. She had to get away from here. Get away from her mother and her vicious, destructive bitterness.

Chapter Twenty-Two

———◆———

IT WAS GRAHAM AND SUSIE who found Dee in the street; she was sobbing and shivering uncontrollably. Graham took off his jacket and put it around her while Susie, despite her own shock, tried to comfort her.

'We can't leave her here like this, Graham,' Susie said, biting her lip. It had been a terrible scene and she was very shaken and upset herself. Graham had told her he didn't get on with his mother but she had never realised that the woman was such a harridan. Now she felt sorry for both Graham and his sister.

'Dee, try and calm down, please. We'll take you back inside. You can't stay out here,' Graham pleaded, trying to sound calm himself despite his anger.

'No! No, I can't go back in there,' Dee cried desperately.

'Please, Dee? We can't leave you like this and I know

Jean is worried about you. I'm going to take Susie home, she's very upset too.'

At the mention of her friend's name Dee quietened a little. 'I . . . I didn't think . . . I just had to get away from Mam and from . . . everyone. They were all staring at us!'

Graham nodded. 'I know. Come on, let's go back in. You're freezing.'

Reluctantly she let her brother and Susie lead her back into the hotel foyer.

'Oh, Dee! Thank God you found her, Graham!' Jean cried, breaking away from her husband and his father. They'd been searching for her in the hotel's lounges and corridors.

'I found her outside in the street,' Graham informed them.

Jean was in tears, thinking her friend had run off to God knows where. When she saw this Dee made a huge effort to pull herself together. 'Jean, don't cry! Please, please don't cry! I'm so sorry I've upset you. I'm all right now. It was just the shock. You can't cry on your wedding day, it's bad luck.'

'It's not your fault, Dee. It's not you who's upset her,' Tony said, putting his arm around his wife. He was furious at all the trouble Flo Campbell had caused. He wished she'd never been invited.

'No, this is all Mam's fault! She's a bloody disgrace! I'm sorry, Tony.' Graham was still seething.

Ernest Littlemore took the situation in hand. 'Tony, take the two girls over to the manager's office and ask can they sit in there for a while to compose themselves while we all go for a quiet drink in the residents' bar to steady ourselves.'

'If you don't mind, Mr Littlemore, I'd like to get Susie home. She doesn't really know anyone and it's been a bit of an ordeal for her too,' Graham said.

Ernest nodded. It had been an ordeal for everyone and he'd never hear the end of it from Mavis. There would be numerous references to the 'common' people Jean's family had insisted on inviting. People who didn't know how to behave in the company of respectable folk.

'Could I ask a favour?' Graham added. 'Could you make sure that Dee gets home all right?' He was concerned for his sister.

'Of course. I'll arrange for someone to drive her home whenever she wants to leave.'

Graham thanked him and shook his hand before guiding Susie towards the door just as Tony returned. Both he and his father walked towards the door marked 'Residents' Bar'.

'I could murder that bloody woman, Dad! I wish she'd never been invited,' Tony exploded as his father ordered two brandies and they sat down in an alcove.

'I have to say I'm inclined to agree with you. We'll never hear the end of it from your mother and it has certainly upset poor Jean and Dee. What in God's name did Dee's father do to cause the woman to be so vituperative?'

Tony had never mentioned Bob Campbell's affair

but now he told his father the whole sorry story.

'I see. Tragic, all of it. No wonder Dee was so upset. Today must have been an ordeal for her even without that outburst from her mother. If that woman isn't careful she'll lose all three of her children. Hatred like that is destructive. The man was a fool but he paid dearly for his mistake.' He finished his drink and got to his feet. 'I'd better get back or your mother will be annoyed. You wait in the foyer for your wife and Dee and if Dee wishes to go home then let me know.'

The manager had been very accommodating. Both the bride and her bridesmaid had been clearly upset. He'd settled them both with a small brandy each, told them to take as much time as they needed to compose themselves, and closed the door behind him. In his experience it wasn't unheard of for someone to cause a scene at functions like this and he was sure that the groom or his father would recompense him for his consideration.

Jean had wiped away her tears. 'You gave me a fright. It was all so . . . unexpected and so *awful* and I knew you were terribly upset but I didn't know where you'd gone. I was so worried about you!'

'I'm sorry but I just *had* to get away. Oh, Jean, what a thing to happen. It was *vile*. Why did she cause such a terrible scene? She must have known it would upset everyone. I know she'd had too much to drink, and that's not like her, but she still must have realised that she was ruining your day. And . . . and why did she have to bring Billy into it? She knew how much it would hurt me. She *knew*. I can't forgive her, Jean. I can't.'

Jean nodded. Privately she thought Flo Campbell hadn't cared what she'd said or whom she'd hurt. She thought the woman was eaten up with bitterness. She was jealous that Jean's parents were reasonably happy. Oh, her da had his faults, he liked a drink and sometimes he spent too much on the horses but that was all. He was open about his faults, he'd never hidden them the way Dee's da had done. Flo was jealous that her da had won that money and had been able to give her a wonderful wedding and jealous of the fact that she had Tony. It was as if she didn't really understand or care how much losing Billy meant to Dee. She seemed incapable of thinking about anyone other than herself and how she had been wounded and betrayed. However, Jean couldn't voice these thoughts to her friend.

'And now she's driven Graham away. I think he's serious about Susie and I'm glad. Someone in this family deserves to be happy.'

'But what about you, Dee? If she keeps on like this what kind of life are you going to have?'

Dee managed a weak smile. She felt weary and numb. 'Don't worry about me, Jean. I'll be all right. You had better get back to your husband and your guests and I'm really sorry about . . . everything. Promise me you'll put it out of your mind and enjoy what's left of the day.'

Jean slowly finished the brandy. She did feel much

better now. 'I will. What do you want to do? Will you stay on or do you want to leave?'

Dee leaned back in the chair. She didn't want to stay. She couldn't face going back into that room full of people. People who were enjoying themselves and who might well now look at her with curiosity or, worse, pity. She didn't want to see the disapproval on Tony's mother's face or hear what Ada had done with her mam. In fact she never wanted to see her mother again.

'I'll go home, Jean, but I can't go on the bus dressed like this. Do you think perhaps Tony's father might pay for a taxi? I know it will be terribly expensive but . . .'

Jean stood up; she could fully understand Dee's decision. 'Don't worry about it. I know a car has been ordered to take my lot back home. The driver can take you and then come back for them. By that time things should be winding down and Tony's dad is going to take us back to Moss Lane.' They were going to spend their first night in their new home before setting off for a few days' honeymoon in the Lake District. 'You stay there while I go and find Tony.'

Dee finished the last couple of drops of brandy, thankful and relieved to be able to leave. She didn't particularly want to go back to that house alone but she couldn't face the alternative.

The car was comfortable and warm and she dozed fitfully on the way home. The driver had been informed by Ernest Littlemore that she was upset and he therefore didn't try to engage her in conversation. The house was in darkness and he made sure she was safely indoors before driving back to town.

She turned on the light in the sitting room and looked around. The room looked the same as it always had done but now it seemed to her that there was no feeling of warmth or comfort or familiarity. It was cold and cheerless, just a room. This house was no longer the home it had once been. It was just a house and a house full of rancour and perpetual recriminations. Sometime, either tonight or tomorrow, her mother would return, nursing a hangover, and she knew there would be no apology to her for the terrible thing she had done or the cruel words she'd shouted for everyone to hear. Dee sat down in the armchair and wrapped her arms around herself. It was as if all her mam's fury and malice hung in the air, was being exuded from the walls, and was pressing down on her. She shivered. Jean had her new home to go to while all she had was a room in this house that her mother had steeped in hatred and unhappiness.

She got to her feet. She couldn't stay here. She switched off the light and went slowly upstairs. She had come to a decision. She'd go back to the peace and tranquillity of Ireland. She'd go back and she'd marry Niall Clarke for she couldn't face a future here. There was nothing left here but memories of things and people she would rather forget.

She slept heavily, exhausted by the traumas of the day, and when she awoke next morning she could hear no sounds coming from downstairs. She got dressed and went down but there was no sign of her mother.

She wrote three notes: one to Jean, one to her mother and one for Celia Ellerby. She intended to post the notes to Jean and Celia later that day, after she'd sent a telegram to Niall and withdrawn her savings from the Post Office. Then she would go to the travel agent's to book her flight. She put all three envelopes in her handbag and set off for the bus stop. She could see no sign of life as she passed the Williamses' house. Probably Ada and Harry had brought her mother and brother home with them and kept them overnight. She was past caring.

When she arrived back later that afternoon she could see that someone had been in the house: probably Davie, judging by the trail of crumbs and the jar of strawberry jam, the lid of which hadn't been replaced. He'd most probably gone back to Ada's. She went upstairs and sorted through her clothes, packing only those she judged to be suitable for her new life. There was no point in taking flimsy, elaborate dresses and shoes. She would have no use for them. Her savings and her ticket were in her bag. She would have to leave soon for her flight was due to take off at five o'clock. She propped the note for her mother up against the kettle and, after taking a last look around the untidy kitchen of Buttermere Close, she let herself out.

As she sat in the airport lounge she wondered what lay ahead of her. Could she settle in a different country with different customs? Spending a holiday and spending the rest of her life there were two very different things. And what about Niall? She knew more about him now through their correspondence but she had no idea of his character except the little she had been able to judge on her visit. Well, she'd made her decision. She'd sent the telegram so there was no changing her mind now.

She'd never thought to be making this journey again, let alone so soon, she mused as the plane took off, climbing slowly and steadily into the grey, leaden sky. Looking out of the window she could see the lights along the docks and at the Pier Head and of the ships below her in the river Mersey as it wended its way towards Liverpool Bay and the Irish Sea, and she wondered if she would ever see the city of her birth again. Oh, they'd been overcrowded in the house in Cobden Street but they'd been far happier there: her childhood had been content and secure in that little house in the slums. The new house in Kirkby should have been the start of a better life for them all but instead it had turned out to be the beginning of a life of heartbreak and disillusionment, disappointment and grief.

She got a taxi to Heuston Station and was relieved that she was just in time to catch the last train to Tullamore that day. As she settled herself in a seat by the window she realised she was hungry; she'd had little to eat all day, but she would have to wait. She managed to doze fitfully but when she finally arrived at Tullamore Station she was tired, famished and full of trepidation. It was late and what if Niall hadn't been

271

able to come to meet her? What if there had been a barge expected? What if he hadn't even received her telegram? To her relief as she stepped off the train he came towards her.

'Give me your case, Dee. You look very pale, are you feeling ill?' he asked, his voice full of concern. She didn't look at all well. She was ashen and drawn. Her telegram had come as a complete surprise and he had been wondering what had happened at the wedding that had prompted her to decide to come almost immediately after it was over. Something terrible, judging by her appearance.

At the note of genuine solicitude in his voice the tears welled up in her eyes. He hadn't asked why she'd made such an abrupt decision, or why she'd arrived at this time of night, which she had fully expected him to, he'd just expressed concern for her health. She was sure now she'd made the right decision, sure he was the right person to provide the comfort and escape she so desperately needed.

'No, I'm not ill, Niall. Just tired and hungry and very upset,' she replied as they walked out of the station yard. She had decided on the train that she would be totally honest with him. She wasn't going to start this new life keeping secrets.

He put his arm around her shoulder. 'We'll go first to the hotel and get you something to eat and then I'll take you back to Mrs Mulcahey's house. I called over when I got your telegram and asked her could she put you up. She doesn't take visitors during the winter months but I told her it wouldn't be for long.'

She felt a little better hearing that. She'd been so distressed and confused that she hadn't given a single thought to where she would stay until she'd been on the train. Then she'd decided she would have to stay at one of the hotels in town even though it would probably be expensive.

'I owe you an explanation, Niall. You must be wondering why I suddenly decided to come over . . . and I . . . I've come to stay.'

He looked down at her. 'Let's wait until we reach the hotel and you've got a hot drink inside you,' he suggested. He could see she was indeed upset about something and he didn't want her to try to explain on the street, but whatever it was that had brought about this decision, he was glad of it. She'd said she had come to stay and that obviously meant that she would marry him. Despite the cold, damp autumn night he couldn't help but feel happy and relieved.

Part V

Chapter Twenty-Three

⬧━━◆━━⬧

1967

JEAN PUT THE BAGS of shopping down on the kitchen
floor and looked around with some irritation. The
kitchen was far from tidy. Couldn't Tony have at least
put his breakfast dishes in the sink instead of leaving
them on the table? She'd had a busy day and she was
tired. She pressed her hands into the small of her back
and sighed. No use standing here pulling faces and
complaining about her husband's untidy habits, she
told herself, better get on with things.

Her mam had told her that marriage wasn't always a
bed of roses, it was often a matter of compromise and
there were times when she thought this was very true.
She smiled to herself. But she was very happy with
Tony, she wouldn't change him for the world.

She collected the dishes and put them in the sink

and then began to unpack the shopping. She would have the whole evening to herself as Tony was working on the renovations to a big salon down in Chester, which meant him staying overnight there once a week, although he complained that the whole thing was getting out of hand and he wished the job was finished. She wished it was too, she didn't like being in the house on her own, she missed him. But there were plenty of things to keep her occupied this evening, she thought.

When she'd tidied the kitchen and made herself a sandwich and a cup of tea she went through to the living room. The late evening sun streamed in through the window and she smiled to herself. She loved this room, it was so bright and cheerful even on dismal winter days. She opened the window as wide as it would go, breathing in the smells of the garden. Tony cut the grass: it was his only contribution to keeping the garden looking neat; he just didn't have green fingers, he'd told her laughingly when she'd come home with a book on herbaceous border plants. But she enjoyed gardening, she found it relaxing and always felt a glow of satisfaction when she looked out of the window and saw the riot of colour in the two small borders. But there was no time for standing gazing out at her handiwork this evening, she had her accounts to do and she needed to make a list of the supplies she required for the shop; they were running very low on both shampoo and bleach and she might even have to send Bernice to the wholesalers if they couldn't deliver quickly enough.

An envelope propped up against the clock on the mantelpiece caught her eye and she smiled. The post must have arrived before Tony had left; judging by the stamp it was from Dee. She sat down at the dining table with her ledger and all the bills and receipts and opened Dee's letter. The accounts could wait for a few minutes.

Dear Jean,

I'm sorry I've been so slow replying to your last letter and really I've no excuse except that I have been making the most of the good weather by doing some badly needed decorating – although Niall says he doesn't know why every room in the house has to be painted every year! I suppose he has a point but it gives me something to do, although you'll be pleased to know that I have applied for a job. One of the solicitors in town is looking for someone to come in a few days a week to do letters and filing and such. Mrs Mulcahey heard about it and as I'm always complaining to her that, much as I love living here in the country, I do get a bit bored now and then she thought it would interest me. Niall really doesn't want me to work, I think he thinks it will detract from his position or some such nonsense but it would at least give me an interest. We are still trying for a baby for, as you know, it's so important to Niall, but still no luck. I keep telling myself I'm still young and that we have plenty of time, and maybe having a job will help take my mind off it.

Jean nodded to herself as she read this. She'd often wondered what Dee did with herself all day not having a job and living so far away from a town. Dee's nearest shop, a post office cum grocery, was over three miles away. She glanced momentarily out of the window, thinking back to how utterly taken aback and worried she'd been when she'd returned from her honeymoon to learn that her friend had packed up and gone to Ireland to marry a man she barely knew. She'd written to Dee, begging her to reconsider. She'd even thought of going over herself to try to persuade Dee to come back, but Dee had been adamant. She couldn't put up with her mother any longer. She hated that house; there was no future for her in Liverpool.

After Flo had recovered from her hangover, which had been compounded by the guilt and shame she felt for the dreadful scene she had caused, she had rushed down to her mam with Dee's letter. Her mam had been just as astounded that Dee had left but had reminded Flo that Dee was twenty-one and could do as she pleased and that it really was time Flo stopped and gave a great deal of thought to the way she was behaving. Flo hadn't been very pleased to hear that, Jean thought wryly, but her mam had never been one to mince her words.

Dee went on to recount some of the trivia in her life but ended by saying she would let Jean know how the interview went. Jean folded the letter and put it to one side; she'd write to Dee tomorrow evening. She wished Dee had a phone, it would be so much easier to keep in touch, but apparently very few people in the rural areas over there had telephones.

At the other end of the table there was a small pile of mail that Tony had obviously opened and she pulled it towards her: a couple of bills and an invitation to a dinner dance at the Adelphi Hotel to be given by one of the firms that Littlemore & Wilson regularly dealt with. That looked interesting. They really didn't go out a great deal as they had been concentrating on furnishing the house. When they did it was usually to the local cinema or occasionally a dance at the nearby Orrell Park Ballroom, but it was years since they'd been to anything as grand as this. She'd splash out on a new dress, she thought, putting the stiff gilt-edged invitation back in the envelope.

She spent the next hour and a half working on the accounts and then she got up to make herself a drink. The dinner dance was in a fortnight so there was plenty of time to look for a suitable dress, but she'd have to take Tony's best suit to the dry-cleaner's. She'd drop it into Johnston's on Walton Vale tomorrow and she was sure their finances could stretch to him buying a new shirt and tie. Probably his mother and father would go to this dinner dance as well and she wasn't having Mavis making any unfavourable comments about the way either of them were dressed. She'd get the suit out now so she wouldn't forget to take it in the morning. She went upstairs to their bedroom and got it out of the wardrobe and found a carrier bag. She folded the trousers after checking the pockets and extracting a book of matches and a grubby handkerchief, and then turned her attention to the jacket. In the inside pocket was a folded piece of paper. She was about to put it on the bedside table beside the matches when out of curiosity she unfolded it. It was a receipt from the hotel he stayed at in Chester, the Grosvenor. Well, at the price they were charging she was thankful that Littlemore & Wilson were paying. She'd begun to fold it up again when something caught her attention. It was made out not to the company but to Mr and *Mrs* Littlemore. She stared at it. It must be a mistake. The receptionist had just been careless, but why not to the company and why had she put 'Mrs'? As he'd been checking out it must surely have been obvious that he was on his own. Or was he? She sat trying to find rational explanations but with a growing sense of trepidation and dread. He wouldn't cheat on her, he loved her, he told her so often. They hadn't been married three years yet. No, it was impossible. Yet she couldn't put it out of her mind. She had to *know*. She couldn't rest until she knew.

She found the phone number at the bottom of the receipt and with hands that were trembling a little she dialled. When she got through she asked to be put through to Mr Tony Littlemore's room. She affected what she hoped was a refined and efficient tone and said she was his father's secretary and had an urgent message for him regarding the work schedule for tomorrow.

'Will you hold the line, please, Miss . . . ?' the voice at the other end queried politely.

'Williams,' she replied, using the first name that came into her head.

'Trying to connect you, Miss Williams,' came the precise but slightly bored reply.

She waited as the phone rang out and at last it was answered. It was Tony's voice. She didn't know whether to speak or not. She didn't want him to know she was checking up on him.

'Hello. Hello, Miss Williams? Do I know you?'

Jean bit her lip. If she spoke he would instantly recognise her voice. Oh, she felt such a fool. Such a suspicious fool. She shouldn't have phoned. Then she heard a woman's voice. It was asking him who it was, and calling him 'darling'. She dropped the receiver as if it were red hot and sat down on the edge of the bed. She could hear the dialling tone and realised he'd hung up.

She replaced the receiver. She felt sick, physically sick. He was there in that expensive hotel room with *someone else*, someone who had called him *darling*. He'd been lying to her about having to stay overnight and this was the third week he'd been away and with *her*. Why? Why, when he'd sworn he loved her? How could he do this? She had never felt so hurt and let down in her entire life. She'd believed and trusted him implicitly. They'd been so happy – or so she'd thought. Obviously she'd been wrong. Should she have seen this coming? Had there been any tell-tale signs in his behaviour? None that she could think of. He'd always had an eye for a pretty face but he'd always told her that there was no harm in looking, he'd married her and she was the only one he loved.

The room had suddenly become chilly and she realised she was shivering. She lay down and pulled the quilt over her and began to cry, tears of abject misery and despair. She'd never loved anyone but him but the feeling obviously wasn't mutual. He had needed someone else and he hadn't given her or their marriage vows a second thought. Oh, she wished Dee was here now. She could have cried out all her despair and anguish to her friend. She missed Dee at the best of times but now, when she deperately needed a shoulder to cry on, Dee was so far away.

She'd cried herself to sleep and when she woke it was with a headache and a heavy feeling of despair. Her confusion was such that it was several seconds before she remembered why she felt like this and the tears again welled up in her eyes. Dejectedly she at last got up. She had to go and open up the shop; Pauline didn't have keys. And somehow she had to get through the day.

Despite the extra care she'd taken with her make-up to try to conceal her swollen eyes she had had to tell Pauline that she didn't feel well, that this head cold had come on suddenly late last night.

'Why don't you go home? We can manage, there's only about an hour this afternoon when it should get really busy and when I've explained I'm sure the clients won't mind a bit of a wait. Go home and go to bed. You really do look awful,' Pauline had said sympathetically.

She'd stayed until lunchtime but all she could think of was that she'd have to confront Tony. The effort of being cheerful and interested in what her clients had to say was too much and so she'd left the girls to cope with the busy Friday afternoon. She made herself a cup of tea when she got in and took it out into the garden. The bright sunlight and the vibrant colours of the flowers didn't lift her spirits as they usually did. There was nothing that could make her feel that way again, she thought miserably.

She heard him come in and she froze, her stomach churning. Now she would have to face him. She would have to confront him. She turned and slowly went back into the house. He was standing in the kitchen holding a huge bouquet of flowers.

'I called at the shop first but Pauline told me you'd come home. That you'd got a terrible cold, so I got you these to cheer you up. You don't look very well, luv.'

She could hardly believe what he was saying. He was trying to behave as if nothing had happened, that he was actually concerned about her. 'I haven't got a cold. I was just too upset to carry on,' she informed him, her voice full of the anguish she couldn't hide.

'Who . . . what's upset you, Jean?'

'Oh, for God's sake, Tony! I . . . *I know*! I know about you and . . . *her*!' she blurted out, unable to control the anger and hurt. 'I found a receipt in your pocket for the Grosvenor and . . . and I phoned. I *heard* her! She called you *darling*!' Tears spilled down her cheeks and she was shaking. She'd never felt so awful in her life.

285

Tony paled visibly. That phone call! That bloody phone call! 'You . . . you were checking up on me? Well, that's very nice!' he blustered.

Rage overcame her despair. 'You were cheating on me, Tony! I shouldn't have needed to be "checking up" on you. I should be able to trust my husband. "Forsaking all others", wasn't that what you promised? How could you? How could you go to . . . to someone else?'

Tony could see the position he was in and immediately changed tack.

'Jean! Jean, I'm so sorry! I never meant to hurt you, truly I didn't! It was just a stupid . . . fling!'

Jean shook her head in disbelief. 'A *fling*! It's been going on for weeks, Tony! How could you do this to me? You said you loved me. I trusted you but you've been lying to me all the time,' she cried pitifully.

He moved towards her but she stepped back. 'I do love you, Jean. I really do. Please believe me. I never meant it to go so far. It . . . it was a flirtation that got out of hand. She means nothing to me, *nothing*!'

Jean was sobbing. How could she believe anything he said now? 'Why, Tony? Why?'

'I don't know, that's the God's truth. I never meant it to happen.'

'You never meant to get found out!' she shouted, fury building in her.

He threw the flowers on the table and took her in his arms. 'Jean, I'll never do anything to hurt you ever again, I swear it! It was one stupid mistake. It's you I love, you must believe me.'

She buried her face in his jacket. 'How can I ever believe you again? I feel so hurt, as if I . . . I'm a failure. Such a failure that you *wanted* someone else.'

'It wasn't like that. I don't *want* anyone else, just you. I love you and I'll never hurt you again. Please, can you forgive me?'

She didn't know what to say. Part of her wanted to believe him but the other part didn't. 'I . . . I don't know, Tony, really I don't.'

'Please let's try again. Let's put it all behind us. I don't want to lose you, Jean. I couldn't live without you,' he pleaded.

She didn't want to lose him either, but she had the feeling that there would be more arguments, more recriminations and more apologies ahead. She wanted to believe he meant what he said but she'd been let down so badly that she knew it would be quite a while before any semblance of trust could be regained.

When she didn't reply and she didn't respond to his embrace he thought what a complete fool he'd been. He really hadn't meant to hurt her. She was a great girl in so many ways. It had just been a bit of fun, a bit of excitement to liven up what was becoming, frankly, a rather tedious life, a life that seemed to be all work and no play. But he knew she didn't think of their life together that way, and she would never see his adultery in that light.

Chapter Twenty-Four

———◆———

D EE SCRUTINISED HER APPEARANCE in the dressing-
table mirror. It was so long since she had attended
an interview that she wondered was she too informally
dressed? She wore a pale blue short shift dress with a
matching jacket that she had made herself, after taking
the bus up to Dublin in the spring to do some shopping
and coming home laden down with parcels. Her navy
shoes and bag had been polished and she'd pinned a
navy artificial daisy to the lapel of the jacket. Her hair
needed cutting, she thought, thinking of the days when
Jean had kept it so well trimmed. Now it meant a
special trip into town to get it cut. She'd tied it back at
the nape of her neck with a pale blue ribbon. At least
she was neat and tidy. Had she aged? she wondered,
peering closely at her skin looking for tell-tale lines. It
was hard to believe that she was now twenty-four. She
sighed, thinking of all the hopes and plans both she and

Jean had had for the future when they'd left school all those years ago. They'd hoped for an exciting future; they'd planned to travel. Well, she'd better travel into Tullamore if she wasn't to be late for this interview.

Niall was painting the sign on the lock as she came out of the house.

'I'm off then, are you going to wish me luck?' she called to him.

He put down the paintbrush and crossed over to her, stepping quickly across the narrow ledge at the base of the closed lock gates instead of crossing by the bridge.

He smiled at her. 'Good luck, I'm sure you'll get the job, even though I'm not mad about you working.'

'Niall, we've been through all that. It's only three mornings a week,' she reminded him as she wheeled her bicycle on to the towpath.

'Sure, I suppose it will keep you from driving me mad with all the painting and decorating and refurbishing,' he joked. 'Take care, there are some terrible potholes in that road.'

She kissed him on the cheek and then rode off slowly towards the road that would take her eventually into town.

He watched her until she rounded the bend and was lost to sight. He couldn't imagine now what life would be like without her. He had fallen deeply in love with her over the last three years. He'd never stopped thanking God for the day he'd received her telegram. It had taken him completely by surprise. He hadn't had a reply to his letter and he had wondered if he would ever hear from her again. Had his proposal seemed too outlandish, too old-fashioned? Had she indeed been shocked and upset? Then out of the blue she'd sent word she was arriving the very same day and asking would he meet her at the station. It hadn't been an unhappy marriage, he thought. She fitted in well, she liked the lifestyle and although he knew she didn't love him in the same way that he loved her, she was fond of him and had changed his life completely. He turned back towards the bridge; the summer months were always busy and he wanted to get the painting finished for there were three boats due this afternoon.

Dee cycled on towards the village of Rahan. She'd become used to cycling everywhere, there was no public transport and they didn't have a car. She enjoyed it in the spring and summer when the breeze fanned her face and the sun was warm on her back but it wasn't as pleasant in winter when the wind and rain stung her cheeks and made her shiver. As she rounded the next bend in the road she caught sight of the little stone church in the middle of the field where she had been married. She smiled ruefully; it had been a very different wedding to Jean's. The tiny church had no stained-glass windows, no statues or elaborately decorated and draped altar, just a simple table covered with a starched white cloth and a silver cross. It had been a very simple service too: just herself and Niall and their two witnesses and of course the minister. She had worn her best suit and blouse and had purchased a hat at the drapery in town.

She had asked Mrs Mulcahey, who had welcomed her back and had been delighted to learn that she was to become Mrs Niall Clarke, to stand for her and had been rather taken aback when the woman had regretfully declined, informing her that Catholics were forbidden to set foot in a Protestant church. It was something she had got used to in the time she'd been here but she still found the power the Church wielded to be a little oppressive, although it didn't affect her directly.

She had found everything so very different at first and it had taken her time to get used to Niall and his ways but he had been very good to her. He understood her need to be in a place where she could escape from her past. Where life was so different and quiet. A place where she could find the peace she needed. They got on well together and now she supposed she did love him but not in the same way as she had loved Billy.

By the time she reached the town she was hot and a little breathless so she got off the bicycle outside the courthouse and walked the rest of the way. The office of Mr James Heffernan was at the bottom of the hill on the ground floor of what had been a lovely Georgian house but was now offices. She leaned her bike against the iron railings and smoothed a few stray wisps of hair back from her forehead before going up the stone steps and ringing the old-fashioned doorbell.

'Ah, Mrs Clarke. Very punctual, and isn't punctuality the courtesy of princes. Come on in,' the elderly solicitor greeted her, ushering her inside and into a rather dark and cluttered room. She sat down and he rummaged through the papers on his desk until he found what he was looking for: her application. 'I need some extra help in the office, Mrs Clarke, as my nephew is joining me in the practice next week. He's my sister's son, all the way from Brisbane, Australia. Sure, he's fully qualified but didn't he take it into his head that he wanted to go travelling halfway around the world. Now he's finally decided to come to the old country and get some experience in Irish law.'

Dee smiled. 'Won't he find things rather quiet here?'

'Ah, he will but I'm after thinking it's what he wants now. I know it's what his mother wants, she doesn't approve of all this gadding about – wasting his life and opportunities is the way she views it. So, there will be myself and Kevin Buckley in here from next week.'

Dee nodded and he then went over her qualifications and experience, and went on to offer her the job. He informed her of the salary and her duties and finished by impressing upon her the confidentiality of her work.

'I'm well aware of that, Mr Heffernan, and I don't gossip. In fact I don't know anyone in town to gossip to and I'm not related to anyone either,' she replied seriously.

He nodded. That fact alone had made him view her application favourably, for in the country areas nearly everyone was related in some degree to everyone else and things that were supposed to be confidential often leaked out. 'You speak a little French, I see,' he added.

She smiled. 'Just a little. I attended evening classes for a few years when I lived in Liverpool.'

'Sure, there won't be any call for it here in the office, although my sister would be interested to know of your accomplishment.'

She looked puzzled. 'Your sister?'

He leaned back and scrutinised her through his heavy horn-rimmed glasses. A pleasant enough young woman, well mannered, city born and bred but obviously intelligent and therefore slightly bored living way out in the country. Apart from the time she spent here working for him perhaps it would be of interest to her to keep up her French lessons. 'My eldest sister. She spent many years in France at a convent in Lisieux. She's home now; she's at the convent here in town. Sister Maria Theresa, she'd only be delighted if you were to call on her. She grew to love France, finds the climate here a wee bit damp.'

Dee frowned. 'Would they let me in? I'm not a Catholic, as you must have realised.'

He should have known that, most of the lock-keepers were Protestant. 'We'll find a way around that. Now, I'll see you here tomorrow morning, Mrs Clarke.'

Dee stood up and shook his hand, thinking that one of her first tasks would be to give the place a tidy and a good going-over with a duster.

As she cycled home she thought it had been a very productive afternoon. She now had a job and a small wage of her own. She was curious to meet Kevin Buckley and hear all about his travels. She would be interested to meet Sister Maria Theresa too; perhaps she could persuade her to give her lessons. There was no harm in improving her French, which was considerably rusty. She might even try to teach Niall, it would be an interest they could share and these days there were more people taking boating holidays on the canal and some of them were foreign. It would be good if she could speak to the French visitors in their own language.

When she arrived home there was no sign of Niall and she realised he must have gone down to the far lock. The post was on the kitchen table. She made herself a cup of tea and sat down. There were two letters for her, one from Jean and the other from Graham. She opened her brother's letter first. Jean had given him her address and he occasionally wrote. He and Susie had been married eighteen months ago; he'd sent her a photograph. Neither her mother nor Davie had attended although Susie had insisted they be invited, despite Graham's protests. She scanned the lines in his scrawled hand and smiled. Susie was expecting a baby. They were both delighted and Susie's mother was already knitting matinée coats. Sadly Dee wondered whether being a grandmother would change her mother's attitude. Would Graham even inform her of the fact? There was virtually no contact between them. She'd write to him later and congratulate them.

She opened Jean's letter and immediately could tell

there was something wrong. The pages were covered with blotchy marks as if tears had fallen on them. As she read of Tony's affair and her friend's shock, disbelief and heartbreak, she shook her head sadly. Oh, poor Jean. She didn't deserve to be hurt like this. She loved Tony so much and she worked so hard both in the salon and to keep her home clean and comfortable. Dee had assumed they'd been very happy. Why had he done such a thing? Surely he must have known it would break Jean's heart? How could Jean ever fully trust him again? Bitterly she thought of her father. Why did some men seem to need more than the love of their wives, regardless of the consequences? She prayed Jean wouldn't become as unforgiving as her mother. But as she read on it seemed as if her friend *had* forgiven him; he'd sworn it would never happen again and that he really loved Jean. She felt doubtful but she of course wouldn't convey her doubts to her friend. She would have to write and bolster up Jean's spirits. That's what friends did.

Chapter Twenty-Five

━━━◆◆◆━━━

JEAN HAD RECEIVED A very supportive letter from Dee in which she had also informed her that Graham and Susie were expecting a baby. When Jean had relayed this news to her mother Ada felt the time had come to have a serious talk with Flo. She had been a little worried about Jean lately too, she seemed a bit down and was quieter than usual but her daughter had assured her that she was fine. They were always rushed off their feet at this time of year with people wanting perms, tints or new styles before going off on holiday.

'You work too hard, Jean. I'm sure you and Tony could take a week off and have a bit of a holiday yourselves,' she'd suggested.

'I'm fine, Mam, just a bit tired. Stop fussing,' Jean had replied. Tony was being very attentive and loving and she was trying desperately hard to trust him again, although on the now very infrequent occasions when he was out late on business all the old fears and doubts would resurface. 'Do you suppose Flo Campbell knows she's going to be a granny?' she'd asked to divert Ada's attention from herself.

'I very much doubt it,' Ada replied. 'She flatly refused to go to that wedding even though I told her she was a fool and that she'd regret it.'

'So, will you tell her?' Jean had asked. She'd begun to wonder should she and Tony try for a baby. They'd been married long enough now (as Margaret often pointed out) and she had the house fully furnished. Her sister now had two sons and both she and her mother had started to drop not very subtle hints.

Ada nodded, determination in her eyes. 'I will indeed.' Even though it seemed everyone else avoided Flo these days, Ada had not given up on her old friend.

When Jean had gone and Harry was ensconced in front of the television watching *Till Death Us Do Part* and roaring with laughter at Alf Garnett's antics, she walked the short distance to Flo's house. Even before she reached the back door she could hear the raised voices. There was obviously an argument going on between Flo and Davie. She sighed heavily. Davie Campbell and her own son Peter were now eighteen. Both were apprentices at a factory on the industrial estate and both had started courting. She herself was delighted, she was looking forward to the day when she'd finally get Peter off her hands and she and Harry could take things a bit easier. Flo wasn't taking the same attitude. Young Davie still spent a great deal of time in her house and Ada thought that, despite everything, he was a good lad.

As she walked into the kitchen she scowled at them both. 'What's up with the pair of you now? You can hear the row halfway up the close.'

Davie flushed. 'The same as usual, Aunty Ada.' It was a form of address he'd adopted years ago.

She could see he was ready to go out. 'Oh, get off with you, lad. Flo, put the kettle on,' she instructed, sitting down at the table.

Davie thankfully made his escape as Flo filled the kettle, her lips pursed in a tight line.

'I'd thank you, Ada, to mind your own business,' she snapped.

'I'm just trying to stop you making the same mistake, Flo. Leave the lad alone. He's growing up and there's nothing you can do about it.'

Flo banged the cups down on the saucers. 'I'm not having him turn out like the other one!'

'There's nothing wrong with your Graham, Flo. He's settled down. A steady, respectable husband he is now and—' She was going to add 'a prospective father' but Flo laughed cuttingly.

'Steady and respectable like his father was, I suppose?'

'Flo Campbell, you are my oldest friend and we've been through a lot together so you're going to listen to me for once. You've driven both Graham and Dee away and now you're hell bent on doing the same to young Davie. They are all decent, good kids. You can't go on like this. You can't tar those two lads with the same brush as Bob. If you do you're going to end up a sad, lonely old woman and those kids are not going to care if you are alive or dead! Is that what you want? You've let all the anger and bitterness take over your life. You're far from happy and you never will be unless you give yourself a chance. Give the kids a chance, Flo. It was the carry-on out of you at our Jean's wedding that made Dee run off and marry a man she hardly knew. That Susie is a nice girl from a decent family but you refused to even meet her, let alone go to the wedding. I don't understand you, Flo, I really don't.'

'I can't do anything about that, Ada. I never wanted all this to happen but I can't forgive and forget, so don't ask me to,' Flo replied curtly. Ada's words had hurt.

'If you can't forgive, Flo, at least try to forget. Find the good in Graham and Davie, not the worst. I've got Dee's address, you know that, and I've begged you time and again to write to her.'

Flo shook her head vehemently. 'No. She went off with barely an explanation, just a few lines on a piece of paper. No forwarding address or even a phone number, nothing! She didn't give me the opportunity to apologise for the way I behaved. I intended to, Ada, you know that—'

'But *she* didn't know that, Flo,' Ada interrupted.

'Well, it's too late now. She's been gone nigh on three years and not a word.'

Ada was exasperated. 'Flo, you seem to be forgetting that it was all *your* fault!'

'It was all her bloody father's fault!' Flo cried.

Ada finally lost her temper. 'For God's sake, Flo, will you shut up about Bob Campbell! Everyone is sick to death of it all. I came to tell you that you are going to be a granny. Your Graham and Susie are expecting, but I can see I wasted my time in thinking it just might be the time for a bit of reconciliation. Well, it's your loss, Flo. And in years to come when you're sitting here all on your own and even more miserable than you are now, just remember you had the remedy in your own hands but you were too bloody pig-headed, too eaten up with resentment, too damned selfish to do anything to change it. If I were you I'd sit down and write to both Dee and Graham and try to make amends and instead of continually nagging and arguing with Davie, let Davie bring the girl home, make her welcome. It's all in your hands, Flo.' Ada paused for breath. Flo stared at her, her eyes wide with astonishment, partly at Ada's vehemence but mostly at this last and totally unexpected piece of news.

'Right, I've said my piece, now I'll have that cup of tea,' Ada said firmly.

After she'd gone Flo sat in the kitchen, feeling dazed and confused. Ada had been a close friend and confidante for years but she'd never spoken to her as strongly before. She didn't want to dwell on a lot of what her old friend had said, particularly about being left entirely alone with no one to care if she was alive or dead. She couldn't bring herself to write to Dee, she felt her daughter's desertion too deeply. Surely Dee could understand her bitterness? Dee had been just as dreadfully hurt by what her father had done. But no, Dee had run off and now lived in a different country. But what about Graham? He had obviously settled down. Ada had said his wife was a nice girl from a good family and now . . . now there was a baby on the way. Ada loved her two grandsons and spoiled them dreadfully. Would the new grandchild help to heal the rift between herself and Graham? Perhaps if she sent a card, it would be a start. And what about Davie? She had to admit he wasn't a bad lad. Maybe she should take Ada's advice and tell him to invite the girl home? The fear she had of him behaving in the way Graham had during those last months her eldest son had spent at home seemed to have clouded her judgement. She didn't want Davie to start drinking heavily and staying out; if he did, she wouldn't be able to stand it. Nor could she face the rows that would follow. She knew she had changed. She wasn't happy and hadn't been for so long. She covered her face with her hands. She felt so weary, so depressed and so utterly lonely.

In her heart of hearts she knew Ada was right. It was all her own fault. She had driven them away with her temper and hostility and selfishness but could she put it all aside? For the first time in years she told herself she would try.

Chapter Twenty-Six

———◆———

DEE SHIVERED AS SHE came out of Mr Heffernan's front door. The wind was icy and she'd be freezing by the time she reached home. Each Thursday night she came to her employer's house where her new friend and teacher Sister Maria Theresa would be waiting. They spent an hour just talking but in French, and then she would spend another hour doing grammar. She had become grateful and fond of both her employer and his elderly sister in the eight months she had known them.

She enjoyed her work and she enjoyed the company of both men. She'd found Kevin Buckley to be an outgoing young man with a shock of auburn hair and green eyes and an easy, pleasant and considerate manner. He'd travelled extensively throughout the Far East and India and had spent some time with relatives in America. When she'd joked that he must be finding

Tullamore a bit of a backwater, he'd replied that quite the contrary, he found it very restful. He'd grown up listening to his parents memories of Ireland and he felt quite at home with his uncle, despite the climate.

James Heffernan had told her he didn't know how he had ever managed without her, she was so efficient. All the previous helpers he'd had in the office since his secretary had retired due to ill health had been rather slapdash, but now his files were always in order as indeed was all his paperwork and the office looked neat, tidy and considerably brighter with the small pieces of bric-à-brac she had either brought from home or found buried in the drawers of an old desk: a spider plant in a bright majolica pot; an old-fashioned brass ink stand and desk set she had polished up; multi-coloured pots to hold pens and pencils; and a couple of framed hunting prints she'd hung on the wall.

She had been a little wary of the small elderly nun at first, particularly as Niall had said she might be looking to convert her, but she had soon found this to be just unfounded speculation on his part. Sister Maria Theresa was a quietly spoken but very pleasant woman and she was also intelligent and well read, having taught at the convent school in Lisieux. Dee enjoyed listening to her reminiscences of her many years in France and realised that she had loved the country and had not particularly wished to return to Ireland.

'But could you not have asked to stay?' she'd ventured.

'Ah, child, I took a vow of obedience. I do as I'm told

and I go where I'm sent,' Sister Maria Theresa had replied. Dee's admiration for her had increased; she knew she would never have the strength of character to obey someone so unquestioningly but the nun had told her it was quite easy when the vow had been made to God. Dee puzzled a great deal about how the Mother Superior of the order could be absolutely certain it was the will of God that someone of Sister Maria Theresa's age should be uprooted and sent back to a country where the climate would most definitely not be beneficial to her health. She gave up in the end, although she still privately thought the nun would have preferred to have stayed in France.

She must miss the warmth at least, she thought to herself as she prepared to mount her bicycle while Kevin Buckley held open the gate for her. He rented a small house in the town but he quite often visited his elderly aunt and uncle, particularly on the evenings Dee came.

'Goodnight, Dee. Take care on the road. I hope those two didn't bore you with all their reminiscences,' he said.

'Not at all. I think you can learn a great deal by listening to older people and neither of them have had what you would call dull lives.'

He grimaced. 'I wouldn't call Aunt's life exactly exciting.'

Dee smiled at him. 'Maybe that's why she chose it. Maybe she didn't want a life full of excitement.'

'You could be right. See you in the morning.' He

waved as she pedalled away. In the time he'd known her he'd grown to like her. In fact he had to admit to himself he liked her a great deal more than was right and proper. She was a married woman, and apparently quite happy with Niall Clarke. He had no right at all to think of her as anything other than a secretary but she was one of the main reasons why he walked the short distance to his uncle's house on Thursday evenings and on the days she didn't work the office seemed dull and dismal.

They were a devoted pair, the elderly nun and her bachelor brother, Dee thought as she rode home with the cold wind stinging her cheeks. Apparently they were the only ones left of a large and scattered family and when her employer joined them at the end of the evening for a cup of tea, before Dee left and he escorted his sister back to the convent, they often spoke of their childhood, which she found fascinating. They belonged to another age and to another and very different way of life, she thought.

She was numb with cold by the time she got home. 'I'm absolutely frozen! I wouldn't be surprised if we have sleet or even snow during the night,' she commented to Niall as she sat down on a stool as near to the fire as she could get, holding her hands out to the blaze.

He'd been reading the *Tribune* but had put it aside when she'd come in and he now got up. 'I'll put some more turf down on the fire and I'll heat up some of the vegetable soup you made, that should warm you up.'

He looked at her fondly. 'Would you not think of missing a few weeks during this bad weather? I worry about you out on the roads.'

She smiled at him. 'I know you do but we've had worse weather than this and I've been all right. Mr Heffernan has been so kind to let me go to his home for my lessons and I think they both look forward to my visits. Besides, the winter is nearly over now. It's almost March.'

He nodded. 'It is, aren't there both snowdrops and crocuses out under the hedge beside the road.'

As she sat with the mug of soup she began to feel the warmth slowly creeping back into her. 'They were talking tonight of when they were both young and of the terrible state the country was in then. I knew something about the War of Independence but I didn't know there was a civil war too.'

Niall nodded, his expression grim. 'Times were desperate then. One half of the country agreed with Michael Collins and was for the treaty and the other half didn't. You had father against son, brother against brother. Families divided for ever. I'm glad I wasn't around then although there wasn't a lot of trouble hereabouts. Mind you, what there was, wasn't my old grandfather in the thick of it.'

'Really? Go on, tell me about it!' she urged. He'd never spoken about this before. 'Which side was he on?'

'The losing side, wouldn't you know it. But when he died he was given a grand send-off, so he was. Half the anti-treaty supporters in the country turned up to the funeral.'

'You mean Catholics as well?'

He nodded. 'We might be different religions but in the matter of national politics we're all Irish.' He looked suddenly serious.

'What's wrong?' she asked.

He sighed heavily. 'I don't think the troubles are over yet. In fact it looks as though trouble is only just getting started in the North.' Seeing the worried look she gave him he put his misgivings aside. 'Ah, don't go worrying about it, it won't affect us down here.' He got to his feet and checked his watch.

'Is there a boat due tonight?' she asked, placated by his words. Sometimes the barges came through at night.

'There is. They should have left Shannon Harbour by now so they'll be a good few hours yet.'

She got up and took the empty mug into the kitchen, peering out through the window into the darkness. 'Make sure you wrap up well, Niall, it looks as if it's starting to snow,' she called.

He came and stood beside her. The kitchen was at the front of the house, overlooking the lock. 'I think you're right, Dee. Don't wait up.'

She left him to his newspaper and went to bed, wishing he didn't have to wait up until the early hours and then go out in this weather to open and close the lock gates. Still, it didn't happen very often these days. The cargoes carried for centuries by the barges were now being transported far more quickly by rail or road and there was talk that the traffic would end altogether soon. Then there would only be pleasure craft going up and down the canal and people didn't take holidays in the winter which meant he wouldn't have to go out at night or in the snow at all.

She was tired and she slept well, only being slightly disturbed once when she heard muffled voices from outside. It was still dark when she woke and glanced at the luminous hands of the alarm clock on the bedside table. With an effort she got up and pulled on her dressing gown. Niall's side of the bed was unslept in: the boat he'd been waiting up for must have been delayed.

She went into the living room and stirred up the embers in the hearth and then placed a few pieces of turf over them to rekindle the fire. She went into the kitchen and switched on the light and filled the kettle. Glancing through the window she was relieved to see that there was no heavy covering of snow and there were raindrops on the window pane. It must have turned to sleet and then rain, she thought.

She took her tea back into the living room and pulled back the curtains. The sky was beginning to lighten despite the clouds and it cheered her. Winter was nearing its end and the mornings were becoming lighter earlier but she'd still have to put on her boots and mackintosh. Often over these cold months she and Niall had discussed saving up for a small second-hand car. He'd said he'd feel far happier if she could drive to town and back and she'd agreed that it would be far quicker, less effort and she'd stay warm and dry into the bargain – but she couldn't drive! He'd told her that was no problem, he'd teach her. She'd laughed, telling him they'd no doubt end up arguing. She smiled as she thought of it; still it would be great not to have to cycle all that way, especially on a morning like this.

She'd just put the dirty dishes in the sink when she looked up and saw Dermot Mulcahey, Nora Mulcahey's husband, running across the bridge towards the house, gesticulating wildly, followed by his wife whose hair was still in curlers. 'What on earth's wrong now?' she said aloud, going to the front door.

The wind whipped the folds of her dressing gown against her legs and large drops of rain fell on her hair as she went out.

'What's wrong? What's happened?' she called.

Mr Mulcahey ignored her and ran to the side of the lock, peering down. His wife caught Dee by the shoulders and pushed her back towards the house.

'Come away, Dee! Come back in the house! Oh, Mary Mother of God!'

Dee was confused and struggled to release herself from the older woman's grip. 'What is it? Tell me?' she cried, a feeling of dread beginning to take hold of her.

Mrs Mulcahey shook her head and forcefully dragged her back inside the house and shut the door. 'There's no helping him now, Dee. God have mercy on him, the poor lad! We all know he couldn't swim.'

Dee felt numb. Niall! She was talking about Niall!

'Oh, my God! It's not . . . it can't be . . .' she stammered.

Mrs Mulcahey pushed her into the kitchen. 'Wasn't Dermot out with the auld dog and he . . . he saw him. It must have been after the barge went through last night. He must have been crossing on the ledge and slipped and fell. It would be slippery with the sleet and rain.' The woman herself was shocked but she felt desperately sorry for both Dee and Niall. There was fifteen feet of freezing cold water in the lock and even if Niall Clarke had been able to swim the sides were sheer with no hand- or foothold. No one would have heard his cries, and then the cold would have set in . . .

Dimly Dee heard the shouts and cries of other men as the neighbours were alerted and rushed to the lock. Mrs Mulcahey guided her into the living room; she didn't want the girl to see them as they struggled to get him out.

As the full horror and realisation hit her, Dee began to sob. For the second time in her life her world was crashing around her.

''Tis a shocking tragedy, Dee!' The older woman held on to her, tears running down her own cheeks. She'd known Niall all his life; he was too young to die. And Dee was so young to be made a widow and they'd seemed happy together.

Nora pulled herself together. This wasn't doing the girl any good. She had to try to be a comfort to her, what relations Dee had were all far away on the other side of the Irish Sea. She made a pot of tea to which she added a drop of the whiskey she found in one of the presses in the kitchen and she coaxed Dee to drink.

'It will help,' she urged.

Dee felt as if everything she had successfully banished from her mind, her father's death and all its consequences, had come sweeping back over her and now . . . now, to add to it . . . Niall had gone too. Her security, the peace of mind she had achieved and the love he'd had for her had gone. She shook her head slowly. 'Nothing will help, not now.'

'Ah, don't say that Dee! God is good, you're young. Is there anyone you want me to get in touch with? Your mother?'

'No! There's a . . . friend but . . .' She couldn't think straight, not now, maybe tomorrow or the next day.

Dermot Mulcahey, accompanied by John Delaney, a neighbour, came into the room and Mrs Mulcahey nodded sadly. Her husband seemed relieved that he didn't have to tell Dee the news.

'I'm so sorry, Dee. It's a desperate thing altogether. A shocking accident, that's what it is,' Mr Delaney said quietly.

Both men looked at each other, wondering what to do next. Someone had gone for the Guards and they'd wondered should they send for the Protestant minister. Had he been of their religion the first thing anyone would have done was to go for the priest.

Dermot sought his wife's gaze. 'The Guards will be here soon enough and we . . . we were wondering about the minister?'

She nodded. 'Best send someone into town for him, up to the Rectory at Hop Hill and, Dermot, someone should call and tell Himself, Mr Heffernan.'

They both departed and she spent the next hour sitting with Dee as first the Garda sergeant and then the local undertaker arrived. Dee was still confused. They'd sat here last night, just a few hours ago, discussing his grandfather and his funeral and now . . . they would have to bury him too. He'd fallen and drowned just a few feet away while she had slept. Why hadn't she woken when she'd thought she'd heard voices? Had that been Niall calling for help? Oh, God, she prayed not.

'Mrs Mulcahey, I'm never going to forgive myself. I slept while he . . . he . . . I heard voices but I thought it was the men on the barge. If . . . if it was Niall calling for help . . . I . . .' She began to sob, unable to continue.

Her neighbour was horrified. 'Hush now, Dee! It *was* the boatmen, didn't I hear them myself? And we wouldn't have heard him if he'd . . . It was windy and raining and there would still have been water coming into the lock, you know how long it takes to finish filling up. And we don't know, he might have hit his head when he fell, Sergeant Molloy will be able to tell us.' She prayed that that had indeed been the case, drowning was a terrible death.

To Dee's immense relief the Garda sergeant confirmed what Nora Mulcahey had hoped and prayed for. There was a deep gash on Niall's head. He would have been unconscious when he went into the water.

'Thanks be to God for that mercy, hasn't she been tormenting herself thinking she'd heard him calling out for help.'

'It would have been all over in seconds, Mrs Clarke, and that's the truth of it. God rest him,' Fergus Molloy said firmly. He'd been a Guard for over twenty years and in that time the canal had claimed a few victims, but he'd never expected Niall Clarke to be one of them, he'd been born and reared beside it.

'Will you be letting everyone know when the arrangements have been made?' Nora Mulcahey asked as she showed him out. 'We've sent for the minister but I'm not quite sure about Protestant funerals. Will there be a removal before the burial?'

He shook his head. 'No. They don't have the same customs, Nora. When Himself arrives you'd better ask him how things are to be done for I doubt she's in any fit state to be thinking of such things now, poor woman.'

She nodded, wiping away her tears, and went back to Dee to await the arrival of the minister.

Chapter Twenty-Seven

———◆———

DEE HAD BEEN GRATEFUL for the Reverend Thomas's visit when he called later that morning. He was the man who had married them and he had known Niall for many years. He was deeply shocked and saddened, he told her. He asked if any of her family would come over to support her in this terrible time and she had begged him to contact Jean, her closest friend. He'd promised he would do it immediately and suggested they wait until Jean arrived before burying Niall. He'd also offered to make all the arrangements if she couldn't face it and she'd been very grateful for that too.

'It's the shock of it all, you see. I just don't seem to be able to concentrate on anything, it . . . it all happened so quickly,' she tried to explain.

'It did indeed and we have to thank God that it would have been over for him quickly too.'

'If you don't mind, I don't think I could stand to have the service in the church in Rahan. It was only three years ago since you married us there.'

He nodded; he remembered it well. 'Then we'll have it in the church at Hop Hill – there will be people from the town who will want to attend – but I'm sure he would have wished to be buried in the churchyard at Rahan. It was the church he always attended,' he reminded her gently.

She agreed, they'd obviously never discussed such things but it would be only right for his final resting place to be near to here and not in town.

When he'd gone Nora Mulcahey tried to get her to rest but she couldn't and a little later a car pulled up outside the house.

'Who will that be?' the older woman wondered as she went to answer the door. Very few people had cars and this one was big and expensive-looking.

'Dee, 'tis Mr Heffernan and his sister and nephew come to see you,' she announced as she ushered them into the living room and then went out to the kitchen to make yet another pot of tea and search the presses for Dee's best china.

Dee made an effort. 'It's so very kind of you to come all the way out here to see me and so soon.'

'Sure and what else would we do? When we heard the desperate news I went straight down to the convent to inform Maria and we agreed we should come. We're all so sorry.'

Dee nodded, the tears welling up in her eyes again.

'I can hardly believe it. It was all so . . . so sudden and I keep asking myself why? Why Niall?'

Sister Maria Theresa reached out and took her hand. 'It's a terrible shock for you, child.'

'I've had so much unhappiness in my life that I've been asking myself what is it that I've done to deserve it?'

The elderly nun shook her head. 'There is no fault in you. Tragedies happen in everyone's life. You'll overcome it, Dee, believe me. You'll find the strength; the good Lord will give you the strength. He never gives us a cross too heavy for our shoulders to bear, you must believe that.'

'I'll try but I feel as if I've no strength at all. I don't know how I'm going to get through today or tomorrow or next week.'

'But you will, Dee. I have the utmost faith in you,' Sister Maria Theresa said firmly.

'And you're not to be worrying your head about coming in to work, Dee. You must take your time,' James Heffernan added.

Kevin was feeling utterly helpless. He too was deeply shocked by the tragedy and he hated to see her so distraught. He longed to try to comfort her but there was nothing he could do. 'And if there is anything I can help you with, anything at all, you have only to ask, Dee.' What else could he say?

'Thank you. Reverend Thomas is going to make all the arrangements for me, the service, the hymns, the obituary notices – everything.'

James Heffernan nodded. He was wondering what her position would now be regarding the Lock House and indeed the position of lock-keeper. One went with the other. He would look into it. He would get in touch with someone from the Grand Canal Company, or the Office of Public Works, or whoever's jurisdiction these things came under now, and find out. He doubted very much that Niall Clarke had made a will but his personal effects would automatically go to her, it was the house he was unsure about.

Mrs Mulcahey served the tea and after reminding her of his offer of assistance Kevin, James Heffernan and his sister left.

'That was kind of them to visit,' Nora Mulcahey said. They might attend the burial but she knew none of them would attend the service at Hop Hill.

Jean received the phone call from the Reverend Thomas that afternoon. Dee had given him the address and the phone number of both the house and the salon. When there had been no reply from the house he had reluctantly decided he had no alternative but to phone Jean at work.

Pauline had answered the phone and had passed it over to Jean with a mystified shrug. 'It's a Reverend Thomas for you, Jean.'

Jean dried her hands and wrapped a towel around the head of the client whose hair she was trimming. 'Excuse me a moment, Mrs Peel.'

Pauline could see instantly there was something very

wrong. Jean had sat down and she'd gone pale. She was nodding in reply to something that was being said and then with three words she finished the conversation. 'I'll be over.'

'Bernice, will you put my client under the dryer, please,' Pauline instructed as she went to Jean's side. 'What's the matter?'

Jean looked up at her with tears in her eyes. 'It's Dee's husband, Niall. He's dead. He's dead. He drowned in the lock.'

'Mother of God!' Pauline exclaimed.

Jean got to her feet. 'I said I'd go over. Oh, poor, poor Dee!'

Pauline recovered herself. 'I'll finish Mrs Peel and Bernice and I will manage the rest of the afternoon's clients and tomorrow's. Monday and Tuesday are fairly quiet so go home and get organised. That poor girl will need you.'

'I'll go to see Mam first but thanks, I honestly don't know what I'd do without you both.'

All the way to her mother's house Jean could think of nothing but how unfair life was to Dee. Just when she seemed to have put the tragedies of the past behind her this had to happen.

When her daughter walked into the kitchen Ada instantly knew something was wrong. For Jean to leave the salon on a Friday afternoon there had to be. 'What's wrong?'

'Oh, Mam. I've just heard that Dee's husband drowned early this morning.'

Ada's hand went to her mouth as Jean slumped down on a chair at the table. 'Dear God! How did it happen?'

'They think he slipped and hit his head and fell. Poor Dee. Why do such terrible things always happen to her, Mam?'

Ada shook her head sadly. She had no answer. 'I'll put the kettle on, luv.'

'I told the Reverend Thomas I'd go over. She'll need someone, Mam.'

'Will Tony go with you? It's a long journey,' Ada asked as she got out the cups.

'I don't know. It depends how busy they are and maybe it would be best if I went alone. I think he'd feel as if he was in the way and I don't want to remind Dee that I still have a husband and she hasn't. I'll see if I can get a flight tomorrow, then I think I have to go the rest of the way by train. She doesn't have a phone so I'll send her a telegram. It might help her if she knows I'm on my way over.'

'Do you want me to tell Flo?' Ada asked.

Jean frowned. 'I don't honestly know. You know how things are between Dee and her mam.' She sighed. 'Oh, do what you think best, Mam.'

'You have this cup of tea to steady you and then you'd better get off home, luv, but I'm glad you came to tell me. I'll send a card and will you put all our names on the wreath?'

Jean nodded. 'I'll get off the bus and call into the travel agency on Longmoor Lane. I remember Dee saying how good they were when she first went over. I can't say I'm looking forward to it, Mam. What can I say to her? What can I possibly do to help her?' she pleaded.

'Just being there with her will help, Jean,' Ada said firmly.

When Jean had gone Ada decided that Flo ought to be told about the tragedy at least and so went down to her house.

'I thought you should know, Flo, that's all,' she stated when she'd relayed the news.

'What should I do, Ada? She's cut herself off from me. Should I write or not?'

'It's up to you, Flo.'

Flo bit her lip and looked worried. 'She might not want me to even know.'

Ada shook her head and sighed heavily. 'How did you ever get to this stage, Flo? She's your only daughter and she's had so much heartbreak in her life.'

Flo looked utterly dejected. She had been trying hard lately to mend the bridges between herself and both her sons. With Davie she was succeeding but with Graham it was proving harder. At least Susie had come to see her. It would take him time, the girl had told her. She had to admit to herself that she had totally misjudged Susie. She'd liked her. As Ada had said, she was a nice girl. Was it time to try with Dee or would Dee refuse any olive branch she held out? 'Should I go over with Jean? If she sees me, if I can talk to her . . .'

Ada was relieved. At least Flo seemed to be making an effort. 'I know what I'd do, luv. She's lost Billy and now this lad she married has died tragically and Jean said she was happy enough with him.'

Flo was still uncertain.

'Pack a bag, Flo. I'll see to your Davie, he spends enough time in our house anyway. I'll go to the phone box and ring our Jean. She was hoping to get a flight tomorrow, maybe they'll be able to arrange one for you too. That poor girl needs her mam at a time like this, even if she doesn't want to admit it.'

Flo still hesitated. 'But what if she . . . she won't see me?'

'At least you will have *tried*, Flo. She won't be able to accuse you of not caring enough to try,' Ada said firmly.

Jean wasn't at all sure that this was the time for a reconciliation, nor was she entirely convinced that Flo genuinely wanted to put the past behind her.

'Mam, this isn't the time for another scene. If she starts going on about Dee's da or Billy Grainger I'll kill her, I really will! That is the last thing poor Dee needs,' Jean had told her mother when Ada phoned.

'She won't, Jean. I think she's finally learned her lesson.'

'Well, if Dee won't see her or speak to her I'm not going to tell her she's wrong,' Jean stated emphatically.

'Just see how things go, Jean,' Ada urged.

Prudently Jean sent Nora Mulcahey a telegram, cursing the fact there seemed to be very few people who had a phone in Dee's part of the world, which made it a long and expensive message. She asked could Flo stay with Nora and begged her to warn Dee that her mother was coming too. She just hoped Ada was right about Flo's change of attitude.

The lack of phones wasn't the only thing she was annoyed about. When she'd told Tony what she was doing he had been a little put out, asking was it really necessary for Jean to drop everything every time there was a tragedy in Dee's life. She considered this to be extremely callous of him and had said so and there had been an argument, which hadn't helped. Now she was going to Ireland barely on speaking terms with her husband and with Flo Campbell in tow, who might well prove to be a very loose cannon indeed.

Both women were tired and tense when they finally arrived in Ireland late the following day. Flo had been terrified on the plane and it had grated on Jean's nerves until the stewardess had given Flo a brandy, but thankfully at least she'd relaxed more on the train journey.

Jean went first to see Nora Mulcahey to introduce Flo and to ask how Dee was. A little calmer but still very shaken and upset, she was informed. She left Flo in what seemed like capable hands and walked across the stone bridge that was illuminated by the light above Dee's front door. She shuddered involuntarily as she glimpsed the cold dark water in the lock where Niall Clarke had met his death. It was so dark and so quiet here, she thought. That in itself was enough to depress you.

To her surprise the door wasn't locked and she went

into the small hallway that led to the living room. It was warm inside the house and she could smell the turf smoke. Dee was sitting beside the fire, seemingly just staring into the flames.

'Dee. It's me, Jean. I came as quickly as I could,' she said quietly, not wanting to startle her friend.

Dee turned and looked at her and then managed a tired smile. 'I thought at first I was dreaming.'

Jean went and took her hands. 'It all must seem like a nightmare but I'm here now and I'll help you get through it.'

Chapter Twenty-Eight

———◆◇◆———

THEY HAD TALKED LATE into the night and Jean felt that her journey had been worthwhile. Dee was now much calmer. She had confided that she hadn't felt the same way about Niall Clarke as she had about Billy Grainger, although Jean realised that Dee had at last seemed to have accepted that loss. She had needed to get away, she had loved the serenity of life here and Niall had been kind, considerate and gentle with her and of course he had loved her. She admitted to Jean that she had come to love him in a way. Not with an all-consuming passion but a quieter, more companionable affection born of respect and common interests. And now she would miss him terribly. Jean made no attempt to ask her friend had she thought about the future, it was far too early for that. She had promised to stay for the funeral and when that was over she would perhaps broach the subject. There was one subject she knew she had to tackle and she wasn't looking forward to it. She would have to chose her words carefully.

She made them both a hot toddy and put more turf on the dying fire.

'This should help us both to get some sleep. I don't suppose you got much last night?' she said, handing Dee the mug. She was worn out but she wasn't going to say so.

Dee shook her head. 'I was exhausted, Jean, but I just couldn't stop thinking of him . . .'

'Hush. Wherever he is now he's at peace. People seem to have been very good.'

'They have. They have very different customs here. Catholic funerals are huge affairs and are carried out very quickly. Usually the day after the person has died. But Reverend Thomas suggested we wait until you arrived, at least, so I would have someone to support me.'

Jean sipped the hot whiskey. 'I'm sorry I didn't come on my own, Dee. I intended to but . . .'

'Why did she come?' Dee asked Jean wearily.

Jean took a deep breath. 'She wanted to, Dee. I wasn't very sure about it. Mam gave her a right dressing down a while ago about . . . about the way she's carried on and she seems to have taken notice, she has been in touch with Susie. Susie actually went to see her but your Graham isn't as forgiving. Mam said she wants to see you, to speak to you but . . .'

'Where is she?' Dee asked at last.

'With Mrs Mulcahey. If you feel you can't see her,

Dee, I'll go over in the morning and explain. I'm certain she'll stay until I go back though. She is terrified of flying.'

Dee tried to take it all in. Her mother had *wanted* to come. But had she changed? Or was she still as bitter? The last thing she needed right now was to be reminded of all that had happened. But Jean had said she'd met Susie and was trying . . . 'What do you think I should do?'

Jean shook her head. 'I can't tell you that, Dee. You have to make that decision yourself.'

Dee sighed. 'I'll think about it in the morning, Jean. I'm too tired, upset and confused now.'

'I think you're right. You need a good night's sleep. We both do and you might feel better in the morning.'

Despite feeling that she could have slept later Jean was up first. She was in the kitchen trying to find out where Dee kept the tea and sugar and the dishes when Dee came into the room.

Jean smiled. 'I was going to bring you a cup of tea, when I'd found everything. Did you get any sleep?'

Dee nodded. She did feel a bit better this morning. The world had lost that trance-like quality. 'I woke earlier on but as I couldn't hear you moving around I thought you must still be asleep. I . . . I've been thinking about Mam.'

'And?' Jean asked.

'I can't refuse to see her after she's come all this way, Jean, but . . .'

'But you don't want her to start harping on again,' Jean stated firmly.

'No. I really couldn't stand that and I'm not entirely sure that I've forgiven her. She made my life even more of a misery than it was.'

'That's understandable, Dee. In your place I'd be thinking along the same lines. Do you want me to have a word with her first?'

Dee nodded. 'Could you try to explain how I feel right now?'

'She shouldn't need it spelled out for her but I will. I'll go over when we've both had some breakfast.'

She found Flo sitting in the front lounge of the Mulcaheys' house talking quietly to Nora.

'I've just been after telling Mrs Campbell here about how well thought of Dee is and how she loves life here. How is she this morning?'

'She's had a good night's sleep and I think she's a lot calmer. Less confused and stunned.'

Flo looked at Jean with some apprehension. 'What has she said about me Jean?'

Nora Mulcahey decided to leave them on their own. 'I'll get out to the kitchen and ask Dermot to fetch in some turf for this fire before it goes out entirely,' she announced.

'She's a very nice woman. She's been kindness itself,' Flo said.

Jean sat down in the armchair facing Flo. 'She said she can't refuse to see you after you've come all this way but . . .' She was trying to find the right words so

Flo wouldn't feel insulted. After all, the woman was as old as her mother and she would never dream of lecturing Ada.

'But she doesn't want me going on about . . . things,' Flo said.

Jean nodded. 'She is still distressed and in shock and she's the funeral to get through yet.'

'I know, Jean. I won't upset her, I promise.'

Jean frowned, wondering if Flo meant it or how long it would be before she reverted back to her usual self. Still, she couldn't voice those thoughts. 'We'd better go over then,' she said, getting to her feet.

As they crossed the bridge Flo shook her head. 'It seems even worse that he should have died so close to the house – just a few feet away.'

Jean nodded her agreement. 'I don't know how she is going to be able to look out of that window or come out of the front door and not remember. Maybe she'll move, I don't know.'

Dee had made an effort to tidy the living room a little and she'd stirred up the fire. She stood beside it, twisting her hands together nervously.

Flo looked at her daughter and she felt guilt and shame and sadness wash over her. 'Dee, I . . . I'm so sorry for . . . everything. I mean that. I had to come. I couldn't bear the thought of you being here alone after . . .'

Dee managed a brief nod. 'It . . . it's not been easy, Mam, but people have been good.'

Jean quietly went into the kitchen, thinking it would

be best to leave them alone. Yet she remained nearby should Dee need her.

Dee sat down on the sofa and Flo went to her side and put her arm around her. 'I do know what it's like, Dee,' she said quietly, thinking back to the shock and grief she'd experienced after Bob's death, before the hurt, humiliation and anger had set in.

Dee nodded.

'Did you love him very much?' Flo asked.

'I loved him but not in the way I loved Billy. With Niall it was . . . different. Oh, Mam, I'll miss him so much. He was my security, he gave me peace of mind . . .'

'I know what that feels like too, Dee,' Flo added sadly.

Dee looked up at her. 'And we've both had it snatched away, but in different ways.'

Flo sat down beside her and took her hands. 'I can't forgive your Da but I'm trying to forget, Dee. To put it all behind me. There's been too much anger and heartache. I'll never forgive myself for what happened at Jean's wedding. I drove you away. I drove you to marry a man you barely knew . . .'

Tears glistened on Dee's lashes. 'But I was happy here, Mam. I was happy with Niall. I'd made a new life for myself.'

Flo nodded sadly. 'I wish I'd known him. I wish I'd written to you, Dee.'

'We were both grieving and raging, Mam, and we . . . we both had every right to be. We both loved da and trusted him and what he did was . . . terrible but I've tried to come to terms with it.'

'And that's something I should have done for your sake and for Graham and Davie. I've been a fool.'

'Maybe I've just grown up, Mam.'

Flo nodded. Dee had indeed matured. 'Life is hard, luv, and there are times when you wonder what it's all about. Times when you wonder is it worth carrying on but you just have to and you have to try to make the best of it. Ada made me see sense, made me see where all the rancour was leading and when I heard about . . . the accident, I just couldn't leave you to cope with it all on your own.'

Dee managed a little smile. 'I'm glad you came. I've some hard times ahead to get through.'

'And I'll be here. That's something else I regret, Dee. The fact that I left you and Ada to cope with all the arrangements after your da died. I wasn't much use to you then. We should all have tried to comfort each other.'

'Mam, that couldn't be helped. Those tablets the doctor gave you had you destroyed, as did the shock, and now I know how it feels. I feel so . . . empty, so . . . lost.'

Flo nodded. That would pass in time, she thought, but at least Dee wouldn't have the added trauma of finding out that there was a terrible, dark secret in the family.

Dee squeezed her hand. Despite the heartache and grief, she felt that at least she had her mother back. That there was someone who really understood how she was feeling.

Jean came in with a tray of tea and smiled at them both. 'I thought a cup of hot sweet tea would benefit us all.'

Flo smiled back. 'It will, Jean, and I'm glad you're here.'

'I'm glad you're both here,' Dee said tearfully. 'It was good of you to come.'

The following morning Jean was surprised to find Kevin Buckley on the doorstep. Flo was still over with Nora Mulcahey and she'd persuaded Dee to have a lie-in.

'Would it be possible to see Dee . . . Mrs Clarke?' Kevin asked. All the way from town he'd wondered if he was doing the right thing but he wanted to make sure she was all right, see how she was coping.

'She's resting. I'm her friend from Liverpool, Jean Littlemore. I'm staying with her.'

'I'm Kevin Buckley. Dee works for my uncle and myself. I . . . I was wondering how she's managing?'

Jean smiled. 'Come in. It's very kind of you to be so concerned.'

Kevin followed her into the living room and Jean indicated that he should sit down.

'She's still in shock but she is better than she was. Her mother came over with me, she's staying with Mrs Mulcahey.'

Kevin nodded. He was glad that Dee had family and friends around her. 'I'm sure she'll find that a great comfort.'

Hearing voices Dee had got up and pulled on a dressing gown but she was surprised and puzzled to see Kevin sitting with Jean.

'Kevin! I . . . I didn't expect you to come all the way out here. Is something wrong?'

Kevin had got to his feet, feeling uncomfortable that he had disturbed her and obviously caused her some anxiety. 'No, nothing like that. I'm sorry to have disturbed you. I just wanted you to know that I'll be attending both the funeral service and . . . afterwards.'

'That's very considerate of you,' Jean said.

For a moment Dee was confused and then she remembered that both he and his uncle were Catholic. 'Kevin, I'll understand if you only attend the burial.'

Jean frowned. What was all this about? she wondered.

Kevin shook his head vehemently. 'No. I'll attend the service as well. I'm not as . . . staunch as Uncle or Aunt. At times like this I think differences in religion should be put aside. He was a good man, it's a terrible tragedy and I feel there's something wrong with a society that can't accept that and pay proper respect. I'll be there, Dee.'

She nodded. 'Thank you, Kevin. I . . . I appreciate your support.'

'And I'm sure you will be equally welcome to come back here afterwards,' Jean added, realising that Dee's Catholic neighbours would be conspicuous by their absence at the service for Niall Clarke.

Kevin thanked her and then took his leave.

'It was good of him to come to tell you, Dee,' she said as she bustled about making Dee a cup of tea.

'It was and he'll be talked about for attending a Protestant service. Things are . . . different here, Jean. They are good people but . . .'

'They have different ways,' Jean finished. 'Still, he seems very nice and very sincere and he also seems to have a lot of common sense.'

Dee smiled. 'He's always been very considerate. He never seemed to mind how many questions I asked him about the places he'd visited. He's travelled a lot.'

'That probably explains why he's more open-minded,' Jean said succinctly.

Niall Clarke was buried two days later and Dee was thankful for the support of both her mother and her friend. She was genuinely surprised and touched by the number of people who had attended the service in the big church on Hop Hill. Kevin Buckley was the only representative of the Catholic community but she had caught a glimpse of James Heffernan in the churchyard at the back of the little stone church in Rahan. There had been no wake in the Catholic sense of the word but people had called to the house afterwards and both her mother and Jean had dispensed drinks and passed around the plates of sandwiches Flo and Nora Mulcahey had made.

Kevin managed to get a few minutes with Jean before he took his leave of Dee. 'She coped with it all very well, I thought,' he said earnestly.

Jean nodded. 'She did but I think she's exhausted now. I'm going to ask her mother to make her go and get some rest while I help Mrs Mulcahey to clear up. Thank you for coming, Dee explained about how . . . different things are here.'

He nodded, looking grave. 'I couldn't insult her by not attending. I had words with my uncle about it. We . . . we value Dee.'

'Tell her that but don't for heaven's sake say you had "words" with your uncle.'

'I won't. I know it would upset her.'

Jean looked at him closely. 'You're fond of her, aren't you?'

He looked awkward but nodded. 'I . . . I admire her greatly,' he admitted before turning away to take his leave of Dee.

Jean watched him, wondering if Dee was at all aware of his feelings. Very probably not, she decided, and now was not the time to impart this knowledge to her friend.

They were due to return to Liverpool in the middle of the week although Jean wished she could have stayed longer. 'I feel terrible leaving you so soon, Dee,' she said as they went for a walk the morning after the funeral. The weather had become more settled, although there was still a fresh breeze that sent clouds scurrying across the sky, and Jean felt some fresh air would do them both good.

'I can't ask you to stay on, Jean. You've to think of Tony and your business.'

'I know. But will you be all right?'

Dee nodded slowly. 'I think so. I think I might even go back to work next week. It will take my mind off . . . things.'

Jean agreed with her. The worst thing Dee could do would be to stay in that house all day. 'Would you think of moving into the town? It would be nearer work for one thing.'

'I don't know. Mrs Mulcahey advised me not to make any big decisions for a while yet and Mam agreed. I'll give myself time to . . . to come to terms with everything.'

'It would be so much easier if you were on the phone, Dee. I could speak to you often, see how you are and how you're coping. Is there no chance of you getting one?'

Dee wished it were possible, it would help to be able to speak to her friend when she felt low, but she shook her head. 'I don't think so. It would have made life a lot easier for . . . Niall but it's very difficult.'

'But the priest and the doctor and the Post Office have them,' Jean stated.

'They're "priority", Jean.'

Jean sighed. 'Would you at least think of coming over on a bit of a holiday? You can stay with me. You don't have to stay at your mam's house.'

'Maybe after Susie has the baby. I would like to see our Graham and Susie again and Davie.'

Jean knew she couldn't press her any further, it wouldn't be fair. 'I'll hold you to that, Dee,' she said with a smile.

Part VI

Chapter Twenty-Nine

———◆———

1969

DEE CAME OUT OF the depot yard in Harbour Street with Kevin Buckley and they walked slowly towards the junction with William Street. It was another blustery March day but at least when the sun shone there was now some warmth in its rays, she thought. Another long winter was finally over and she'd been without Niall for a year now. She'd found it so hard at first. She would turn to speak to him before remembering. She would automatically look up when standing in the kitchen, waiting to see him come across the bridge. Dee found it easier if she kept herself busy, gave herself no time to think or to dwell on her loss. She hadn't paid her promised visit to Liverpool yet, she'd taken Mrs Mulcahey's advice about not making too many decisions. She'd felt it was too soon. She went to work, had laid out a vegetable patch which she tended diligently, and did some charity work. It all helped and Kevin had been very supportive. Dee glanced at him as they walked along. He'd become a close friend over the months. He'd advised and encouraged her on matters both important and trivial and now she felt she could confide in him totally. He'd been the one who had set up the meeting they'd just attended and he'd been the one who, at his uncle's behest, had looked after her affairs, working quietly in the background on her behalf.

Both Jean and her mother had given all the support and encouragement they could considering the distance. Both wrote regularly and Jean had begged her to go over to spend Christmas with them but she'd made excuses. The weather was terrible for travelling and she had promised to help out at various charitable functions in the town.

Graham and Susie now had a beautiful little daughter, Charlotte. They'd sent photographs and she'd bought frames for them; they now took pride of place on her mantelpiece, beside the one of Davie and his pretty fiancée Liz, and the one of herself and Niall on their wedding day.

She greeted two women she knew but as she was with Kevin she didn't stop to talk. When Niall had been alive she had known very few people in the town but that too had changed since she spent more time in Tullamore.

After Niall had died the Grand Canal Company had

been in the process of being incorporated into the Office of Public Works, for commercial traffic on the canal had ceased; only the seasonal pleasure boats now used it. A relief lock-keeper had been employed during the season which ran from March to September. Kevin had told her not to worry about anything concerning the lock or the Lock House, he had it all in hand. He was liaising on her behalf with the appropriate authority. But she had come to realise that one day she would have to meet that authority's representative to discuss her future and that's what they had been doing that afternoon. They were now on their way back to the office to inform James Heffernan of the outcome.

He eagerly ushered them in and settled her in the chair on the opposite side of his desk that was always used for clients, while Kevin pulled up another chair and sat beside her. 'Well now, and how did it all go?'

'They were very considerate but I know I have to thank Kevin for putting the case to them so succinctly,' she replied, smiling at them both.

'Haven't they been at sixes and sevens themselves over what to do about the canal. So, what did they say?'

She glanced at Kevin who nodded his encouragement. 'They said that if I wished to I could take over Niall's position as lock-keeper with a salary and of course continue to live in the house and maintain the lock. Apparently it's not unheard of for a woman to do the job.'

'It is not. Isn't there a woman keeper down at the Twenty-ninth Lock at Ballycowan? It's always been a tradition that's kept in families,' Kevin added. He'd ascertained all this information before he'd contacted them on her behalf.

James Heffernan nodded. 'So, what did you tell them?' he asked.

'I told them I would let them know. I would like the time to think about it and they agreed, as long as I don't keep them waiting for months. They'd prefer not to have to employ the relief for this season.'

'We suggested that six weeks would be an appropriate length of time,' Kevin added. He'd wanted longer, he didn't want too much pressure to be put on Dee, but they'd not been in agreement so he hadn't pushed the point.

'That seems fair enough,' the older man agreed.

Dee frowned. 'As I told Kevin, the truth of the matter is that I don't know what to do. I don't know if I'm physically capable of the work. I don't know if I want to commit myself, my whole future to remaining there. I've thought about what Niall would have said and I know he would have wanted me to stay. At least there would still have been a "Clarke" operating the lock but then what happens after me?'

James leaned forward, steepling his fingers and looking thoughtful. 'Sure, who knows what will have become of the canal and its traffic by that time. Nothing goes on for eternity. You must consider yourself.'

She nodded and so did Kevin. He had a point. 'So, I have some serious thinking to do,' she said.

'Would it be of any help to talk to Maria?' he suggested.

Dee still met the elderly nun from time to time but her health this last winter hadn't been good. 'If she feels up to it. I don't want to burden her with my problems. I've already taken up a great deal of Kevin's time in this respect.'

'You know I don't mind, Dee. You need to talk important decisions over,' Kevin said quietly.

'She'd only be delighted to see you. She's been feeling stronger this last week, thanks be to God.'

'This climate doesn't help her,' Dee mused.

'Don't I know it, but what can you do? Come up tomorrow evening, I'll bring her out for an hour. The change will do her good.'

'Thank you. Now, I'd better get back.'

Kevin saw her to the door. 'I want you to promise me that you'll talk things over with me as well, Dee. I've all the time in the world to listen and advise.'

She smiled at him. 'You've been so good and so patient with me already, Kevin, and I'm grateful.'

'It's a life-changing decision, Dee.'

'I know, and I promise after I've spoken to your aunt I'll come and talk to you.'

He smiled at her, relieved. He really did want to know of her decision, he had plans of his own.

The next evening Dee was pleased to see Sister Maria Theresa sitting in a comfortable chair beside the fire with a rug over her knees. She did look considerably brighter than the last time Dee had seen her but she noticed that the nun's hands were very swollen with arthritis.

'It's lovely to see you looking so much better, Sister.'

She smiled but then tutted. '*Français, s'il vous plaît, Denise.*'

Dee laughed. Sister Maria Theresa always called her by her full name. '*Comment allez-vous? Bien?*' She reverted to the language she had become so familiar with. 'Did your brother tell you that I have been offered the position of lock-keeper?'

'He did and he also told me you are uncertain what to do?'

Dee nodded. 'I know Niall would have wanted me to accept and stay on, to continue the tradition, and it's so sad that we didn't have children.'

Sister Maria Theresa nodded. 'It is but he has gone and the name will die out. Even if you were to remarry and have children those children would not bear the name Clarke, nor would they be of any blood kin to Niall. So, if you were to decide not to stay, Denise, someone else would take over. Either way, eventually, it will no longer be "Clarkes' Lock", I'm afraid.'

Dee had to agree. 'That's very true.'

'What do you *really* want to do with your life, child? You are still very young. Twenty-five? Twenty-six?'

'I'll be twenty-six in a few weeks' time,' Dee informed her.

'Do you not wish to go back to England? Your family is there.'

Consternation filled Dee's eyes. 'I know but I don't know if I could settle in a city now.'

'You could pay them a visit, just to see,' the nun suggested.

'I only have six weeks to make up my mind,' Dee replied. She smiled a little wryly. 'When I left school I said I would like to travel, that was the reason why I began to learn French. Jean and I promised ourselves we would and that we'd have some excitement in our lives before we settled down.' She sighed. 'But then things didn't quite turn out the way we expected. She opened her salon and met Tony and got married and I . . . I had a very painful experience and life at home became unbearable so I decided to come to Ireland.'

Sister Maria Theresa had been watching Dee very closely but now she leaned back in the chair, wincing a little at the pain this movement caused her. 'I think you are sorry that you never took the opportunity to travel, except of course to come here.'

'It's something I really haven't given a great deal of thought to,' Dee replied.

'Until now? Why not think about it, Denise? Your French is excellent; you could easily find well-paid work. It is a beautiful country with many different regions to explore. Don't wait until circumstances or age or health make it too late. Don't waste the life and the talents God has given you.'

Dee smiled at her. 'I will think about it, I promise.'

'I'll pray for you, child, that you may find the guidance you need to make the decision that is right for you.'

'Thank you,' Dee replied sincerely. Maybe she would write and ask Jean what she thought about the idea. All those years ago they'd planned to go together but that was out of the question now. If she went she would be going on her own and that was a huge decision to take. She had a feeling she might well need Sister Maria Theresa's prayers.

True to her promise she went to see Kevin to tell him what his aunt had advised.

'She advised you to travel?' he said with surprise. It had come as a shock to him.

Dee nodded. 'It was something I always wanted to do but . . . it didn't happen. She said I could easily get a job.'

He'd never harboured uncharitable thoughts about his aunt – until now. 'I never knew that. Do you . . . really want to leave?'

She looked troubled. 'I still don't know, Kevin. Maybe it's still too soon to be making such an important decision but I only have six weeks, you know that.'

'If you decided you couldn't stay on as lock-keeper you could rent a place here in town,' he suggested earnestly.

'I'd have no income, except what I earn working for your uncle. I'd have to find full-time work and you know that won't be easy. Work is hard to find, people still have to emigrate.'

He stood up and thrust his hands into the pockets of his trousers. This wasn't the right time or the right place and he had no idea of how he was going to declare himself. He didn't want to put more pressure on her but he didn't want her to leave either. Reluctantly he decided he couldn't say anything. 'Will you think about it, Dee? I'm certain something could be worked out regarding a full-time job.'

She looked doubtful. 'You know there isn't enough work to keep me employed full time, Kevin.'

'There might be. Uncle James has been saying for a while now that he's thinking of retiring. I know he wants me to take the practice on.'

This surprised her. 'And will you? Don't you want to go back to Brisbane?'

He shook his head. He enjoyed life here and if he went back to Brisbane he'd be leaving her. 'Maybe for a visit in about ten years' time. I'm settled here. I like Ireland and I'm very fond of Uncle James.'

'So, you'll stay?'

He nodded. 'With just me to deal with all the clients I'd need you, Dee. Will you bear it in mind?'

'It's certainly something I hadn't thought about and I promise I will consider it, Kevin. And I'm going to write to Jean and see what she thinks.'

He felt greatly relieved although he sincerely hoped Jean wouldn't come out in favour of his aunt's suggestion that Dee up stakes and go and live and work in France.

Jean read part of the letter out to Ada when her mother called to see her on Sunday afternoon.

Ada looked concerned. 'Why would she want to go and live and work in France? If she's thinking of leaving Ireland, and I can't say I blame her if she is, why doesn't she come home? Flo is a different woman these days, now she's a granny and young Davie is saving up hard to get married. Flo would be over the moon to have her back home.'

'It's something we always said we would do – travel,' Jean said, folding Dee's letter up.

'That was years ago when you were just a pair of kids. You're grown women now and she's the chance of a full-time job with that solicitor.'

'I know but maybe she feels it's the right time. If she leaves it much longer she might never get the opportunity again. I have to agree with you, Mam, I think she should leave that place. She's stuck out there in the back of beyond without even a telephone and I know I could never come out of that front door and not be reminded of the poor lad drowning just a few feet away. I don't think she should stay there and spend her time heaving those gates open and shut and keeping the place looking tidy. She's too young and she'd be just wasting her life. If she's going to stay she'd be better off in town and working full time but it's not my decision. It's not my life.'

'But she's asked you what you think. What will you tell her? And she hasn't got a lot of time to make up her mind, don't forget.'

Jean pursed her lips and frowned. 'I think I'll write and tell her to go for it. She should at least give it a try and if she's not happy then she can always come home.'

Ada nodded. She supposed Jean was right. 'Has she written to Flo and told her all this?'

'I don't know, she doesn't say. But you'd better not go opening your mouth about it, Mam. Flo might get upset if Dee hasn't written.'

Ada looked indignant. 'Would I go doing something like that?'

Jean grinned at her. 'You would, Mam.'

'Don't be so hardfaced, my girl. You're never too old for a clip around the ear even if you are a married woman. Where is he, by the way?'

Jean's grin faded. 'Playing golf. He seems to spend all weekend on the damned golf course these days.'

Ada shook her head. 'Put your foot down, Jean. You should spend the weekends together.'

'Don't forget I work all day Saturday, Mam, and he says it's not just for pleasure. There are a lot of business deals done on the golf course and he can't afford to miss out on them.'

'That's as may be but he could still take you out on a Sunday. He's got the car, you could go off to the North Wales coast, especially now the weather is getting better,' Ada pointed out. 'And of course if you were to start a family he wouldn't be able to go swanning off to the golf club all the time.'

Jean sighed. 'Let's not get into that discussion again, Mam.'

But she did think about it after her mother had gone and she got out the iron and ironing board to make a start on the pile of shirts that needed doing. It wouldn't hurt him to give up his golf for one day. Even after the game had finished he didn't come straight home. He spent just as much time in the club house at what he jokingly called 'the nineteenth hole'. Maybe she'd suggest it when he finally came home. She'd enjoy a run out to Llandudno or Rhos-on-Sea next week, weather permitting, of course. And maybe her mother was right about starting a family too. It was something she would discuss with Tony maybe later that evening.

She'd finished the ironing and put it away and was preparing to reply to Dee's letter when the phone rang.

'Mrs Littlemore?'

She was puzzled, the voice was unfamiliar and sounded stern and authoritarian. 'Yes, this is Mrs Littlemore speaking. Who is calling?'

'I'm Police Sergeant McManus from Mather Avenue. There's no need to be alarmed, madam, but I'm afraid your husband has been involved in an accident.'

Jean went cold. 'Tony? An accident? Oh, my God!'

'Calm down, please, Mrs Littlemore. It's not serious. It's nothing fatal. His car was involved in a collision on Mather Avenue. He's got minor injuries and he's been taken to Mossley Hill Hospital.'

Jean breathed a sigh of relief but her hands were shaking. 'He is definitely not badly hurt?'

'As I said, just minor injuries. I'm sorry to have to inform you by phone but your local station are short-staffed, it being Sunday. Are you all right?'

'Yes, yes, I'm fine. Thank you and thank you for

letting me know. I'll go straight to the hospital,' Jean replied and then replaced the receiver. Oh, thank God he wasn't badly hurt, she thought.

She ran upstairs and changed her shoes, dragged on a coat and came down to look for her handbag. Then she stopped dead. Only now did it dawn on her what the police sergeant had said. A collision on Mather Avenue! What the hell had he been doing on Mather Avenue? The golf club was in West Derby, which was miles away on the other side of the city. She sat down for a minute. She would still have to go, she would have to find out what injuries he had, even though he'd said they were 'minor'. She wasn't even very sure how to get to Mossley Hill from here. She felt upset and very uneasy. There was something not quite right here.

It took her over an hour and three buses to get there and throughout the journey her anxiety had increased. She couldn't get the question out of her mind. Just what had he been doing over in this part of the city when he was supposed to be in West Derby?

In Casualty she went straight to the desk and told them why she had come.

The nurse was very considerate. 'It must have come as a terrible shock, luv, but it's not too bad. In fact it could have been far worse. He's broken his ankle and his wrist, he's got some cuts and bruises and he's a bit concussed so we'll have to keep him in. I'll take you through.'

Jean thanked her, relieved. 'I suppose the police have sorted the car out, they didn't say anything about it on the phone,' she said, wondering vaguely what had happened to his golf clubs.

'I suppose that's all been towed away and of course the passenger escaped with just a few cuts, which is often the case.'

Jean had been walking beside the nurse but now she stopped dead, her heart plummeting like a stone. 'What passenger?'

The nurse looked embarrassed, realising too late she shouldn't have mentioned that.

'What passenger?' Jean demanded. Anger was beginning to stir in her.

The nurse could see Jean was determined. 'I'm so sorry, I really shouldn't have said that.'

'I want to know. All the way here I've been asking myself what he was doing on Mather Avenue when he was supposed to have been at his golf club in West Derby.'

The nurse bit her lip. 'It was a young lady. She was discharged fifteen minutes ago.'

Jean pressed her lips tightly together. He'd had a girl in the car with him. It was happening again. He'd been cheating on her again. 'You will have her name then.'

'I'm sorry but I don't think I can—'

The humiliation and fury bubbled over. 'Yes, you bloody well can! I have a right to know who she is!'

'A Miss Lucy Whiting,' the nurse answered hesitantly. She'd be on the carpet in Matron's office for this.

With her cheeks burning and tears of rage, hurt and

disappointment stinging her eyes, Jean turned and abruptly walked back in the direction she'd come from, heading for the exit, leaving the nurse standing staring after her in shock.

Chapter Thirty

———◆———

SHE DIDN'T GO HOME. Without really realising where she was going she made her way to her mam's house. By the time she reached there it was late and she felt cold and numb with shock and misery.

'Jean! In the name of God, what's the matter?' Ada demanded when she opened the door.

Jean's face crumpled and she flung her arms around her mother. 'Oh, Mam! Mam! I can't believe he's done it again! He swore he wouldn't and I . . . I believed him!' she sobbed.

Ada drew her into the living room, raising her eyebrows and gesturing with her head that Harry should leave. He duly switched off the television and went out into the kitchen to put the kettle on, wondering what had happened to upset Jean so much.

Gradually Ada learned all the details of Tony's first affair and now this latest betrayal. She hadn't known anything about the first one, Jean had kept that to herself. Now she was furious, remembering how that very afternoon Jean had said he spent all weekend playing golf. The bloody liar! She could quite cheerfully murder him.

'I'll kill him! I'll kill him with my own two hands for treating you like this, Jean! You should have told me about the first time, he'd have felt the lash of my tongue I can tell you!' she spluttered. But then she controlled herself, trying to think logically. 'Could he not just have been giving her a lift somewhere?' she ventured, feeling it had to be asked.

Jean raised a tear-stained face. 'No, Mam! He's been lying to me again. He was supposed to be playing golf in West Derby and he was over in that part of the city with *her*. I've been such a fool! It must have been going on for months and I never knew. I'd still not have known only that nurse put her foot in it by letting it slip. I *believed* him! How could he hurt me like this again? Oh, Mam!'

Ada was still fuming but she was going to have to give Jean some support. 'I'm so sorry, luv. Really I am. I never would have thought it of him. You're staying here tonight. You're not going back to that house in this state.'

Harry came in, bearing a tray and looking just as upset as his wife. He'd heard what Jean had said as he'd come down the hall.

'Have this cup of tea, luv, and try and calm down a bit,' Ada urged.

'What'll she do, Ada? I mean that feller's in the hospital,' Harry asked.

'And as far as I'm concerned he can damned well stay there! Let his fancy piece sort it out,' Ada snapped.

Jean sipped the tea. She didn't care what happened to him now, she told herself. As far as she was concerned it was all over. She could never, ever trust him again. He wasn't going to put her through all this hurt and mortification again.

'Shouldn't someone at least let his parents know?' Harry ventured.

'What's wrong with you, Harry? You seem to be thinking more about him than our poor Jean!' Ada exploded.

'I'm just trying to be a bit practical, like.'

'Let his flaming toffee-nosed mother go and visit him and bring him out and I'll tell you this, Harry, I'll take a delight in telling her just how her precious son has behaved. She won't be able to look down her nose at us now, not after what's he's done to our Jean.'

'I can't forgive him again, Mam. I don't want to go back to that house. It will never be home to me again. Can I come back here?' Jean wailed. She was still very upset.

'But all your things are up there, Jean,' Ada reminded her.

'Will you come with me in the morning while I go and pack some things to bring back?'

Ada nodded, sadly. What was the matter with Tony Littlemore, for God's sake? He had a good job, a lovely home, a good wife who worked so hard and had truly loved him. Obviously it hadn't been enough. 'I take it you won't be going into the salon tomorrow?'

Jean shook her head. 'I . . . I'll ask Pauline if she can manage for a few days and then I'll put a notice up, saying we will be closed next week. I can't face people, Mam. I just *can't*. It was bad enough last time, trying to pretend everything was fine.'

Ada's heart went out to her. 'Jean, why don't you go over to Dee next week? Get away from everything. I'm sure it will do you good.'

'I'll think about it, Mam,' Jean promised. Right now she could barely think straight. All that filled her mind was the fact that Tony had hurt her terribly – again – and probably didn't even care.

Ada phoned Mavis Littlemore from Jean's house next day and took great delight in hearing the astonished, disbelieving cry that echoed down the phone line. She told the woman that she had better get herself off to the hospital for Jean certainly was not setting foot there again, nor did Jean want to hear any of his pathetic, trumped-up lies by way of an excuse. In fact her daughter had told her emphatically this morning that she wanted nothing more to do with him. It was over, for she could never believe a word he said ever again.

That afternoon Ernest Littlemore arrived at Ada's house full of sympathy and apologies. He was genuinely upset and shocked at his son's behaviour, he told Ada.

'I've come to see if there is anything I can do. Will she just speak to him? Perhaps it can all be sorted out. She should at least give him the opportunity to try to explain and apologise. It's such a drastic thing – divorce.'

'To our generation it is. We stuck it out no matter what happened but things are different now,' Ada reminded him.

He nodded in agreement. 'I know but please can you persuade her to at least see what he has to say for himself? I'll take her to the hospital and I'll bring her back here. I honestly don't know what's got into him, Mrs Williams. Jean is a lovely girl and I never thought he could behave like this towards her.'

'Ada, go and see what she says. I agree with Ernest. At least let him have the opportunity to explain himself,' Harry said.

'Harry, you know as well as I do that it's not the first time he's done this. She didn't confide in anyone last time and he swore to her it would never happen again and of course she believed him.'

Ernest Littlemore looked even more concerned. He hadn't known that. 'I'm so sorry, I didn't realise. Oh, poor Jean.'

And you can go home and tell that to his mother too, Ada thought grimly. Fine job you did in bringing him up, she added to herself.

'But you should still ask her, Ada,' Harry urged.

Jean had been lying down but after a bit of coaxing from her mother, she reluctantly agreed to go and see Tony.

They drove to the hospital virtually in silence for Ernest just didn't know what to say to her and Jean didn't want to speak about it. He asked her if she wanted him to go in with her but she shook her head, so, after informing him of the ward Tony was in, he promised to wait for her in the car park.

Jean made enquiries and duly found her way to the ward feeling very unsure and miserable.

He was in the bed by the window and she walked slowly towards it. He turned and she could see he had cuts to his face and there were yellow and purple bruises around one eye. One of his wrists was in plaster. When he caught sight of her he tried to pull himself up higher on the pillows. She fought down the feeling of pity that had risen at the sight of his injuries.

'Jean. I've been hoping and praying you would come. It's not at all how it looks. Sit down and let me explain.'

She shook her head. 'No, I'll stand. Why was that girl, Lucy something, in the car with you? Why were you not at the golf club, Tony?' She was surprised at how calm and steady her voice sounded; inside she was shaking.

'I'd been at the club, Jean, I swear I had. You can ask anyone. Ask old George the barman, he'll tell you. I was just giving her a lift home, that's all.'

'All the way to this end of the city? I don't believe you, Tony. You can't honestly think I'd believe that. If she was playing golf why not on a course near here? There must be closer courses than West Derby.'

He looked away, unable to meet her eyes. 'I hardly knew her, Jean. You have to believe that. I'm really sorry. I didn't mean to worry or upset you. She's someone I just . . . met.'

Jean felt all the anger drain away. She felt bone weary. It was always going to be like this. He would always be just 'meeting' someone. He would think that if he said sorry, gave some flimsy excuse and swore he loved only her, she would believe and forgive him and they would go on again – until the next time. But she knew she couldn't live like that. There had to be trust for a marriage to work and her trust in him had been irreparably shattered.

'Sorry isn't good enough, Tony. I'll never be able to believe a single word you say and I can't, I *won't* live like that. It's over. I never want to see you ever again.' She didn't wait for him to speak, she just turned and walked away.

It was Flo who sent the telegram to Dee. Ada had told her what had happened and her heart went out to the girl.

'Poor Jean, I really feel for her, Ada.'

Ada nodded. Flo would indeed know how Jean was feeling.

'She'll get over it, Ada, in time. But don't let it eat away at her. We don't want her ending up the way I did. It will do her good to get away from everything for a while. Dee might be able to talk it all through with her, they've always been close. I'll let Dee know,' she'd promised.

Dee had gone to the station to meet the Dublin train, all thoughts of her own situation dismissed from her mind. She had never thought that Tony would cheat on Jean again. Like her friend she had thought it had been just one stupid mistake. Now they both knew differently.

'I wish I'd taken notice of everyone and gone over for a visit. I would at least have been there on the spot when . . . when you found out,' Dee said when they got back to the Lock House. Jean looked pale, drawn and tired, she thought.

'It's all right, Dee. Mam has been very good. It was she who suggested I come over.'

'She was right. You need some time to think about everything. Is he . . . is he out of hospital?'

Jean nodded. 'I believe so. He's at his mother's house. His father is furious with him, so Mam said.'

'He's a nice man, his father. I remember how kind he was to me when Mam caused that terrible scene. It's going to be very hard for you, Jean.'

Jean sat down on a stool and wrapped her arms around her knees. 'I know, Dee. But I won't take him back. I *can't*. I can't spend my life wondering where he is and what he's doing or who he's with. That would destroy me. I told Mam I want a divorce on the grounds of his . . . adultery.'

Dee looked at her pityingly. Oh, where had it all gone wrong for Jean? Her friend had seemed to have everything. A successful business, a lovely house of her own and a happy marriage but now her world had fallen apart. She knew Jean had loved Tony with all her heart but she could understand that her friend couldn't go on living with him now.

Chapter Thirty-One

DEE SENT WORD TO Kevin that she wouldn't be into work tomorrow as Jean had come to visit. She had explained Jean's situation briefly and hoped he would understand. She was surprised therefore when she saw James Heffernan's car pull up outside and Kevin got out.

'I didn't expect you to come out, Kevin.'

'I just wanted to make sure you were . . . both . . . all right.'

'I'm fine but obviously she's very upset.'

He nodded; from what little he knew he could understand.

Dee pulled the door closed behind her. 'Shall we go for a bit of a walk? She's still asleep, she didn't have a very good night so I don't want to disturb her.'

He fell into step beside her as they walked down the narrow track that led to the next lock. It was a bright, sunny morning with the first hint of the warmth of spring in the air. The hedgerows and trees were still bare but here and there along the bank the first cowslips and primroses were starting to appear.

'What's happened, Dee? Your note just said there had been a domestic crisis, which is a bit vague.'

She nodded. 'Poor Jean. She found out that Tony has been cheating on her – and it's not for the first time. She's devastated.'

He frowned. 'That I can understand.'

'She feels she'll never be able to trust him again and she won't . . . can't live her life like that. She's going to divorce him.'

'On the grounds of adultery, I assume. She's fortunate she doesn't live here. That option wouldn't be open to her.'

Dee nodded. 'I know but her decision affects me too.'

They'd reached a part of the canal where a small stone bridge ran over a culvert which was used to divert water and Dee stopped and leaned against the wall.

'How?' Kevin asked, wondering what she meant.

'Jean and I have been close friends since we were about five years old. We've been through so much together. We've always been there to help each other out in times of . . . trouble.' Dee was remembering how much time Jean had spent with her after she'd found out about Billy. 'I've been trying to think what will be best for us both. Maybe we should make a clean break. Go travelling. We always said we would but never got round to it. But if she doesn't want to come with me,

I'll go back to Liverpool with her. She's going to need someone to get her through this divorce and I would get a job and live with Mam. She's . . . different now.'

He looked at her sadly. 'So, either way you're thinking of leaving?'

She nodded. She hadn't had much sleep herself; she'd tossed and turned thinking what would be best for both their futures. 'In a way I'll be sad to leave. I do love the peace and quiet and everyone has been so good, especially since Niall's death.'

Kevin stared unseeingly at the calm waters of the canal. It was now or never. If he said nothing he would lose her for ever. 'Dee, I . . . I don't want you to leave Ireland.'

'I know. I don't know what I would have done without you, Kevin, this last year. You're a good friend and always will be.'

'Could I . . . ever be more than that, Dee?' he said quietly, not daring to look at her.

She didn't reply. She was taken aback.

He took a deep breath. 'I love you, Dee. I've loved you almost from the first moment I met you. I couldn't say anything, it wasn't right. Niall was your husband but then, after . . . after the accident I began to hope. I'll be taking over from Uncle James in the near future, I could offer you a good life and we needn't live in town. You could still enjoy the tranquillity.'

Dee stared at him in silence. She was utterly confused.

'Dee?' He pleaded, taking her hand.

'Kevin, I . . . I don't know what to say. I'm very fond of you but I've never thought of you . . .'

'As anything other than a friend,' he said.

She nodded but she didn't pull her hand away. She didn't know how to answer him. She knew him far better than she'd known Niall before she'd married him, although the circumstances had been different, and it was true she was *fond* of him but . . . 'Kevin, I don't know what to say. I . . . I'll need . . . time . . . and there's Jean to think of. I can't let her down at a time like this.'

He nodded. At least she hadn't dismissed him out of hand. 'I understand that, Dee. I won't rush you. If you feel you need time to . . . to help Jean get through this or if you decide to travel for a while, I'll understand.' He managed a smile. 'After all, I spent almost two years travelling the world before I found the place where I truly feel at home. I couldn't deny you the same opportunity.' He didn't say that falling in love with her was the main reason why he had decided to settle here, he felt it wouldn't be fair. 'All I ask, Dee, is that whatever you decide to do, please keep in touch? I'll be here and I'll wait for you, that's a promise.'

She nodded. It was good of him not to press her for any kind of a decision. 'I will keep in touch, Kevin. I promise. Whatever we decide to do, wherever we go, I'll write,' she replied sincerely.

They walked back towards the house in silence, both deep in thought, and before he got into the car Kevin kissed her on the cheek.

'Good luck, Dee. Remember I love you and I'll wait for you.'

She watched as he turned the car around and then waved as he drove away.

Jean was up and dressed. 'You should have woken me. Who was that?'

'Kevin Buckley. I sent word that I wouldn't be into work and he came out to see if everything was all right.'

'That was good of him,' Jean said tiredly.

Over the next few days the two girls went for long walks and Jean at last began to see why Dee loved living here. It was as though the serenity of the place calmed you and enabled you to sort things out in your mind.

'I can see now why you came here when you did,' she said as they walked along the rough path that skirted a field that led up on to the bog land. 'It's a good place to sort out problems, there's time to think without everyone around you putting their twopennyworth in.'

Dee nodded. She'd said nothing to her friend about her conversation with Kevin but it had been constantly on her mind.

'I'm still going through with the divorce. I haven't changed my mind. Have you come to any decision about staying on?'

Dee pulled a twig of blackthorn from the hedge. The buds were still tightly furled. 'I've been thinking what would be best for both of us. Should we both make a clean break, do what we always said we would do – go travelling – or should I go back to Liverpool with you? I'd easily get a job, live with Mam . . .'

'Could you stick that?' Jean asked.

Dee threw away the blackthorn twig. 'She's much better now, you know that – thanks to your mam. It's not going to be easy for you, Jean, having to go to court and then sell the house and . . . everything.'

They'd reached the gate that led on to the bog and Jean climbed up and sat on top of it, staring out over the fields. Dee climbed up and sat beside her. From up here you could just glimpse the roof of the Lock House and the flat, grey waters of the canal.

'I know but I'll get through it. If you leave you'll miss all this.'

Dee sighed. 'I know and . . . and there's something else. I haven't said anything up to now because I didn't want to upset you even more.'

'What?'

'When Kevin called we went for a walk so as not to disturb you and he . . . well, he told me he . . . he loved me. I had no idea. It was a complete surprise.'

Jean smiled at her. 'I once asked him if he was fond of you and he admitted it. It was just after Niall died so I didn't feel I should mention it. He's a very nice person, Dee.'

Dee nodded. 'He is.'

'But you don't love him?' Jean said quietly. 'If you remember, you weren't in love with Niall when you married him.'

'That was different, you know it was. I don't know

how I really feel about Kevin. I never thought I could really love anyone after ... Billy, but I grew to love Niall, in a different sort of way.'

'You've changed, Dee. You've grown up and Billy, well, it was a long time ago now.'

Dee sighed. 'I know.'

'What did you say to Kevin?'

'Not much, I was so confused. He said he could offer me a good life here but that he wouldn't pressure me. He just asked me to promise I'd keep in touch – whatever I decided to do.'

'And will you?' Jean asked.

Dee nodded.

'Good. Well, it's time we made some kind of decision about the future. I'll have to go back to sort things out but ... but I think we should take Sister Maria Theresa's advice.'

Dee was surprised. 'What about your business?'

'I'll sell up. It's a busy salon, it shouldn't be hard. I don't want to keep it now. I've been thinking ... wondering what kind of a future I'd have if I kept it going. All I'd do would be go to work and then go back to Mam's house and that's not much of a future to look forward to. For one thing she'd drive me mad in six months. I'd sooner take a chance and go with you. Shall we go to France? At least one of us can speak the language, and if we hate it we can either move on or go back home. I wish now I'd learned a language.'

'You'll soon pick it up. Living and working in a country is the best way to learn.' It seemed a lifetime ago since she'd heard those words, Dee thought. She could think of Billy without any feelings of pain or loss now and she wondered where he was and what he was doing. She would never know.

'Then that's settled,' Jean said firmly, sliding off the gate. She knew there were difficult days ahead of her and there would be heartache and anguish but if she could look forward to a new kind of life in a country where there would be no unhappy memories it would be a start. 'We'll both have to go back to Liverpool first though. You've been promising to go and see your niece for ages and your mam will be pleased to see you.'

Dee thought back to the day she'd flown to Ireland to be Niall's wife. She'd wondered then would she ever see her native city again. Now it seemed she would and she was beginning to look forward to being reunited with her family before she and Jean set off on the adventure they'd planned all those years ago. The time away would give her ample opportunity to make up her mind about Kevin Buckley. It would be a new beginning for them both.

Epilogue

———•◦•———

Sainte-Marie-la-Campagne, 1972

DEE SQUINTED IN THE bright sunlight as she came
out of the dark interior of the house. Even this
early in the morning it was very warm, she thought, as
she crossed the small square that was grandly named La
Place de la Liberté. It was shaded by ancient plane trees
whose dusty leaves hung limply for there wasn't a
breath of wind to stir them. The brilliant reds, purples
and pinks of geraniums and bougainvillea cascading
from the balconies contrasted sharply with the pale,
faded stucco walls of the buildings that surrounded the
square. She never tired of the flowers, she thought as
she headed for the Café des Orchidées where she and
Jean had a coffee each morning before Jean headed for
the Salon Paradis where Jean worked and she made her
way to the rue Afrique du Nord to the offices of Claude

Minot, the solicitor or 'Notaire' as he was called.

Her dark hair had been streaked by the sun and had been cut short by Jean. Her short, simple blue and white cotton dress looked fresh and cool. She was barelegged but wore flat white shoes and her skin had been deeply tanned by the sun.

'*Bonjour*, Marcel. *Comment allez-vous?*' she greeted the waiter pleasantly, finding a table in the shade and putting her bag on the floor.

'*Un petit café*, Madame Clarke?' he enquired, smiling. He always asked even though she had black coffee every morning. When they had first arrived in this small town in the countryside twenty kilometres from the bustling Côte d'Azur, they had caused a flurry of interest: two young English girls, one apparently a widow and the other a divorcee and both of them attractive. Their arrival hadn't pleased some of the older women but as they'd settled in and it became obvious that they were not out to entice all the men from their respective spouses they had been accepted. Madame Clarke spoke fluent French and Madame Littlemore's command of the language had greatly improved. She was also popular in the salon where she worked, especially with the younger women, for she had lived and worked in Paris for a short while and was *au fait* with the most modern hairstyles.

Dee settled back to wait for Jean, who had gone to see if there was any post for them. She smiled to herself, thinking how pleasant and different life here was. On Sundays they sometimes took the bus to the coast where they would sit in a café and observe the rich and famous. Then they would head for the beach to sunbathe and swim in the warm blue waters of the Mediterranean. They had been here for almost eighteen months now. They had gone first to Paris where they had rented a minuscule apartment and Jean had found work in a small salon and she had been employed as a receptionist in what was really not much more than a Bed and Breakfast establishment. They'd never intended to remain in the city for long and had moved on, working their way south until they'd ended up here. They'd liked the small town so much that they'd decided to stay on, renting the ground floor of Madame Camaieux's house, she being a widow.

Marcel brought her coffee and a *un grand crème* for Jean who was now crossing the square, waving two envelopes.

Dee knew that one of them would be for her, a letter from Kevin. As she'd promised she written to him regularly and he always replied promptly. He kept her up to date with the events in Ireland. James Heffernan had retired the previous year and Kevin had taken over. A look of sadness filled her eyes as she remembered the letter he'd written last year informing her that his aunt, Sister Maria Theresa, had died. She felt she owed the quiet, gentle nun a great deal. There was a new lock-keeper at the Thirtieth Lock although the canal was only used by pleasure craft these days. There were no more commercial barges. Through their correspondence they'd grown closer in a way, even though they were hundreds of miles apart. She'd gone home in April for Davie's wedding and at her request Kevin had come over from Ireland for the event. She'd realised then how much she'd changed, how much she'd missed him and when she'd returned to France she'd given her feelings for him a great deal of thought. She was twenty-nine and now she knew what she really wanted from life. There were no more doubts about the future.

'Two letters today. Phew, it's going to be another scorcher!' Jean remarked, sitting down opposite and fanning her face with one of the envelopes. The blue of her eyes was accentuated by her tan and her short hair had been bleached by the sun to a silvery blond. She wore a short white skirt and a pink and white cotton top and had carefully placed her crisp green and white overall on the back of the chair.

'Is it the letter you've been expecting?' Dee asked, sipping her coffee. Jean had been on pins awaiting the reply to the application she'd sent off almost a month ago. She'd put Kevin's letter in her bag. She'd read it when she got to her little office, before Monsieur Minot arrived. She didn't want to spoil Jean's moment.

Jean had already scrutinised the envelope closely and nodded.

'Well, go on, open it and put us both out of our misery. The suspense is killing me,' Dee urged.

Jean hesitated. 'I'm nervous. It's going to be a big change.'

Dee sighed. 'Jean, how often have we discussed it? Discussed *everything*. You don't want to go back to Liverpool, you were emphatic about that. Your Decree Absolute is through, your mam would drive you mad, you want the opportunity to see more of the world, and it's a great opportunity to do just that.'

Jean still hesitated. 'I know but I don't want you to feel that I'm trying to influence your decision in any way.'

'You know you're not. I told you last Sunday that I've made up my mind. I'm going to write to Kevin today and tell him I've finally decided to go back to Ireland and to . . . him. It's true, absence does make the heart grow fonder. I know now that I really do miss him. I love him and I want to spend the rest of my life with him.'

'You are *sure*?' Jean pressed.

'Absolutely certain! Now, will you open the damned letter?'

Jean carefully opened the large envelope and drew out a sheet of headed paper. The name 'Steiner' was embossed elegantly in gold and pink across the top.

'Well? Have you got an interview?' Dee asked as Jean scanned the typed letter, her eyes shining with excitement.

'Yes! Yes, I've to go to London to their salon in Mayfair next week and if they find me suitable I'm to go to Southampton to join their staff in the salon on board the *QE2*. Oh, Dee! Just think, I'll be working on that fabulous new ship! I've read that all the décor is just state of the art. I'll be going to New York and on world cruises too!'

Dee reached over and grasped her hands tightly. 'I'm delighted for you, I really, really am! They can't possibly find you *unsuitable*, not after having had your own salon and with all the experience you've had working in Paris and here, and now your French is good. Isn't it a great way to see the world and get paid too?' She was overjoyed for her friend; she knew how much Jean wanted this opportunity.

'Just think of all the people I'll meet too, from all kinds of backgrounds,' Jean enthused, the excitement bubbling up inside her.

'Oh, your mam will be so proud of you – and so am I,' Dee added.

Jean nodded, thinking what Ada's reaction would be to this news.

'And you never know, you might meet someone. Someone special that you can trust.'

Jean grimaced. 'That's not very likely. You know what they say about sailors and there being a different girl in every port.'

'Who said anything about it being a sailor?' Dee protested.

Jean smiled. 'Well, I'm not going looking for romance. I'm going to see the world, enjoy myself and if I happen to meet someone . . . well . . .'

Dee smiled back. 'I just want you to be happy. I want us both to be happy.'

Jean nodded. 'We will, Dee. Just wait and see, the future is looking very bright for us both now.'

Dee looked around for Marcel. 'I know it's a bit early but I think this calls for a small celebratory pastis or Cognac, don't you?'

Now you can buy any of these other bestselling books by **Lyn Andrews** from your bookshop or *direct from the publisher*.

FREE P&P AND UK DELIVERY
(Overseas and Ireland £3.50 per book)

A Daughter's Journey	£6.99
Days of Hope	£6.99
Far From Home	£6.99
Every Mother's Son	£6.99
Friends Forever	£6.99
A Mother's Love	£6.99
Across a Summer Sea	£6.99
When Daylight Comes	£6.99
A Wing and a Prayer	£6.99
Love and a Promise	£6.99
The House on Lonely Street	£6.99
My Sister's Child	£6.99
Take These Broken Wings	£6.99
The Ties That Bind	£6.99
Angels of Mercy	£6.99
When Tomorrow Dawns	£6.99
From This Day Forth	£6.99
Where the Mersey Flows	£6.99
Liverpool Songbird	£6.99
The Sisters O'Donnell	£6.99
The Leaving of Liverpool	£6.99
Ellan Vannin	£6.99
Mersey Blues	£6.99

TO ORDER SIMPLY CALL THIS NUMBER

01235 400 414

or visit our website: www.headline.co.uk

Prices and availability subject to change without notice.